The Obituary Tango

The Obituary Tango

A selection of works
from the Caine Prize for
African Writing

First published in 2006 by Jacana Media (Pty) Ltd
10 Orange Street
Sunnyside, 2092
Johannesburg
South Africa

ISBN 1-77009-211-0
     978-1-77009-211-2

Cover design by Disturbance

Printed by CTP Books, Cape Town

See a complete list of Jacana titles at www.jacana.co.za

Table of Contents

Introduction

In 2005 for the first time the Caine Prize judges had over 100 qualifying stories to read (108 in all – by coincidence the same number have qualified in 2006). We have the impression that more and more short stories by African writers are being published, both in Africa and elsewhere, and we believe the Caine Prize has played a role in stimulating this welcome development.

Our winning story in 2005, 'Monday Morning' by Nigerian writer Segun Afolabi, was first published in *Wasafiri* (issue 41, Spring 2004), the review edited by Susheila Nasta, which also published the shortlisted story by Jamal Mahjoub from the Sudan, 'The Obituary Tango' (issue 42, Summer 2004). *Wasafiri* is one of three excellent UK-based journals from which we regularly receive entries, the others being *Banipal*, edited by Margaret Obank, and *Sable*, founded more recently and edited by Kadijah Sesay. Muthal Naidoo's 2005 shortlisted story, the delightful 'Jail Birds', came to us from the South African writer-led journal *Botsotso*, which is another regular source, as of course is the Kenya-based magazine *Kwani?*, founded and edited by our 2002 winner, Binyavanga Wainaina. The Cape Town journal *Chimurenga* has provided a shortlisted story this year.

The sponsors who keep these periodicals going deserve every commendation. Academic publishers also play a key role. The Ugandan writer Doreen Baingana was shortlisted in 2005 for the second year running, this time for her story 'Tropical Fish', which reached us from the *African American Review* (vol 37, no 4, 2003) and has since become the title-story of a collection of her short stories, very beautifully produced by the Massachusetts University Press. 'Tindi in the Land of the Dead', the shortlisted story by Nigerian writer Ike Okonta, was published in *Humanitas* (vol 2, no 1, 2000) by the George Bell Institute of Queen's College, Birmingham.

2005 was the first time for three years that none of our shortlisted stories came from internet magazines – though there was a record number of entries from that sector.

Talking of publishers prompts me to pay tribute to Irene Staunton, who achieves so much in difficult circumstances with Weaver Press in Zimbabwe. She published our 2004 winning story in her anthology *Writing Still*, and she has already produced another anthology of Zimbabwean short stories, *Writing Now* (Weaver Press, 2005), some of them qualifying for the attentions of our judges this year.

As in previous years our writers had other successes. Doreen Baingana won the Commonwealth 'Best First Book' Prize (Africa Region) for her collection, *Tropical Fish*. Segun Afolabi's 'Monday Morning' will be the title story of the collection of his short stories about to be published by Jonathan Cape. And Chika Unigwe, from our 2004 shortlist, was shortlisted in 2006 for the Dutch equivalent of the Orange Prize for her novel translated into Dutch, *de feniks*.

The principal funders of the Prize were once again the Ernest Oppenheimer Memorial Trust and the Gatsby Charitable Foundation. They have kept the Caine Prize afloat for yet another year. Without them we should simply not exist.

The Celtel Caine Prize African Writers' Workshop 2006

This year saw the fourth of our workshops for African writers, which we held for the second time at Crater Lake, near Naivasha, in Kenya. We thought it right to keep faith with Crater Lake – a tented camp inside the rim of an extinct volcano, isolated, tranquil, beautiful, just an ideal venue for a workshop – despite the brutal killing in July 2005 of its manager and co-owner, John Goldson. His successor and the devoted staff looked after us superbly. They relished the writers' presence and could be espied listening behind the scenes to our readings in the evenings and devouring transcripts in their off-duty moments. We mourn John's death as they do. We planted trees at Crater Lake in his memory, and we dedicate this volume of stories to him and to them.

This year's workshop produced really excellent stories and they all appear here. It was the first in a series of Celtel Caine Prize workshops. Celtel have very generously undertaken to finance our workshops for an initial period of three years. Celtel Kenya organised a public reading by our writers in Nairobi when the workshop was over. Celtel's sponsorship of the workshops will bring real benefit to African writing and enable us to plan seriously ahead.

Once again we depended heavily on the 'can-do' skills and resourcefulness of the *Kwani?* Trust staff to organise the workshop on the ground; and we benefited again from the generosity of Kenya Airways in bringing participants out from the UK.

An absolutely crucial factor in the success of our workshops is the participants' knowledge that the stories they write there will be published in our annual anthology alongside the previous year's Prize shortlist. For this we thank our publishers, Jacana and New Internationalist, most warmly.

Nick Elam
Administrator of the Caine Prize

Caine Prize Stories 2005:
Winner and Shortlist

Monday Morning
(Winner)

Segun Afolabi

'I WANT TO PISS,' the boy said in their language. He held his mother's hand as they walked, but his feet skipped to and fro.

The mother scanned the area, but she could not find a place for her son; there were too many people besides the trees, talking, laughing. 'Take the boy to the edge of the water so he can piss,' she said to her husband.

The boy and his father hurried towards the lake. The father was glad to see that his son could find relief. They did not notice how people looked at them with their mouths turned down. Sour. The eyes narrowed to slits.

The breeze blew and the ducks and swans floated past. The boy was afraid of them, but his need to evacuate was too urgent. Steam rose from the stream that emerged from him as it fell into the water, and he marvelled at this. There was so much that was new to understand here. He had seen on television at the hostel how water could become hard like glass, but the lake was not like that. The swans pushed their powerful legs and the ducks dipped their heads beneath the surface. The father held on to his son's jacket so he would not fall in. There were bits of flotsam at the bank where the water rippled. The boy looked away, a little disgusted, and gazed into the clean centre of the lake.

They came away from the water's edge and joined the mother and the boy's brother, and the boy from the hostel whose name was Emmanuel. The father looked at his wife and children. He wondered at how beautiful everything was in this place with the whispering leaves and the green grass like a perfect carpet and the people so fine in their Sunday clothes. He thought, with God's help it can surely happen. You are distraught, time passes and you are away from it. You can begin to reflect and observe. It was difficult now, to think of artillery and soldiers and flies feeding on abandoned corpses.

The little one laughed and said, 'My piss made fire in the water,' but the mother slapped his shoulder. 'It's enough,' she said.

They joined the people on the path as they strolled through Regent's Park. Only Emmanuel voiced a desire to walk on the grass, but he did not dare because the father had forbidden it. He was a feeble man, Emmanuel thought, so timid in this new place, but his sons were different. Bolder. They had already grasped some of the new language. A breeze gathered up leaves and pushed the crowds along. A clump of clouds dragged across the sun. People pulled their clothes tight around themselves. The mother adjusted her scarf so there were no spaces for the wind to enter. She reached across with her good hand to secure her husband's baseball cap. The area in the centre of his scalp was smooth as marble and he felt the cold easily. She shoved her mittened hand back into her coat pocket and watched the children as they drifted away. After a moment she called, 'Ernesto, come away from there,' to her eldest boy. They had wandered towards an area where people were playing a game with a ball and a piece of wood, and she did not want there to be any trouble. Not today, not on Sunday. She knew his friend was leading him to places he would not have ventured on his own and she feared there would be difficulties ahead. The youngest boy skipped between them: the mother and father, his brother, the brother's best friend. He was her little one and she would hold on to him for as long as she was able.

The father sighed and called out to his children. The cold was setting in again and their walk was too leisurely. They would have to return to the hostel before the sun disappeared. He called to Ernesto, 'Come, it is time for us to go. Tell your brother.' It would take at least half an hour for them to walk back.

Ernesto turned to Alfredo, the little one, who giggled as they played a game among themselves – *Kill the Baron*. The friend, Emmanuel, ran about them, laughing, until the father called again. 'We are going back, you hear me? Ernesto, hold your brother! We go!'

Emmanuel looked at him. He did not speak their language, but regardless, he thought the father was a stupid man – too fat, too quiet. The boy had lost his own father in his country, in his own village home. Now he could only see the faults in them, the other fathers, their weaknesses, what they did not understand. He had thought his father remarkable at one time, but with his own eyes, he had seen him cut down, destroyed. They were foolish and clumsy, despite their arrogance. He would never become such a man himself.

The children trailed behind the mother and father as they navigated paths that took them to the edge of the park. As they came to the road, Alfred raced to walk beside his mother, and a passing car screeched to a halt.

'Keep 'em off the road, for fuck's sakes!' the driver shouted.

The mother held her son, and the father looked at the driver without expression. The boy had not run across the road, but the driver had made an assumption, and now he did not want to lose face.

'Keep the buggers off the road!' he shouted again, and again there was no response.

The father glanced at the mother who only shrugged and held her boy. Emmanuel turned to the driver and waved an apology on behalf of the father, grinning to indicate he understood. But he did not know the appropriate words, and the driver failed to notice or did not care for the gesture. He sped away, complaining bitterly to his passenger. There were people on the pavement who had seen the incident, who now stood watching. The mother and father did not understand the signs and gestures the people used. They did not feel the indignation. They knew only that they were scrutinised and they were sometimes puzzled by this, but they were not overwhelmed.

They trudged along the main road near the building where the books lived. The huge railway stations teemed with people. In the mornings sometimes, the father walked in the vicinity of the stations. At night the area was forsaken, but during the day, workers emerged in their thousands. Often he looked at them and it seemed impossible that he could ever be part of this. The people moved as if they were all one river and they flowed and they did not stop.

'Here is the one!' Alfred squealed to Emmanuel when they came to the glass hotel. 'I will live here!'

'You're crazy,' Emmanuel said to the boy. But he could not fail to notice the guests in the lobby, the people sipping tea in the café, the warm lights, the congenial atmosphere.

The sign at the building read Hotel Excelsior, but this was not a hotel. The orange carpet was threadbare, the linen was stained with the memory of previous guests, the rooms sang with the clamour of too many people.

When they arrived, the mother knew it was not a place to become used to. They had their room, the four of them, and it was enough: the bed and the two narrow cots. There was warmth even though the smell of damp walls never left them. They could not block out the chatter and groans of other occupants. In the mornings the boys feasted on hot breakfasts in the basement dining room where there was a strange hum of silence as people ate. They were gathering strength after years of turmoil in other places. This was the best part of the day.

As they approached the hostel the sky was already turning even though it was still afternoon. Men and women walked up and down the road, but they did not have a destination. They glanced at the family with eyes like angry wounds. A women knelt on the pavement with her head upturned, swaying, and when the family passed, Alfredo could see that she was dazed. The mother cupped her hand against his face so he could no longer look at her. Another man guided a woman in a miniskirt hurriedly by the elbow. He was shouting at her. He crossed the road so he would not have to meet the family and then re-crossed it after they had passed. Every day they saw these people, the lost ones, who seemed to hurt for the things they were looking for but could not find. The mother wondered sometimes, have they never been young like my boys? Where does innocence flee? She wanted to be away from this place, away from the Excelsior. She wanted her family's new life to begin.

The father had begun to work. He could not wait for any bureaucratic decision when there were people who relied on him for food and shelter, for simple things: his mother, his sister and her family, his wife's people. It had begun easily enough. A man at the hostel had told him there was work on a construction site in the south of the city. They did not ask for your papers there, he said. It was a way to help yourself, and if it ended, well, there were other places to work. It was important not to be defeated, he warned, even though you were disregarding the rules. The man had been an architect in his own country, but now he did the slightest thing in order to help himself. He was ebullient, and when the father looked at him and listened, he was filled with hope.

Four of them journeyed from the Excelsior to the building site in the south. Every day they took their breakfast early and joined the people who became a river on their way to work. The job was not complex, but one could easily become disheartened by the cold and the routine. The father dreamed of the day when he could return to his own occupation, to the kitchen where he handled meat and vegetables and the spices he loved so much. He had not touched any ingredients for many months now and sometimes he was afraid he would forget what he had learned. It was however already ingrained in him and he could not lose it, this knowledge, but he did not know it yet.

He moved building materials from one place to another, and when they needed a group of men to complete a task, he became essential. But he did not know the English words. Most of the others did, but there was no one from his country here. Sometimes they would slowly explain to him the more difficult tasks, and every day it seemed, the work became more intricate. The father moved his head so they would think he had understood, but he did not understand one word. He began to sense that words were not necessary; he could learn by observation and then repeat what he saw. In his own country he had not been an expressive man. Even as a child he had only used words when absolutely necessary and people often thought he was mute or he was from another country or his mind was dull. But all of that did not matter; he had learned to cook and he had discovered the love of a woman who did not need him to be someone he was not.

The woman touched the man at the meat of his shoulder and, when he felt her, his body relaxed. It was not like coming home when they returned to the Excelsior; the strangeness of the place and noise of the people there discomfited them. A woman was crying behind the door of the room opposite theirs and they wondered, had she received some terrible news? Would she be returning to the place she had run away from? The hostel was a sanctuary, but it was also a place of sadness for many, and often it was only the children who gave it life.

'Tomorrow,' Emmanuel said to Ernesto, and he touched him lightly on the back and then ran to another floor of the building where he and his mother lived. He did not acknowledge the father and the mother. Alfredo turned so he could say goodbye to his brother's friend, but the boy was already gone. He could not understand how Emmanuel had spent the day with them and could then disappear without a word to him. He too wanted a friend, like the children he had played with in his own country.

'Why does he go so fast?' he asked. He felt the smart of Emmanuel's abruptness in his chest.

'He has his own mother,' the woman replied. 'Maybe he feels bad for leaving her all day.'

Alfredo thought about this, about how he would feel if he had left his mother alone in the hostel, and he understood his mother's words. He said, 'We will… When… When will we go to the glass hotel?' The words emerged so quickly from him in his agitation that they fell over one another.

'We will go one day,' the father said as they entered the room. 'You will see.' It was his secret plan to take his family to the hotel one weekend, when a person could eat a two-course meal at a special rate. He would work on the construction site until he was able to pay for things they needed, for the money he would send back home. Then they would spend the day at the glass hotel. Perhaps there would be a swimming pool for his sons. He touched the boy on his head so he would not feel bad about the place they were in, the unfriendly Emmanuel, the people they had left behind.

At night the father dreamed he was in his old kitchen, with the heat and flies and the cries of the chickens outside. The mother flew to the beach on their coast and noticed how the moonlight glinted off the waves. Ernesto dreamed of his school friends before they had been forced to scatter, before the fighting had begun. Only Alfredo remained in the new country in his sleep; he was in the glass hotel, in his own room.

The night moved on and then other dreams began, the ones of violence: of rebels and rape and cutlasses arcing through the air. The father began to shudder in his sleep, and then his wife woke. When she realised it was happening again, she reached out and petted him with her club, her smooth paw. She did not know that she was doing so; it was instinctive. Ordinarily she concealed the damaged limb. They had severed her hand in the conflict, but she could still feel the life of her fingers as she comforted her man. In the new country, they had offered her a place to go, for trauma, but she did not want that; she had her boys, her quiet husband. There was a way to function in the world when the world was devastating, everyone careless of each other and of themselves. She knew that now. She had been forced to learn. In a moment her husband was still again and she lay back with her eyes closed, but she did not sleep.

It was a simple thing, a misunderstanding, that caused the confusion the next day. The father travelled south, to the construction site. By the end of the week he was certain that he would have earned enough to send several packages home. But mid-morning the inspectors arrived.

The foreman took him aside. 'You have the correct papers?' he asked.

The father looked at him and nodded. He did not understand what was happening. He continued to work as the inspectors wandered around.

He could not see the other men from the hostel, but he would look for them soon so they could take their lunch break. It was colder today, but he had been working so hard that he had been forced to remove his sweater.

They came up the scaffolding, two men with their briefcases and the foreman beside them. From the corner of his eye the father could see the men from the hostel across the road. They were waving to him frantically. The inspectors approached another man and talked quietly with him. They stood where the ladder was situated. The father could not see another way down. He thought, I am in a place I do not understand. The ground is vanishing beneath me. He pictured the boy, his youngest, and he pushed away the fear. He ran to the edge of the platform and grasped the metal pole. He did not look down in case he faltered. He held the pole and allowed gravity to carry him, not knowing how it would end. His hands were cut and then his torso rubbed against the brackets. He remembered his sweater lying on the platform. He did not have the strength to manage a smooth descent and his shirt and trousers were torn, but he did not notice these things. His mind was on his folly. If he were caught he would jeopardise everything for his family and he did not know if he could live with himself after that.

He hobbled across the road where the others were waiting for him. He looked behind once to see if he was being followed, but no one was there.

'That was close,' one of the men called and clapped him on the shoulder. They all laughed, but he did not laugh with them. He only smiled. His hands and arms were aching and the blood had soiled his clothes.

When the mother saw him, she became very quiet. No one spoke. They only fussed around the wounds and the blood and torn clothing. Their fear was like a fist of bread they could not swallow. The youngest boy began to cry. His brother, Ernesto, was frightened, but excited too. He went and told his friend what had happened. It was like an adventure; the blood, the daring escape.

Emmanuel smirked; it only confirmed his thoughts. He said, 'He is stupid, your father.' He could not help himself. It was the way he was now. Angry. He did not know that he blamed his own father for dying, that it was a wound inside himself that would fail to heal.

Ernesto looked at him, disbelieving, and then he walked away. It was too much, the injured father, the distraught brother, the hurtful friend. Too

15

many things were happening at once and he could make no sense of it. When he returned to his room, his father was resting on his brother's cot. He saw him there, a man who was not slender, a man who hardly spoke. He began to wonder about Emmanuel's words. Was there any truth in them? A seed had been planted now.

Alfredo sat beside his father looking from the carpet to his mother, back to the carpet again. The mother's silence disturbed them all. She tidied the room and soaked the soiled clothes in the bath and seemed not to care about what happened. Even the father eyed her cautiously, but he did not say anything.

'God will help us,' the father whispered, so that only the youngest one heard.

The boy was quiet. At length he asked, 'Where is God, papa?' The father sighed and looked at his son. 'He is in the room. He is here with us, all around.' He lifted his arms and waved his fat finger to illustrate.

The boy looked around the room, but he did not understand. His brother followed his gaze, but he did not know what they were looking at.

'You are a chef, you are not a labourer!' the mother shouted. 'You cannot cook with your hands torn like this! Do you understand?' She had gone from silence to blind rage in an instant. She shook her fist, but held the arm where her hand had been severed tight against her stomach. She did not care if the other people heard through the thin walls. She was tired of holding everything in. 'How can we make a new life if you cannot work because you are injured? Did you think what would happen if they caught you with no papers, what would happen to us, the boys? We cannot go back to that place where they are killing us! Soon they will allow us to stay and you can do whatever job you like. But still you cannot wait. You are ready to risk everything.'

The boys looked from their wounded father to their mother as she stood over him. They took in the damp walls, the orange carpet with the kink by the bathroom door, the window that overlooked the street where the girls walked at night and people roared sometimes in their misery.

'I am going to see Emmanuel,' Alfredo said after no one had spoken in minutes. He closed the door quietly and ran through the corridor and down the stairs. He did not stop running when he came to the street or to a busy road where cars and buses clamoured. A tall man, wrapped in a soiled duvet, strode along the street peering into rubbish bins. Shrieking. Alfredo continued to run. He mingled with people as they waited for permission to cross the road. A woman moved away from him as if he were a street urchin. When he reached the other side he began to run again. He did not look behind for fear of seeing his father or his mother or anyone from the hostel. He ran and ran until he arrived at the hotel and when he was through its glass doors he stood still and breathed deeply.

He said he had been going to see Emmanuel, but ten minutes later, his friend knocked at the door looking for Ernesto. All the anger in the room vanished. They searched the lounge where the television was, and the breakfast room, the reception, but they could not find him. No one had seen him disappear. The mother was shaking and the other son was mute with anxiety.

'We must look outside. Alfredo!' the father called. 'He cannot go far from here. Where did he go? Alfredo!' He was bellowing now. He was not aware of the strength of his own voice. Ernesto looked at him, his eyes wide with trepidation.

The man at the reception desk said the staff would scour the hostel to make sure Alfredo was not hiding anywhere. 'Where could a little boy go?' he asked.

Emmanuel thought suddenly that he knew where he was. He said in English, 'Maybe he goes to the hotel,' and he pointed.

They did not know the boy was already in the elevator of the glass hotel, rising above the street, looking out at the city they had recently arrived in. There seemed to be nothing between him and the world outside except a thin sheet of glass. When he peered down at the retreating traffic he found he was not afraid. He came out on the top floor and approached the long corridor. He began to try the handles of all the rooms he passed. He was looking for his own room, but he knew he needed a key. He did not know whom to ask. A man opened a door he had tried and squinted at him and closed it quickly. Otherwise it was quiet. He saw no people. He was anxious now and tired and he did not know what to do.

A woman opened a door near the end of the corridor and a cloud of light fell across his path. She did not notice him. She removed some objects from a trolley and then re-entered the room. He came to the door for a moment, waiting for her, but he was very tired now. He sat on the carpet in the corridor, trying to remain alert, but his head hung down.

'Who are you?' the woman said to him.

He jerked his head up. He was not sure whether he had fallen asleep, whether time had passed – had she simply come out as soon as he had sat down? He looked at her, but he could not understand all the words she spoke.

'Are you lost?' she asked. 'Are you looking for someone?' She did not seem angry, but he did not know how to make her understand.

He said, 'The room,' with all the English he could muster, but he knew it was not enough.

The woman gazed at him and spoke some words in her own language and he was amazed he could understand her completely. He had thought his family were the only ones in this new place.

'Come,' she said. She pushed the door of the room she had been cleaning and showed him in: the wide bed so perfectly made, the large face of the television set, the gleaming marble in the bathroom. He walked to the window and knelt in a chair and looked out at the vast city. He could not hear the sounds of traffic far below, he could not see the river of people entering the railway stations, he could not see the lost ones shuffling to and fro on the street. He saw only rooftops and sunlight and all the space in the world between the earth and sky that seemed like emptiness, that was untouched and beautiful. He turned and climbed onto the bed. He did not worry about the woman or his mother and father or when he should return to the hostel. He was too tired for any of that. The boy slept. Again, he did not have bad dreams. He did not even dream of his own country. He saw the green grass in the park that Sunday afternoon, his mother's five fingers reaching for his face, his father and brother, even the angry friend, Emmanuel, sitting on the bed in the hotel room, looking for the face of God.

Segun Afolabi was born in Kaduna, Nigeria and grew up in various countries, including the Congo, Canada, East Germany and Indonesia.

Afolabi has been writing for over ten years and has had stories published in *Wasafiri, London Magazine, Edinburgh Review, Pretext* and others. A collection of short stories provisionally titled *A Life Elsewhere* is due out in spring 2006, and a novel, *Goodbye Lucille,* will be published in spring 2007. Both will be published by Jonathan Cape.

A graduate from University College, Cardiff, Afolabi has previously worked as an assistant content producer and sub-editor for the BBC.

Tropical Fish

Doreen Baingana

PETER ALWAYS PLOPPED DOWN heavily on top of me after he came, breathing short and fast, as if he had just swum across Lake Victoria. My worry that he was dying was quickly dispelled by his deep snores, moments after he rolled off me. I was left wondering exactly what I was doing there, in the middle of the night, next to a snoring white man. And why was it that men fell asleep so easily, so deeply, after huffing and puffing over you? There I was, awake, alone with my thoughts, loud-in-my-head and never ending, like a ghost train. Sex was like school, something I just did. I mean, of course I wanted to. I took myself there, no one forced me.

Peter was pink actually, not white, except for his hair, what was left of it. It had suddenly changed colour from the stress of his first rough years in Uganda trying to start his fish-export business. He was only thirty-five, but to me at twenty, that was ancient. When naked, though, he looked fourteen. He had an adolescent plumpness, a soft body, almost effeminate, with pale saggy legs. His skin felt just like mine. We met through Zac, a campus friend who also worked for Peter's company. Peter exported tropical fish bought from all over the country: Lake Victoria, Albert, Kyoga and River Nile. He paid next to nothing to the local fishermen, then sent the fish in tank loads to Britain for pet shops. Very good profits.

Zac and I were both at Makerere University, what used to be called 'the Harvard of Africa', south of the Sahara, not counting South Africa, which didn't leave much else. But that was back in the Sixties, before Big Daddy, Idi Amin, tried to kill off as many professors as he could. Most ran into exile, and the 'economic war' did the rest of the damage. But we didn't complain, we were lucky to be there.

I was drinking Waragi in Zac's room when Peter came in one evening. I liked Zac because he knew he wasn't going to become some big shot in life and so didn't even try. Apparently he supplied Peter with ganja. Because of my lifelong training to catch a suitable mate, when Peter walked in I found myself immediately turning on the sweet, simpering self I preserve for men. I recede into myself, behind an automatic, plastic-doll smile. Peter looked amused by the crabby room. He looked around like a wide-eyed tourist at the cracked and peeling paint, the single bare bulb, a tattered poster of Bob Marley on the wall, the long line of dog-eared Penguin Classics leaning sideways on Zac's desk, the untidy piles of handwritten class notes. Zac was finishing his B.A. in literature.

Zac got off his chair quickly and offered it to Peter. 'Hey, man.' Zac had convinced himself he was black American. We laughed at the nasal way he talked, the slang from videos, his crippled-leopard swagger, especially for someone so short. I kept telling him, 'Give up, Zac, no one's impressed,' but that was his way.

Peter refused the chair and gingerly settled onto Zac's single bed, which was covered with a thin brown blanket. The *muzungu* wanted to do the slumming right. I was sitting at the other end of the bed. Its tired springs creaked and created a deep hole in the middle as he sat down. I felt myself leaning over as if to fall into the hole, too close to Peter, into his warm personal space. I shifted away and sat up on the pillow, pulling my legs up into me. Did he think I didn't want to sit too close to him, a white man? There was a short, uncomfortable silence. But with the two men there, I didn't have to start the conversation.

Zac said, 'How about a drink, man? Peter, meet Christine, the beautifulest chick on campus.' He was trying to be suave, but it sounded more like mockery. I smiled like a fool.

Peter turned and smiled back at me. 'Nice to meet you, Christine.' No teeth showed, only the small, gray shadow of his mouth. I put a limp hand into his outstretched one. He squeezed it hard, like a punishment. His skin was hot. I murmured something back, still smiling about nothing, then took a large swallow from my drink, keeping my face in the glass.

Zac reached into a small dark cupboard. Inside were two red, oily-looking plastic plates, a green plastic mug, a dusty glass with two or three spoons and forks in it, a tin of salt, and another of Kimbo cooking fat. He took out the glass, removed the spoons and blew into it. With his finger, he rubbed off a dead insect's wing stuck to the inside. "I've got to wash this. I'll be right back," and he left me alone in the tiny, shadowless room, with Peter. It was my first time alone with a white person. There was a nervous, bare-bulbed silence.

With an obvious smirk, Peter turned to look around the shabby one-desk, one-chair, one-bed room. I wished I could open the window and let in the coolness of the night. But I didn't want to move, and mosquitoes would quickly drone in. It was raining lightly outside, pitter-patter on the glass, which made the small square lights of the next hall shimmer like a black and yellow curtain, far away and inaccessible. Whisks of white hair at the back of Peter's head stuck out unevenly over his collar. The light's shine moved the bare, pink hilltop of his head as he turned to me.

'So, do you go to school too?'

'Yes.' Soft and shallow.

'Yes? And what do you study, Christine?' Like a kind uncle to a five-year-old.

'Sociology.'

'Socioo-logy?' He stretched out the word and couldn't hide his amusement. 'That's quite impressive. You must be a very intelligent girl.' His smile was kind in an evilish, shadowed-mouth way. I smiled back, showing him that *I*, at least, had big bright teeth. There. I don't think he noticed.

Luckily Zac came back at that moment. I quickly swallowed the rest of my drink and left. In the warm, just-rained night, the wet grass and soaked ground smelt fertile. I dodged the puddles in the cracked pavement, which twinkled with reflected streetlamp light. Not that I really noticed, I was too busy beating myself inside. You smiling fool, why didn't you say something clever? Almost walking past my hall, I wondered why I was so unsettled, even intrigued.

That weekend, Zac told me Peter wanted us to visit him at his house in Tank Hill.

'Me? Why?'

'The *muzungu* likes you.' He chuckled shortly, dryly.

'Don't be silly. I'm not going.'

'Come one, we'll have fun. There'll be lots to drink, eat, videos too. Bring Miriam if you want.'

We went in the end, of course, because Peter lives on top of Tank Hill, one of Kampala's seven hills, like Rome. Up there, diplomats' huge mansions hide behind high cement walls lined across the top with shards of cutting glass. Rent is paid in dollars only. Swimming pools, security guards. And he wanted me. Nothing would happen if I went with Zac and

Miriam, my tall Tutsi friend, whom Peter would prefer anyway, I told myself. She had the kind of looks whites like: very thin, with high angular cheekbones and jaw, large slanting eyes. And she was so daring, did whatever she wanted with a bold stare and brash laugh. No simpering for her. She even smoked in public. So I was safe.

It was fun, sort of. Peter was overly attentive, serving drinks, plumping pillows, asking questions. We ate in courses, brought in by his houseboy Deogracias, an old man with crooked, spindly legs attached to big bare feet like boats. Black on bright pink. Deo spoke to us in Luganda, but not to Peter, of course. As if we were at his houseboy level. Later, I told Zac and Miriam I found Deo's familiarity vaguely offensive as if he was saying, I've seen your kind pass through this house before. They both laughed it off, 'Christine, you're too much. What's wrong with being friendly?'

Peter chose *Karate Kid* for us to watch, saying it was our type of movie. How would he know? I concentrated on gin-and-tonics. This was a whole world away from home, from school. The brightly painted, big-windowed house smelt of mosquito repellant from emerald rings smoking discreetly in every room. Bright batiks on clean white walls, shiny glass cupboards full of drinks and china. Everything worked: the phone, the hot water taps, a dustbin you clicked open with your foot. No need to touch. As soon as the power went off, a generator switched itself on automatically, with a reassuring low hum.

We turned off the lights to watch the movie, and Peter somehow snuggled up close to me. I pretended not to feel him, as I sank into the comfort of having all my needs satisfied. Nothing to worry about. The drinks eased me. When the movie was over, the lights stayed off. Peter prepared a joint and we all became giggly. Everything slowed down pleasantly. He moved back close to me and started stroking my trousered thigh up and down, up and down, gently, absentmindedly. It was soothing. I sat still. I didn't have to do anything.

Zac talked in a monotonous drone about the hidden treasures of Egypt, the esoteric wisdom that Aristotle stole, or was it Plato, and then the Egyptians forgot everything. Peter asked, 'Whey didn't they write it down?' and we all laughed for a very long time. Miriam got up and weaved around the room, holding her head, saying, 'I feel mellow. Very very mellow.' Over and over, giggling. Peter led her to his spare bedroom that was always ready, with clean sheets, soft lamps and its own multi-mirrored bathroom. He brought Zac a bedcover for the sofa, and then took me to his room as though it was the practical, natural thing to do. It felt sort of like a privilege. The Master Bedroom.

In the bathroom he got me a new toothbrush from a packet of about twenty, already opened. 'You have many visitors?' I wondered out loud. He laughed and kissed me on the mouth. 'Women?' I mumbled, as he ate up my lips. I thought about the wrapping: coloured blue plastic over the cardboard box, each toothbrush wrapped again in its own plastic, and lying in its own little cardboard coffin. I wanted to keep the box, but didn't dare ask. He would have laughed at me again.

I lay on the bed in my clothes. Peter took off his clothes and draped them neatly folded over a chair, pointing two small pale buttocks toward me as he leaned over. Then he took my blouse and pants off methodically, gently, like it was the best thing to do, like I was sick and he was a nurse, and I just lay there. In the same practical way he lay down and stroked me for a few appropriate minutes, put on a condom, opened my legs and stuck his penis in. I couldn't bring myself to hold him in any convincing way. I thought I should moan and groan and act feverish, overcome by a wild rage of some sort, like white people in movies. But I was feeling well-fed and well taken care of, a child full of warm milk. One thought was constant in my head like a newspaper headline: I am having sex with a white man. It was strange because it wasn't strange. He was done in a few minutes. He tucked me under his arm like an old habit, and we sank into sleep.

Peter became my comfortable habit. On Friday evenings I escaped from the usual round of campus parties to go to my old white man; my snug, private life. No one scrutinised me, questioned my motives or made any judgments, up on Tank Hill, except Deo. He was a silent, knowing, irritating reminder of the real, ordinary world, my place in it. But when Deo had cleared up the supper things and left to go scrub his huge, bare boat-feet with a stone, I was free to walk around the large, airy house naked, a gin-and-tonic melting in my hand. This made me feel floaty, a clean open hanky wandering in the wind. I didn't have to squash myself into clothes, pull in my stomach, tie my breasts up in a bra, worry about anything, be anything. Who cared what Peter thought? He said nonsensical things like, 'You're so many colors all over, how come?'

'What about your red neck?'

'That's 'coz I'm a redneck, luv.'

'I thought so.'

'Come here, you!' Our tussle ended up in bed.

My eldest sister, Dorothy, might have heard about Peter from someone. She was a born-again Christian, like I was once.

'Saved,' with too clear and rigid a sense of right and wrong. But she wouldn't say, 'Stop seeing that white man.'

Instead, she told me of a dream she'd had: that I was being given drugs by some white people.

'They only want to use you,' she said.

I didn't answer. What could I say, that it actually was okay? Her self-righteousness made me want to go right back to Peter's.

For some reason I told him Dorothy's dream. He laughed at me. I heard 'superstitious, ignorant blacks!' in his laugh. Maybe not, but like with most things between us, I wasn't going to try to explain it, what one can see or read in dreams. I don't mean that they're true. But we couldn't climb over that laugh to some sort of understanding. Or didn't want to try.

One weekend, Zac told me they had gone to the Entebbe Sailing Club with another girl, some young ignorant waitress, or something. 'Why are you telling me?' I scoffed. Didn't he think I knew Peter? I didn't like the sailing club anyway; it was practically white only because of the high membership fees and selective sponsorship rules. I became very black over there. Zac was surprised I didn't seem to care about other girls. Why squander feelings, I told myself. What was more annoying was Peter's choice of those waitress types.

Deogracias called him Mr Peter. I asked him, after two months or more, what his last name was. He said, 'Call me Mr Peter,' and chuckled. He enjoyed the lavishing of respect I knew he didn't get from anyone back home. Mr Smithson, I read on a letter of his. How ordinary. Whenever he whined about the insects everywhere, the terrible ice cream, and only one Chinese restaurant, I wanted to tell him I knew he was lower-class, Cockney, and doing much better here, practically stealing our fish, than he ever would in Britain. So he should just shut up. But of course I didn't. Our Lady of the Smiles and Open Body.

When Peter called one Friday evening, I was having my period. I felt I shouldn't go. What for? But I couldn't tell him that, not so bluntly. How could we openly admit that he wanted me for sex, and I knew it, and agreed? Over the phone, moreover? It was easier for me to say nothing, as usual. I took a taxi to his house, and he paid for it. Peter had already started on the evening's drinks with *muchamo*, roasted meat, on his verandah. A Danish man was visiting, one of the usual aid types, whom Peter had just met. These ex-pats quickly made friends with each other; being white was enough. They grouped together at Half-London, a collection of little shops lined along a dusty road at the bottom of Tank Hill. At each storefront, melting in the hazy heat, plastic chairs sat under gaudy red-and-white umbrellas advertising Coca-Cola and Sportsman cigarettes. *Ye Ssebo!* There was lots of beer-drinking and prostitute-hunting. A let's-pretend-we're-local hangout I avoided.

I put off telling Peter about my period, but felt guilty, for some reason. Finally, in bed with the lights off, he reached for me as usual, but I moved away a little. 'I'm having my period.'

'What?' I had never said no to him.

'You know… my period. I'm bleed–'

'Oh, I see. Well–' He lay back on the bed, a little put out. But he fell asleep pretty soon all the same. Instead of relief, I felt empty, a box of air.

That Christmas, Peter went off to Nairobi. He left very cheerfully, wearing a brightly flowered shirt, the sun glinting off his sparse white hair and pink baldness. The perfect picture of a retiree set for a cruise. He was off to enjoy the relative comforts of Kenya, the movie theatres, safari lodges, maybe Mombasa's beach resorts. He had sent off a good number of rare fish; it was time for a holiday.

In town, as Peter dropped me off, he kissed me on the mouth in the middle of Luwum Street, in front of the crowds, before breezing away. I was left in the bustling, dusty street, feeling the people's stares like the sun burning. Who was this girl being kissed in broad daylight by some old *muzungu*? Aa-haa, these *malayas* are becoming too bold. Couldn't she find a younger one at the Sheraton? One man shouted to Peter, for the crowd, in Luganda, 'She's going to give you AIDS. Look how thin she is!' Everyone laughed. Another one answered, 'It's their fault, these *bazungu*, they like their women thin. Let them fall sick.' General laughter.

I walked down to the taxi park, ignoring them. A girl like me didn't spend her time in the streets arguing with *bayaye*. I had better things to do. Over Christmas I didn't, but he would come back. Call me when he needed me, and I would escape to the big white house, the gin-and-tonic life, my holiday. Well, campus too was a kind of holiday before real life ahead of me: work, if I could get it, at a government job that didn't pay, in a dusty old colonial-style office, shoes with fish soles, a roasted maize cob for lunch, debts, kids, becoming my parents. One option was marriage to someone from the right family, the right tribe, right pocket-book and pot-belly, to have him pay the bills. With my degree I would be worth exotic cows, Friesians or Jerseys, not the common long-horned Ankole cattle. But I didn't have to think about that for two more years. For now, I had my game: being someone else, or no one, for a few hours.

Peter brought me bubble-bath soap from Nairobi because I said I'd never used it before. He prepared the bath for me. Water gushed out of both taps forever. Abundance, the luxury of wasting. If you've never fetched water, known how heavy the jerrycans can be, how each drop is precious, you can't really enjoy a bubble-bath. To luxuriate in a whole bathtub of water, just for you. The lovely, warm green froth a caress all over.

Peter undressed and joined me, his penis curled up shyly in his red pubic hair. He spread my thighs gently and played with my lips. I closed my eyes, shutting out everything but his careful, practiced touch. Sank, sank, into the pleasure of it. The warm water flopped around, splashing out onto the white bath mat and shiny mirrors. Peter crept up over me and entered slowly, and I thought, maybe I do care for him, maybe this is all that love is. A tender, comfortable, easing into me.

I found out I was pregnant. We used condoms most of the time. I didn't say anything when we didn't. My breasts started to swell, and my heart grew suspicious, as though my belly had secretly passed on the message. When my period was more than twelve days late, I told Miriam. I couldn't tell Peter. It didn't seem to be his problem, not a part of our silent sex-pact. This was personal. Miriam's sister Margaret, a nurse, worked at a private clinic in the city. Nobody stopped me, they all knew it had to be done. I tried not to think about it. At the clinic, the anaethetist droned at me in a deep kind voice as he injected me. When I wouldn't go under quickly, he asked, with a knowing half-smile, if I drank a lot. I was going to remain conscious but wouldn't feel anything, he said. Just like real life. The doctor was cream-gloved, efficient, and kind, like Peter. I fell into pleasant dreaminess. Why did I always seem to have my legs spread open before kind men poking things into me? I let them.

At the clinic, I read an article about all the species of fish that are disappearing from our fresh water lakes and rivers because of the Nile Perch. It was introduced by the colonial government Fisheries Development Department in the fifties. The Nile Perch is ugly and tasteless, but it's huge, and provides a lot more food for the populace. It was eating up all the smaller, rarer, gloriously coloured tropical fish. Many of these rare species were not named, let alone discovered, before they disappeared. Every day, somewhere deep and blue, it was too late.

Margaret gave me antibiotics and about two years' supply of the pill, saying curtly, 'I hope we don't see you here again.' I was rather worried, though, because the doctor said I shouldn't have sex for at least two weeks. What would I tell Peter when he called? Maybe I should say what happened. Now that I had dealt with the problem, I wasn't bothering him with it. I just wanted to tell him.

I went to Peter's office without calling, not knowing what to say. It was on Barclay Street, where all the major airline and cargo offices were, convenient for business. It was surprising how different Peter was at work: his serious twin, totally sober, a rare sight for me. He got authority from somewhere and turned into the boss, no longer the drunken lover. Once, at night, he told me how worried he was because all the workers depended on him – what if he failed? This talk, the concern, made me uncomfortable. This wasn't my picture of him.

The first time Peter took me to his office, on my way back to school, an Indian businessman came in to see him. The Asians were coming back, fifteen years after Amin gave them seventy-two hours to pack up and leave the country. They were tentatively re-establishing themselves, which didn't please the Ugandan business class too much.

Peter led the short, bustling, black-turbaned man into his back office, where I was sitting. The Indian glanced my way and back at Peter, summing up the situation. After a curt, 'How are you?' he dismissed me and turned to business. Jagjit had come to sell Peter dollars, which was illegal except through the Bank of Uganda, but everyone did it anyway, by *magendo*. He produced a thick envelope and drew out old, tattered green notes. Peter checked each one carefully, rubbed it between his palms, held it up under the light, turned it over, and scrutinised it again until he was satisfied. There was one note he put aside, then went back to after checking them all. He said, 'Sorry Jagjit, this one's no good.' It was a $100 bill. That was about 1,000,000 shillings.

'No, no that can't be. I got this from Sunjab Patel – you know him – over in Industrial Area.' Very fast, impatient.

'Yeah, but *I'm* telling you it's not worth anything. Look here–' and they compared it to another, straining their necks from note to note. Finally, Peter picked up the false note, and with his usual smirk, slowly tore it in two, his eyes steadily watching Jagjit's face. He was too shocked to protest, his large brown eyes fixed on the half-notes in each of Peter's raised hands. Peter held the torn pieces over the dustbin and let them float down slowly into it. All of us watching. 'You've got to be careful. *Anyone* can cheat you around here,' he said, and shrugged.

Peter turned to his safe, snug in a corner, and pulled out a canvas bag, which he emptied onto the table. Jagjit counted the many bundles of weary-looking notes. He was flustered; whether embarrassed or annoyed, I couldn't tell. Out he rushed, after one last look at the torn note, as if he wanted to grab it from the rubbish. Poor him, I thought, but then again, he deserved it for giving me the once over and deciding I didn't count.

Peter shook his head slowly. 'The bastard.'

'I don't think he knew.'

Peter reached over and took the half notes from the dustbin, patted them off, and laid them together on the table.

'Peter!'

He smiled to himself, then looked up. 'What if I gave it to you?'

'What!? What would *I* do with it?'

'My little Christian Christine,' and he chuckled some more.

This time, Peter was busy with a group of men who were loading a pickup parked on the street. I was startled again by the way he was at work: stern and controlling, giving direction in a loud voice, striding up and down. Then he saw me.

'What are you doing here?' Brusque and impatient.

'I was just passing by.' I felt horribly in the way.

'Okay, okay. Wait.'

He waved me on into his back office. After a short while he followed. But, somehow, I couldn't say it, so I asked him for a piece of paper and biro, which made him even more exasperated. I wrote down, 'I have just had an abortion.'

Peter took the paper, smiling impatiently, thinking I was playing a childish game. His usual smile got stuck for an instant. A hint of what looked like anger flickered across his boyish face. He didn't look up at me. He took the biro from me, wrote something down, and passed the note back across the table. It read, 'Do you want some money?'

I read it, glanced up at him quickly, then away, embarrassed. Back to his five little words. I shook my head no, my face lowered away from him. No, not money. I had nothing to say, and he said nothing back. After a bleak silence, like the silence while we made love, far away from each other, I got up to leave.

'I'll call you, okay?' Always kind.

'Okay.' Always agreeing. Yes, okay, yes.

The men working for him moved out of my way in that over-respectful way they treat whites, but with a mocking exaggeration acted out for their black women. As usual, I ignored them, but shrank inside as Peter kissed me dryly on the lips, in front of them all, before I left.

The street was hard and hot. Filled with people walking through their lives so purposefully, up and down the street, so in control. But they seemed to be backing away from me. Did I look strange? Was there blood on my dress? The hot, dusty air blown up by the noisy, rushing traffic filled my head like thunder.

Did I want money? What did I want? Bubble baths, gin-and-tonics, ganja sex, the clean, airy white house where I could forget the hot dust outside, school, my all-too-ordinary life, the bleak future? A few hours free from myself. Was that so bad? Had I wanted *him* to care, of all people? He was trying to be kind, I supposed. I'm sure the only Africans he knew needed money. Six months of sex, and did I want money? What did we want from each other? Not a baby, obviously. Nothing that permanent. Our baby. What a joke. I discarded my baby like I did my body, down a pit latrine crawling with cockroaches.

I waded through the taxi-park bedlam into a *matatu*, and was squashed up on all sides by strangely comforting fat hips, warm arms, moist breaths. The old engine roared to a start, blocking out the radio's loud wail of *Soukous*. The driver revved the engine repeatedly to get passengers to come running, as if we were leaving right away, only to sit for another fifteen minutes. The conductor screamed for more people, ordering us to move over, squash up. We all wanted to get home, didn't we? Hawkers pushed cheap plastic into our faces through the windows, their spit landing on our cheeks. The voice of one of them pierced through the noise, pleading insistently for me, me, to buy some Orbit chewing gum for my young children at home. 'Aunty, remember the children, be nice to the children!'

We finally moved away, swaying and bumping up and down together with each dive in and out of potholes, each swerve to avoid the oncoming cars that headed straight toward us like life. I closed my eyes, willing the noise and heat to recede to the very back of my mind. The glaring sun hit us all.

Doreen Baingana's short story collection, *Tropical Fish: Stories out of Entebbe,* was published in February 2005 as the winner of the Associated Writers and Writing Programmes Award in Short Fiction in 2003. Doreen also won the Washington Independent Writers Fiction Prize in 2004.

She was a Writer-in-Residence at the University of Maryland, College Park. Doreen has an MFA from the same university, teaches at the Writers Centre in Bethesda, Maryland and works part-time at Voice of America Radio. She was born in Uganda.

This story was originally published by Harlem Moon and is reproduced here with permission.

The Obituary Tango

Jamal Mahjoub

WAIT A MINUTE, LET ME FINISH what I was saying before I lose track of my thoughts. No, it has nothing to do with growing old. Salwa said the same thing to me years ago, when the children were barely walking and she was suffering the way all women suffer when they start to lose their looks: 'You never finish your sentences. You never say what you set out to say.' Of course she was right then and she would still be right now, if I had not divorced her. I would be the first to admit it. I blame the age we live in. Who has the time these days to finish anything, I ask you? It's like a disease. I mean a condition that everyone suffers from but no one talks about. Your thoughts skip from one subject to another so lightly that you barely realise. Like a bird pecking at seeds scattered on the ground, here there, everywhere. Before you know it you have to tell the entire history of the world, the discovery of America, the invention of the lightbulb, who built the pyramids, just to get to the end of the story you are trying to tell. Which, by the way, I now hear the Arabs are claiming, typical of them. No, not the lightbulb, the discovery of America. They claim everything for themselves as though nothing could ever be achieved by anyone else. Imagine if it was proved that actually it was the Jews who did it? Where would that leave us? The point is that everything changes, even the hard facts of history. The things we were taught in school, what we used to take for granted, no longer hold.

Okay, so let me get on with it then. I had to take a taxi because I was late and getting to the airport in this city is like training for the army. I mean the running up and down stairs, the suitcases, no one to help you. People half, a third of my age are struggling. They have heart attacks younger and younger, and no wonder. They rush about red faced with huge sacks strapped to their backs like cockroaches fleeing a kitchen that has just been sprayed. Why the airport? My daughter's wedding. She finally decided to make her parents happy and marry someone who is as least vaguely from our part of the world. No Catholics, Protestants, or Jews, heaven forbid, she got over that in her rebellious phase. So, I should be pleased, but the fact of the matter is that I am worried. I mean, Yemen? Do I really want my grandchildren to grow up with a father who lounges about all day chewing cud like a goat? This is genetic. My son, Abdin, you remember him? He tells me they can't help it. It is in their genes. I don't care which part of their anatomy it is in, frankly, I'm against it. But what to do?

She says she is happy. Love. These things are out of our hands. Try to interfere and see where it gets you. Remember Mustapha Medood, whose son stabbed an English boy for seeing his sister. They had an old Hadendowa sword hanging on the wall, for decoration. Tourists buy them. They look quaint. So he pulled this dagger from the sheath. Sword, dagger, what's the difference? It went straight through that poor boy's heart. He died before the ambulance arrived. Things being how they are in this country, it is not a place to have accidents with swords. The lawyer was very good. He pleaded temporary insanity. I hear the son is living in the States now. Boston, or New Jersey or somewhere. Blood. That's what comes from trying to interfere. No, I can live with the grass chewing, thank you.

Where was I? The airport? Not so fast. First I call a minicab. You know how hard it is to find a real taxi. When they see one of us standing in the street they go strangely blind. And besides, they charge too much. I call this company which is run by Somalis, or maybe they are Nigerians. Gangsters in any case. I say I need a car to take me from SW19 to Heathrow and they take ten minutes to check the price. I can hear wailing Bedouin music in the background. These people are tribal. No matter where you set them down on Allah's earth they squat like they never left the dustbowl they came from. As if the airport were a destination they had never heard of. Finally they decide they can take me. I am honoured. I don't tell them this because they get upset easily and think nothing of throwing the phone down on you, customer or no customer. You have to agree on the price beforehand otherwise the drivers hold you to ransom on a lonely road. It's so much like being back home.

Anyway, the car arrives and I look at the driver and see it is one of their Africans. Tell me what it is with these English people that they won't

work any more? None of them. Don't get me wrong. I don't mind being
driven by an African, except that they get lost all the time. They nod, yes
mate, and off you go. They drive you halfway to the sea before turning
around and asking if you have any idea where you are. The thing about
Africans is that they never admit they are wrong. Never. You remember
Shahin Tawil? The one who was in that scandal years ago. You remember,
he was selling arms export licences to the Argentinians who were using
them to fire Exocet missiles at the Royal Navy. I know it was a long time
ago, but the stain of the episode never left him. What else do you
remember about him? I ask you. He had a miserable little place in North
London somewhere. He drank heavily, and he used to visit English
prostitutes. A very unwholesome man altogether. He was actually beaten
half to death by one of these drivers. Why? He asked that same question,
believe me. These people drive all day, their nerves are taut like the strings
of a *kamanga*. One snaps and they attack, like those dogs the Nazis had. I
have no doubt that Tawil was drunk, of course, but still. A driver has
responsibilities. Tawil had to flee for his life. He ran through the streets
screaming for help. This is London. You think anyone stopped to help?
Would you? One drunken African being chased by another? People
stepped out of their way. This one might have been a Sikh now that I
think about it, but turban or not, none of them can find their way. So I
was not overjoyed to see this man sitting in the driving seat. And besides,
they don't like us. They may come from the same continent, but they take
one look and say to themselves, 'Arab, Muslim.' They watch television like
everyone else. They see planes crashing into high buildings, women being
stoned to death, suicide bombers blowing themselves into tiny fragments
in the back of their Ford Mondeos. One of them accused me of being a
slave trader. You took my ancestors! he screamed at me. All because I
wouldn't let him keep the change. I mean, a five pound tip? He jumped
from the car. He had gold teeth, an enormous ring through his nose and
dreadlocks like black mambas shaking in my face. Leaping up and down
in the street like a dervish. I doubt he could even recognise his ancestors
if they were lying underneath his wheels.

Still, I thought, finding Heathrow airport could not be that difficult. As
we are driving along I began to notice something about this man. Firstly,
it was his accent. You know it's an instinctive thing with us. We recognise
one another instantly. My son could tell you something about genetics, but
that boy's life is like one of those South American melodramas they play in
the afternoon. Salwa became addicted to them years ago when she heard

they were all about sex. She and I stopped having relations after the children were born, well almost. What is the point, she used to say, you lie on top of me but you dream of other women. I gave you your children. If you want more, find yourself another wife. I took her advice, of course. That's what television does to a woman's head. She wanted romance. I ask you. A woman in her forties with two children. Romance? The point is that my son, ever since he dropped out of university with nothing in sight, no plan, no ambition beyond spending his father's hard-earned money, does nothing but accumulate the names of women in his address book. I cannot begin to imagine how many bastard grandchildren I might have spread across the south west of England. Years of expensive private tuition, grammar schools and so forth because the boy could not find out which end of the book is which without help. Now all he does is watch television all day. Claims that he learns more from that apparatus, lying on his back, than he ever did in university. You could have saved all that money, he laughs in my face, lighting one cigarette from another.

Genetics, tribal instinct, whatever. As we drive I become aware that there is something familiar about the driver's accent. Not only the accent. I sit forward to get a better look at his face. I speak to him in Arabic. He looks at me in the mirror. I'm sure I know you, I tell him. We were at school together. Years ago and far away. He shakes his head, but I am certain. I am thrown by the fact of seeing him in this environment. Behind the wheel of an unmarked minicab is the last place I expected to find this man. I notice other things. His clothes are shabby. He needs a haircut. His face has lost its shape somewhat. Also, he drives with the ease of a man who does not know the meaning of hurry. Timetables, appointments, flight departures, closing gates, none of it means the slightest thing to him. I watch the vehicles passing us by left and right, sounding their horns, raising their fingers in obscene gestures. We seem to be trapped in a bubble, sinking slowly. I am barely aware of all this though, because I realise that I am in the company of a piece of living history; my history.

Beshir Awadallah Yusif. El Haj. This man was a hero to us, we looked up to him. He wasn't even that much older than I was, five, six years, maybe, no more. Enough to make an impression at that age. He was a hard worker, of course, diligent, dedicated, and smarter than most people in that school, including the teachers. He read all the time, night and day. We were poor in those days, all of us. I used to live a few streets away from him. We had toilets that were buckets. A hole in the ground. A man would come every evening to empty it. My own children laugh when I tell them this.

But it makes a difference. These things are what form you as a person. My kids can have whatever they want, all they have to do is ask, but the truth is they don't have anything of substance, you understand? I don't envy them growing up in a world like this. What is there to hold on to? El Haj, we called him that because he seemed old beyond his years, he would be there every evening sitting outside under the streetlights to read. They couldn't afford to have the lights on in the house. Most houses had one, maybe two bulbs, but it cost money to replace them so they remained dark most of the time. Who read in the evening? Most people were unable to read in broad daylight. Everyone respected him. Eccentric fellow, had his own sense of style. He used to wear a hat. Nobody wore hats. This was a real hat. It was one of those like a golf player wears, with a fluffy thing on top. Someone must have given it to him. Do you remember the hat? I asked him, and he smiled at me in the mirror. He remembered the hat.

I was humbled. The whole world fell away, the fancy suit I was wearing, the airline tickets clutched in my hands. I felt none of it. Do you have any idea what the chances are of us meeting like this, in a taxi, thousands of miles from where we were born? Our lives have passed by, governments have risen, dictators have fallen and here we are. Not a very high probability, he agreed. Probability. I couldn't even spell a word like that. I forgot all about my daughter's wedding, the herder she had decided to throw her life away for, my worries about my son, my own health problems. All such thoughts left me. It was as if I were on top of a very high mountain, looking out over my entire life.

You see, I realised early on that I would never get very far with those books. I left school and went straight to work. I lifted myself up. I did it the hard way. No, I don't regret a thing. You are forgetting that I can remember what it was like when we had nothing. I remember the stink of rotten water thrown in the streets, that grey colour of death. I took chances. I spied opportunities it would have been foolish of me to ignore. I made a life for myself and a lot of people have benefited from that.

I envied him. I can admit that now. I never used to be able to, but nowadays who cares? He is driving me to the airport in a car that he rents from a nomad gangster. He, the great wise man of our new age. He went to university. He went abroad. He lectured to audiences all over the world. They sat quietly and listened to this man who used to squat over a bucket and read by the stars when the power went. He rose to great heights. His name was in the papers. I saw him on television once and barely recognised him. Big hair and a colourful shirt like he had just stepped from behind a burning bush. He was being photographed on the White House lawn shaking hands with presidents, and now here he was driving an unmarked minicab through streets he did not know. Of course he had opportunities. He must have had, rubbing shoulders with the rich and famous. But he would have said no. A man of principle. I felt elated and terribly sad. In the back of my mind, I realised, I had somehow always relied on him being there, putting the world right, you see? But look, everything changes. If you don't move with it you get left behind, like one of those insects they find trapped in stone. I was saying this to my neighbour, who by the way is not from here at all, I don't know where he is from, I can hardly understand a word he says. I said to him that when I was a young man Russia stood for something. I don't know what we were talking about. I said, they were powerful. They had missiles and a huge army and everyone was terrified of them. The great Russian bear. Those Volga cars that roared along like furious giant beetles. El Haj used to be a communist, I was sure. Everyone was in those days, the political ones. The Soviets were our only hope, he explained. The Americans were backing the Israelis, bombing Vietnam. They assassinated Lumumba. They should never have gone into Afghanistan, he said. That was the key to their downfall. They charged in as the mighty Soviet Union and they came crawling out as caviar peddlers and whores. This was precisely my point. Today Russian women are spreading their legs, excuse me, all across the planet. The smart ones get themselves set up as wives over here, though I've heard that these are the ones too ugly to make it as whores. They have it all organised. They send you a picture of a nineteen-year-old beauty – wonderful. Your spirits rise just to gaze upon a healthy woman like that. And the thought of having all that sweetness in bed next to you each night is enough for many a lonely man to sign away their lives, which is exactly what happened to our friend Ragab. You remember him? He was so happy. For three months he was floating on clouds. Then they sent him a woman who would make that door look beautiful. She was so big he had to buy a new bed. She terrified him. He was physically scared of her. She kept insisting that he send money here, there and everywhere. Her mother was ill, her sister had just had a baby who was sick, etc. In the end, he said there was an entire village living off the wages of one poor African professor at a small English university.

The great dream had been eclipsed. El Haj's visions for the African continent had come down to 'sell everything, even your grandmother'. What did it all mean? You know, I am a religious man. No, seriously, not a drop has passed my lips in more than a year. Not since the by-pass operation. Did I tell you about the pilgrimage? What a mess. I thought I would die in the crush. Loss of dignity is part of the experience I was told. Try telling that to my children. 'Religion is fear,' my son says. Where did you learn that, I asked, watching naked women on television? No, he says, if there was an almighty God then he should be able to tell the difference between someone who is pure at heart and a fat hypocrite who gets on his knees because he is feeling old and mortal and regrets a lifetime of sinful behaviour. I love him, but if he wasn't my son I would have his liver ripped out through his throat with a fishhook.

We played by their rules, El Haj said. That was our mistake. Back when we had a chance to change things we played by their rules. We wanted what they had. We wanted Regents Street and Piccadilly Circus. We wanted Oxford and Cambridge. We wanted Westminster. Instead of thinking for ourselves. Nowadays, he said, no one even remembers that there was such a thing as a colonial period. The English today are tired of hearing what their forefathers did. And besides, they say, look what happens when you are left to your own devices.

He was confessing that he had become irrelevant. No one was interested in his ideas anymore. Time had passed him by. Not even the English, who had educated and trained him. They had experts of their own, he said, who told them what they wanted to hear. And it was true that we had seen our fair share of lunatics, bloodthirsty despots building palaces in the sand, gold taps in the bathroom when most of them had grown up without knowing what flowing water was.

I felt uncomfortable with this turn in the conversation. After all, he might accuse me of having played a part in this disaster. Still, it was a joy to hear him talk. It brought back so many memories. Of Salwa when she was young, when the children were small and used to play in the sunshine and seemed infused with hope. They would grow up so strong and take care of us when we were old. But life is an awkward bitch, excuse me, never goes where you want it to, never gives you what you ask for, always wants more.

When we get to the airport he refuses to take my money. Pride. The great weakness of our people. We all want to give. Why is that? I'll tell you, because it leaves a door open for fate. Better to live in hope that some day you might receive something in return than to take the money now. This is our greatest flaw, what holds us back. Step aside in this world and someone else will step up. I expected this, which is why I stuffed the money down the back of the seat as I got out. I know, someone else might have found it, but you want me to go through life feeling I am in debt to this man? I couldn't, I couldn't bear it, and besides, I don't know quite how to explain this, but all the time I was with him I had the feeling that he had given up, expected nothing from life. He wasn't playing the game, you know how some people do. No no no, I could never, etc., etc., and then whoops it disappears into their wallet faster than you could swat a fly. No, he was being sincere. He had given up. I don't think he even thought he would live long enough to spend it. I tell you, I had the feeling I was talking to a dead man. As the car was driving off I said to myself that is the last time I shall ever set eyes on that man. The whole time it was like someone else was with us in the car. Then I realised what it was about our conversation. It was like that dance. You know the one? Very famous. I can't remember what it is called. Spanish. The dance is a prelude, usually to sex. In this case it would have been to death. I think also he felt grateful to me. In a way, you see, I gave him the chance to speak out, to summarise the entire course of his life, they way they do in the papers when someone famous dies, only in his case no one will even know he is dead.

So I ran into the airport thanking the Lord for my good fortune, for the fact that I never had my head filled with high ideas about making something of myself. I felt young, elated, I felt like jumping into the air and shouting. I wanted to hug my son and tell him to stay by the television, that sooner or later he would get the urge to go out and earn some money and that he would probably have a stroke of luck, like me with those first aircraft contracts. Who needs an education? Where does it get you? We live in an illiterate world. No one cares any more. Books? What for? The leader of the most powerful nation on earth cannot spell. This is our time, the small people. I thanked the Lord for all of these things. I thanked Allah for the fact that I had my health, that my daughter was to marry a man in the oil business. Did I tell you he got a Christmas card from that man Cheney? No, he's not a Christian, I'm sure of it. It's just something they do, you know, out of courtesy. They send them to all their employees. Chinese, Buddhists, Hindus. It's what they call that thing, globalisation. I tell you, I don't care if he is the leader of a herd of hill goats, just so long as he doesn't get any big ideas about changing the world because that, my friend, is the end, believe you me.

Jamal Mahjoub was born in London, where his father was stationed at the Sudanese cultural centre. He spent his formative years in Khartoum, Sudan, before being awarded a scholarship to Atlantic College in Wales. He went on to study geology at Sheffield University in England. He returned briefly to the Sudan in search of employment, after which he decided to dedicate himself to writing. Since then, he has lived in a number of places, including London, Denmark and currently Spain, as well as extensive periods in France. Mahjoub has worked in a variety of sectors to support his writing, including telemarketing, catering and futon-making and has also worked as a librarian, freelance journalist and translator.

Mahjoub's first three novels were published in the Heinemann African Writers Series. The main subject of Mahjoub's novels is his relationship to the Sudan, as a migrant with mixed parentage. His first novel, *Navigation of a Rainmaker* (1989), relates the journey of a young man returning to the Sudan from Britain in order to claim his heritage, but it is the height of the famine and the traveller begins to see himself as the embodiment of the same malaise that is gripping Africa. *Wings of Dust* (1994) was followed by *In the Hour of Signs* (1996), which deals with the Mahdist movement in the nineteenth century and the birth of the modern Sudan, and *The Carrier* (1998). *Travelling with Djinns* (Chatto & Windus 2003) won the Prix de l'Astrolabe award in France in 2004. The short story 'The Cartographer's Angel' won the Heinemann/Guardian African Short Story Prize in 1993. His most recent work is *The Drift Latitudes* (Chatto & Windus 2006).

Jail Birds

Muthal Naidoo

GAVAZA IS BUSY MOPPING AND CLEANING the cell for a new prisoner, one of these political detainees. *They don't put them in with the others. They keep them by themselves. Each one gets a cell, like in a hotel. Since they released Mandela in February, the jail is filling up with teachers and students. They have nothing to do, so they just make trouble.* Gavaza looks around the gloomy cell painted dark grey, with an open toilet cubicle and a drinking fountain next to the low wall. *They will bring a bed in here. Political prisoners are too good to sleep on the floor. Now I have to look after this one, the first woman to come here. Hai, extra work for me. Why do these people want to fight the government? They should keep quiet and mind their own business. Now I have to keep my eyes on this woman, make her clean the cell, make the bed and not do anything funny. Watch her in the shower; see if she's hiding anything in her bum.*

Simon, one of the warders, calls and Gavaza goes into the charge office. Two white security policemen are there with the woman, small and skinny with grey hair. Gavaza wants to laugh. *What is this old coolie doing here? How did she get involved in all this political nonsense in a bantustan? So old and wearing shorts, hau, hau, hau! She is sitting there very quiet but she doesn't look frightened.* One of the security policemen shouts at Gavaza, 'Search her bag. Look for papers and bring them to me.' Gavaza looks at the cheap suitcase on the bench near the door and then begins to go through it. She sees a box of tissues. She goes through the tissues very carefully. She looks up and sees the woman watching her. There is nothing here. She turns over the clothes, looks through a book and blank foolscap sheets that are inside one of the shirts; looks through the rest of the clothes and can find no papers so she closes the bag. The security policemen, who have been

41

talking to Mrs van Zyl, supervisor of the female section, notice that she has finished and one of them orders Simon to lock up the detainee. Mrs van Zyl, Gavaza and Simon accompany her to her cell. Gavaza wants to laugh again. How can this small gogo be so dangerous? Even I can kill her like a cockroach. In the cell, Mrs van Zyl sees that there is no bed and orders Simon to bring one in immediately.

When Gavaza returns with the woman's supper at five o'clock, she sees that the bed is in and the old coolie is sitting on it. She has put her bag on the built-in seat and the sleeping mat is on the floor alongside the bed. Gavaza gives the woman her supper: six thick slices of brown bread, two big fat sausages, half a tomato and a mug of coffee. When Gavaza comes back to collect the plate and mug, she sees that the coffee mug is empty and half a slice of bread and the tomato have been eaten. The sausages have not been touched. She is shocked. *What's wrong with this woman? Simon told her that security picked her early in the morning and she hasn't eaten all day. And now to leave all this food on her plate! She thinks she's too good, eh? All right, she can starve then.*

When Gavaza takes the food back to the kitchen, the supervisor becomes worried. 'Why didn't she eat?' Gavaza simply shrugs. She can't understand why her supervisor is making such a fuss. So what if the stupid woman didn't eat? But Mrs van Zyl is going on about hunger strikes and inquiries into prison conditions and all sorts of rubbish like that. *I should have quietly put all that food in a bag and taken it home. That's what I'll do next time.* After her chores, Gavaza goes out to hitch a lift back to the village. When she gets home, just after 7 pm, she has to cook for the next day. She has a family to feed. She's up by four in the morning, and by 5 am out on the road hitching again. It takes at least two hours to get to work. She is at the prison by 7 am. She goes to wake the woman and orders her to make her bed. She loses her patience when she sees how the woman is doing it and shows her the right way. At first the woman resists and then she laughs and gives in.

When Gavaza brings the broom, the woman stands to the one side so Gavaza can sweep. *Who does she think she is? She's the one in jail.* Gavaza pushes the broom at her. 'You sweep!' The woman looks a little confused and then takes the broom and sweeps. Gavaza is surprised to see that she can handle a broom. Then she tells the woman to go out into the yard to wash. The detainee sticks out her hand and says, 'My name is Lutchmee.' Gavaza backs away, stares at the hand and tells her not to waste time. *This woman has no respect. I am a police matron. They should give us uniforms. Not*

42

these overalls. She watches as Lutchmee brushes her teeth. The water is boiling hot and she can scarcely rinse her mouth. She asks for a plug for the sink and Gavaza tells her to use the wrapping from the soap to block the hole. Then the woman washes the clothes she has been wearing. To shower, she pushes the button on the wall and the water shoots out from the built-in spout in a short boiling jet. She has to keep her hand on the button if she wants a continuous spray. But the water is boiling hot. Gavaza laughs to herself as she watches the woman trying to run through the spurts. After she has showered, Gavaza sends her back into the cell and goes to help with the prison breakfasts.

In the kitchen, she finds Mrs van Zyl fussing about what to feed the woman. She puts together a plate of porridge and coffee. *Just like in a hotel! These troublemakers get special treatment but people like her who work and do everything they are told are treated like dogs.* She takes the prisoner her breakfast and when she goes back for the plate finds that she has not eaten the porridge. 'I can't eat this porridge. The milk or something has gone off.' Gavaza smells the plate and wrinkles her nose. Again the woman offers to shake hands and repeats her name, Lunchy or something. Hey, these coolies have funny names. *Doesn't she know she must respect me? I am in charge of her.* She gives Lunchy a contemptuous look, collects the plate and mug and goes off to the kitchen.

Mrs van Zyl throws up her hands. The woman is not eating. She will have to report it to the station commander. Gavaza can't understand the fuss. Lunchy was toyi-toying against the government, now why are these Afrikaners so worried about her? They should be glad if she kills herself. But this is not her problem. At lunchtime, the plate comes back again almost untouched. Mrs van Zyl sends for De Lange, the station commander, and Gavaza hears them talking. The station commander complains about having to cater for people with different backgrounds. What does the woman expect? That they should start cooking curries?

Later that day, friends bring a whole lot of supplies for the woman, biscuits, chocolates, juices and a bag of wool. De Lange is so pleased that he picks up the supplies himself and marches off to Lunchy's cell. One of Lunchy's friends, a tall white woman, demands to see Lunchy and even though they all tell her she is not allowed, she pushes her way through and Gavaza has to run after her to try to stop her but the woman storms into the cell right behind De Lange. The kommandant is taken aback and stands open mouthed. Lunchy is glad to see her friend and gives her a big hug. It's funny to see this short black woman embracing this big white woman. As her eyes inspect the cell, the friend tells Lunchy that they have brought her embroidery and Lunchy smiles with gratitude and pleasure. Gavaza is waiting to see what De Lange will do. She is afraid he is going to blame her. But he is just staring at the intruder and motioning her out. Then De Lange finds his voice and tells the white missus she must leave but the missus is very cheeky and the kommandant almost pushes her out. When they have gone, Lunchy starts laughing. Gavaza wants to know what is so funny and she says, 'Rita is fearless. Nobody can stop her once she makes up her mind to do something.'

The kommandant comes back. He is very pleased with all the food that Lunchy's friends have brought and tells Lunchy he is trying to get her transferred to another jail where she can get her own traditional food. Gavaza can see that Lunchy wants to laugh. *No respect, even for the kommandant!* Lunchy tells him she doesn't need special food, they just mustn't give her meat, she's a vegetarian. The baas shakes his head. She will be better off somewhere else. When he leaves, Lunchy looks through the parcels and then offers most of the food to Gavaza. *Hau! I can't take it. If they catch me I'll be in trouble. What's wrong with this woman? She doesn't want even her friends' food.* Then Lunchy takes the wool and a big piece of cloth from the bag that she was so happy to receive and shows Gavaza the embroidery that she is working on. Gavaza covers her mouth and laughs. She calls that embroidery. *Sies!* It is so ugly! Lunchy, thinking Gavaza is glad for her, puts the cloth on the bed and says she is going to start working on it right away. Gavaza leaves shaking her head and laughing. She has to go and help with supper.

The next day, when Gavaza comes to Lunchy's cell, she sees that Lunchy has used some of the wool to make a line and has tied it from the window bars on one side of the cell to the window bars on the other. She has hung her towel, panties, bra, shirt and shorts on the line. Gavaza takes one look at this, covers her mouth and rushes out the cell. She comes back within a few minutes with Simon who tells Lunchy, ' You can't have this line.'

'Why not? I need it to hang up my washing.' Gavaza reaches up to pull down her clothes and Lunchy explodes. 'Don't touch my things!' Gavaza stops in her tracks; Lunchy seems much bigger than she thought. 'Get out of here. I put up the line; I will take it down!' Gavaza and Simon leave. *The stupid woman. Doesn't she know that they will get in trouble if the kommandant sees the line in her cell?* If she doesn't take it down, Gavaza will bring Simon back. When Gavaza takes her lunch plate, she sees that the line has come down and she is relieved. But the woman is sitting there pulled up, not smiling and greeting her as she usually does. Gavaza doesn't mind; that's the way it should be and she thrusts the plate at Lunchy.

But the next day Lunchy is friendly again. Lunchy gestures to all the supplies she has stacked up on the bench. She can't eat all this food and asks if Gavaza knows anyone who needs it. Gavaza looks at the bench covered with plastic bags of biscuits, chocolates and juices. *It's a lot of food but I can sneak it all out over a few days. The family will be pleased.* She tells Lunchy she will see. Then she hands over the plate of food. Mrs van Zyl has been making a great effort to get the woman to eat and Gavaza waits to see what Lunchy will do with the half tomato, some chips, a slice of avocado, vegetable pickles and bread that she has brought. She is sure Lunchy is going to explode again. Such rubbish food! No meat, no pap! But Lunchy looks up with a big smile and thanks her. Gavaza is shocked. *She is thanking me? I would never give anyone food like that. Hau! She thinks I make her lunch. What a stupid woman!* She goes off shaking her head while Lunchy tucks in.

Over the next few days, all the parcels are cleared out and Gavaza's children and grandchildren are very happy with the treats that she brings home. Lunchy asks her about her family and her work in the prison. Gavaza doesn't respond at first but Lunchy keeps pressing and she begins to tell her about herself. Lunchy looks very surprised to hear that Gavaza has being working at the prison for ten years but only earns a hundred and fifty rand a month even though she works seven days a week from seven in the morning to five in the afternoon. Gavaza is fifty-nine years old and looks after women prisoners and does the washing. Her husband, in his sixties, works on a farm and earns a hundred rand a month. They live in the village of Boyi with their nine children, ranging from age nine to forty.

A week after she has been detained Lunchy's lawyer comes to see her and Gavaza is very surprised when Lunchy asks her to come and meet him. He is Advocate David Mabasa. He greets Gavaza and shakes her hand and she makes a little curtsy as she greets him. Gavaza doesn't know why she has been called to meet the advocate. All she knows is that Lunchy is strange and she must expect such things from her. After the visit, when Gavaza takes her plate, Lunchy removes the serviette and is very pleased. She thanks Gavaza copiously. *Oh keep quiet, woman. What are you getting excited about? Potato chips, a tomato, a slice of avocado and two fish sticks! Maybe Lunchy is happy because Mrs van Zyl put a serviette over the food. But she is acting as though I am treating her special. Me? She's mad. Why does she think I am doing special things for her? If it were up to me, she would get the same as others.*

On the second Saturday, Mrs van Zyl gives Gavaza a plug for the washbasin in the yard and Lunchy gives Gavaza a big broad smile and washes herself from the basin so that she won't get burned. At lunch time, Gavaza again brings avocado, tomato, fish sticks, boiled vegetables and a cup of tea. Lunchy starts to dance around like a mad woman singing, 'Tea, tea, gloria tea.' When she tries to take Gavaza's hand to dance with her, Gavaza pushes her aside and she falls on the bed laughing. Gavaza despite herself also laughs. *The woman is mad. What is Gloria tea?* The next day, Sunday, Gavaza comes running in. The kommandant wants all the wool and embroidery. According to Mrs van Zyl, the major from the security branch came last Thursday and saw Lunchy working on embroidery. This morning he phoned and shouted at the kommandant who shouted at Gavaza and the warders and sent them to retrieve the embroidery and search the cell. The major thinks Lunchy has papers and books in the cell. They don't find anything except some scraps that Lunchy uses to wrap her sanitary pads. They take the scraps and embroidery and wool. Lunchy looks disappointed. *Well, she can't have privileges.*

That afternoon, that same tall woman who pushed her way into the cell the week before, comes to visit Lunchy. Again Lunchy calls Gavaza to meet her visitor, Rita. Gavaza doesn't want to but this is a missus and she feels obligated to shake hands with Rita and curtsy. Gavaza sees that Rita has brought a lot of parcels for Lunchy. After the visit, Gavaza brings lunch and when Lunchy sees the plate, her eyes grow big and she smiles. Gavaza sees a lot of vegetables, two baked potatoes, pumpkin, cabbage with cheese sauce, tomato, fish sticks and rice. *A lot of food today but no meat. How can people eat like that?* When Gavaza comes back later to collect the plate, she sees that it is almost empty but Lunchy hasn't eaten the rice. *Hau! But Indian people like rice.* Lunchy is sitting on the bed reading the Bible. *The Bible! But she is not Christian!* Lunchy smiles and says her friend brought it.

The next day, Monday, Gavaza goes off to the kitchen leaving Lunchy washing in the yard. A few minutes later she runs back. Lunchy is still at the washbasin, 'They want everything clean, clean, the major is coming.' Lunchy, towelling off, exclaims, 'Again? That's the third major in the last three days. What do they want?' Gavaza is mopping furiously. She can't trust Lunchy with the job today, not when the Major is coming. 'This is Major from Security. You better watch out.' *Lunchy acts like she doesn't care.*

But when Major van Wyk comes, she'll jump. That afternoon, a major comes to inspect the cell. It is not *the* major from the security branch. Like others, he asks Lunchy about the food. *Hau! Lunchy says it's fine.* He is there for a few minutes and then off to the cells of other political prisoners. Gavaza goes to the kitchen to fetch Lunchy's food and sees that it is almost like yesterday's, except there are no potatoes. *But that mad woman will like it.*

Before Lunchy can eat, a warder comes in and tells her that the doctor is waiting to see her in the charge office. 'Why? I didn't ask for a doctor.' 'Come. Come. The doctor's waiting.' Lunchy follows him and Gavaza goes out with her. Gavaza shakes her head. *First the major — now the doctor. They keep on checking. We are not ill-treating the prisoners? Only security police do that. I wonder how Lunchy will like the doctor; he doesn't know how to talk. He only shouts.* Gavaza watches as the doctor rudely calls Lunchy and talks very roughly to her. Lunchy talks back and looks at him like he's a fool. Gavaza laughs to herself. *Hey, that doctor didn't get it all his way today.* After lunch, Gavaza finds Lunchy with the Bible again. Lunchy spends the rest of the day and next day reading the Bible. *Good. Maybe, it will help her to stay out of jail.*

On Wednesday Gavaza is annoyed with Lunchy. *She wants clean sheets. But it's been raining every day. Can't she see that? She asked for clean sheets on Monday. Tuesday she asked for clean sheets again. And again today.* 'What must I do? It's still raining.'

'Don't they have machines for washing?'

'No, I do washing.'

Then she says, 'The people here are mad, and you will go mad because you work for mad people.' *Hau, she has no respect. How can she talk to me like that?* Then Lunchy tells the warder she wants to see the kommandant. *Hau, she is going to complain. I'd better find some sheets.* Gavaza goes off to the laundry and looks through the cupboards, eventually finds some and takes them to Lunchy. She leaves when Lunchy goes to wash and because she is quite disturbed about the sheet incident, forgets to stay and lock her up and doesn't realise that she has given Lunchy extra time in the yard until one of the white policemen shouts at her. He had been to see why Lunchy wanted to talk to kommandant and found her lounging against the wall enjoying the sunshine. That afternoon Gavaza had to rush off because her daughter was ill.

When Gavaza comes the next morning, she is surprised to see Lunchy wearing a sleeveless shirt. 'Why you dress like that? You want to get sick? It's cold and raining.' When Lunchy says, 'I have hot flushes,' Gavaza frowns and looks about the cell. *What is she talking about? I don't see anything.* Lunchy asks Gavaza about her daughter. She had an upset stomach but she's all right today. Gavaza's nine children all live at home. Six of them are working but make no contribution to household expenses. Lunchy wants to know why she hasn't kicked them out. *Hau! What kind of question is that?* So Gavaza asks, 'And *your* children? Who look after them now?' Gavaza is shocked to hear that Lunchy is not married and has no children. Gavaza shakes her head. *Not married. No children. What kind of woman is this?* 'You looking for man?'

Lunchy laughs, 'What for?' Gavaza shakes her head. *You can't trust women who are not married. They are evil.* After lunch, Gavaza comes to release Lunchy so that she can have her afternoon wash. 'You hurry up. Security major coming just now. You put on nice clothes.'

'Why? He's not my boyfriend.' Gavaza laughs. But the major does not come.

Friday, while Lunchy is showering, Gavaza can no longer stand the sight of her ugly legs. 'Your legs are grey. Why don't you put lotion on your legs.'

'I don't have any.'

'Buy some.'

Lunchy just looks at her.

'Ask the policeman to buy for you. Write note and give him.'

Lunchy is surprised. 'I don't have money.'

She really is stupid. 'Didn't they take your money when they bring you here?'

'Oh I forgot about that. I had twenty rands on me. You mean they will let me have it? Oh good. Bring me a pen and paper.'

'Ask warders. They give you paper, they give you money.'

The next day, Lunchy dances up to Gavaza and pulls her skirt up to her knees and shows off her legs. 'Thank you, Gavaza. Now I can enter a beauty competition.'

On Sunday, while they are making the bed, Lunchy asks Gavaza if she is ZCC (Zionist Christian Church) and if she is going to Moria next weekend. 'Easter not next week. Not for two weeks.'

'Oh good, my brother is coming next week. I thought he would be caught up in the Easter rush to Moria. I was going to tell the lawyer to tell him not to come.' As she was tucking the blankets under the mattress she says, 'Today is Sunday. Don't you go to church?' Gavaza puts her hand to her heart. 'How much it hurts me. I can't go to church. But I worship at home… You too, you better pray in here.' Gavaza is shocked to hear Lunchy say, 'I don't have to. I am not Christian.'

48

'You don't believe in Jesus?'

'No.' Gavaza wants to go down on her knees right there and then. Instead she orders Lunchy out to wash, hurries her and locks her in so she can't spend any time in the yard.

Later that day, Lunchy is still going on about church. 'Why don't you ask the station commander to give you leave to go to Moria? Isn't Easter the most important time for Christians?' Gavaza frowns and snaps at her, 'They don't give time for church.'

Lunchy persists, 'At least they have a service here then?' Gavaza shakes her head in frustration and walks out. *Lunchy has funny ideas. Church service in a police station? What next?* That evening, as Gavaza is leaving to go home, Simon tells her, 'That Lunchy, she sent for the kommandant and told him you are a Christian and he must let you go to church on Good Friday. He didn't like that. He told her that you are a policeman and policemen are on duty twenty-four hours a day. Then Lunchy asked him, "Do you go to church on Good Friday?" De Lange went red. He was so angry. He told her he is the kommandant and this is his police station. She mustn't tell him how to run it. I could see Lunchy was worried. She told him not to blame you. You don't know what she is asking him. You know nothing about this. But the kommandant just turned and walked out. I think he went to call the major.'

'The security major? Hau, hau, hau! That woman is a troublemaker. Why doesn't she mind her own business?'

The next morning, when Gavaza comes to work, she is kept waiting. By the time a warder opens up Lunchy's cell, she is fuming. She has been waiting since seven for them to open up. As she is going into the cell, someone calls her to come and help with breakfast. She shouts back, 'I'm busy.' She tells Lunchy, 'They don't treat me right. They tell me, so many time, I am old. I can't work nice. Hau, yesterday Mrs van Zyl, she come in the yard and she take her finger over the floor like this, then she hold up finger and say, 'Look at this dust. You too old.' Today, I'm not going to help with breakfast. If they shout, I'm going to tell them they must pension me off. Then they will keep quiet. They don't want to hear that.' Lunchy says, 'Good. We black woman must stand up for our rights.'

What does she mean, 'we black women'? For the week, Gavaza finds the kommandant, Mrs van Zyl and other white personnel rather abrupt with her. She is given extra duties and has to stay past five o' clock. On one occasion, Mrs van Zyl asks her, 'You looking for trouble with the security police?' Gavaza is shocked. *Did they report me to the major? Hau, hau, hau! It's all that Lunchy's fault. She is a stupid woman.*

On Saturday, Gavaza receives bad news and is very upset. Lunchy wants to know what's wrong. Gavaza doesn't want to talk to Lunchy; she is in trouble because of her. But Lunchy persists and Gavaza needs someone to talk to. 'Yesterday, my brother, he die. He only forty years. After he get money in bank, he collapse. He give his wife money and she put it in the pocket, then he fall down dead right there in bank. Why she put money in pocket? She put money in pocket and she kill him.' Lunchy gives Gavaza the change from her twenty rand so she can visit her brother's family. Gavaza puts the nine rands in her pocket. *She mustn't think she can butter me up.* Soon afterwards, Gavaza comes back to tell Lunchy that her brother is here. Lunchy is very happy. She has been worried about him. Gavaza knows he went for a big operation and is not so well but he has come all the way from the big city, all the way here to the north, four hours driving. *She is lucky to have her brother. My poor brother, to die so young.* Gavaza doesn't go to the front office when Lunchy's visitors come. She is too sad. When Gavaza takes Lunchy her supper, just a mug of coffee – that's all she ever asks for – Lunchy gives her some of the food her brother has brought. It is delicious, Gavaza enjoys the roti and curry.

On Tuesday morning when Gavaza comes to the prison Simon tells her, 'Major van Wyk was here last night, with his partner. They came to see Lunchy.' Gavaza can't control her anxiety. 'The major! Did he ask about me?'

'I don't know. They took Lunchy into that little office there. They talked to her for a long time. I hear the major talk, talk, talk. Lunchy, she didn't say much but she was arguing. They are coming back tonight.' Gavaza rushes off to see Lunchy to find out what happened. *Did the major say anything about me?* She finds Lunchy sitting on the bed frowning? 'So Major van Wyk come to see you. What he say?' Lunchy looks like she is not going to talk. *It must have been bad.*

Then Lunchy says, 'Oh he had a lot to say. First he took his gun and put it on the desk. Then he said, "I do not wish to hear any sarcastic remarks from you or I will keep you in detention for as long as I like." Then he told me I was one of those who organised the stay away in Gazankulu. I said I was not but he didn't believe me. So I told him, "If you don't believe me, why are you talking to me. Send me back to my cell." Then he said, "I am a Christian."'

'You didn't tell him you not Christian.'

'I didn't but I am very glad I am not. He said, "I go down on my knees every night and thank God that there are cowards in this world." So I asked him, "Are you calling me a coward?"'

50

'He said, "You are afraid and ashamed of what you have done." No I'm not. But I won't confess to things that I have not done.'

'Yes, yes, but what did he say about me?' Lunchy looks puzzled. 'Did he say anything about me?'

'No. Why would he ask about you?'

'So he didn't ask. That's good. But he's coming back tonight.' Lunchy nods. 'Maybe he will ask tonight.'

'Why what have you done?'

'Me, nothing. It's you. You tell the kommandant to send me to church.' Lunchy bursts out laughing. 'Yes, that is a crime isn't it?' Gavaza shakes her head.

Lunchy is crazy.

The next morning, when Gavaza comes in Simon tells her, 'Hau, you should have been here last night. The major, he was so angry. When they come out of the little office after the interrogation, he looked like a tomato. He shouted at me to take Lunchy back to her cell. Then he asked about her embroidery and Lunchy smiled and said "Oh, you took that already." Then the major asked, "What have you got to read?" Lunchy's smile got bigger and she said, "The Bible." The major just marched out without another word. His assistant was dancing around. He looked like he wanted to box Lunchy's ears.'

'Did they say anything about me?'

'I don't know. I didn't hear what they were talking inside.'

When Gavaza goes into the cell, she finds Lunchy happily snuggled in bed. 'Get up, get up. We must make the bed and then you must wash.' Lunchy drags herself out of bed and helps Gavaza make it. 'What happened last night? What did the major say?'

Lunchy smiles. 'He asked me about you. He wanted to know if you belonged to the Christian Women's Association. He said he knows that the Christian Women are planning to blow up the police station.' Gavaza's hand shoots up over her open mouth and she stares wide-eyed at Lunchy. 'They can fire me now and I won't get my pension.' Lunchy quickly says, 'No, no. I am only joking. The major didn't ask about you. He wanted to about the celebration I organised when Mandela was released. He wanted to know about the Youth Group and the teachers' group and mainly he wanted me to give him names so he can go and arrest people and put them in jail.'

'He didn't ask about me?'

'No, no. Anyway why should he arrest you? You're already in jail.'

'What do you mean? I am a police.'

51

Lunchy takes her towel and goes into the yard. Gavaza follows her. 'Why he so angry? Simon tell me he very angry.'

Lunchy laughs, 'He kept on calling me a liar so I jumped up and banged so hard on his desk, his gun almost fell off. I told him I'm not giving names and I asked him to prove that I was lying to him. He got so angry because I was rude to him.' Gavaza can't believe that Lunchy would dare to shout at the major. *They mustn't blame me for that. This woman has no manners.*

A few days later, Gavaza can't find the broom so she brings the mop and hands it to Lunchy. 'You know how to mop?' Lunchy mops the cell and then the yard. Gavaza raises her eyebrows, 'You can work!' Later that day, Lunchy's friends bring her another load of goods. *Lunchy doesn't want them to bring food and she tells them but they don't stop.* But Gavaza is glad. Today they brought two litres of milk and two small cups of yoghurt and Lunchy is happy about that. But now she wants Gavaza to put the milk and yoghurt in the fridge. Gavaza frowns. Lunchy wants her to ask Mrs van Zyl. 'You ask kommandant.'

Lunchy says, 'No I am asking you. You are my *baas.*' Gavaza frowns. *Is she making fun of me?* She tells Simon and Nhlanhla, another warder, about Lunchy's cheek, asking her to get her stuff put in the fridge. Nhlanhla says, 'Tell Lunchy the fridge is broken and you can't help her.' Simon says she should agree, then just smuggle the stuff out and take it home. Gavaza tells him to keep quiet. 'You want everyone to know.' Nhlanhla accuses her, 'You don't share with us. We can report you, you know.' This leads to an argument and a lot of shouting. Gavaza is angry with Nhlanhla and says, 'I will ask Mrs van Zyl if she can keep the stuff in her fridge,' and rushes away to the kitchen. When she goes to fetch the milk and yoghurt, Lunchy is so pleased, she begins to thank Gavaza profusely but Gavaza just takes the milk and yoghurt and ignores her. *I am not doing this for her.*

On Good Friday, Gavaza arrives late and is very cross. She has more duties because some of the other matrons haven't come to work. She tells Lunchy she is not going to do the extra work. Lunchy stops sweeping and leans on the broom to listen. 'Go on, sweep!' Lunchy replies 'Yes *baas,*' and springs into action. Gavaza laughs. Then she tells Lunchy that this morning she called Mrs van Zyl by her first name, Hannalie. 'Mrs van Zyl look up with big eyes and ask "What happen to 'missus'?" I ask if "missus" is her name and Mrs van Zyl give me a dirty look and say, "*Ja.*"' Lunchy laughs and tries to shake Gavaza's hand but Gavaza doesn't allow it. On Sunday, when Gavaza takes Lunchy's plate, she greets her in Tsonga. Nhlanhla who is Shangaan, has taught Gavaza how to greet in Tsonga. Lunchy is pleased and tries to answer but she can't understand what Gavaza is saying. She laughs with Gavaza and tells her, 'You have learned more in one morning than I have in two years. But now I have plenty of time to learn and you can teach me.'

After lunch, a security police officer comes in and asks Gavaza to take him to Lunchy's cell. He tells Lunchy to pack her things; she is going home. Lunchy can't believe it. She turns surprised and excited to Gavaza but she is standing there, a policewoman on duty. *So Lunchy is going home. That is how it has been with this lot of detainees. Keep them for twenty-eight days and then send them home. The security they don't tell us anything. They just come and go, as they like. They bring these people, dump them on us and we have to look after them. Just when you get use to one, they take her away.* Lunchy, who is packing quickly, keeps looking up at Gavaza who ignores her attempts to communicate. Gavaza looks at all the parcels still piled up on the concrete bench. Lunchy says to the officer who is watching and waiting, 'I don't want this stuff. I would like Gavaza to have it.' He shrugs. Lunchy asks Gavaza to take all of it and the stuff in the fridge. Then Lunchy picks up her suitcase. 'This is so sudden. I can't believe I'm going home. Goodbye Gavaza. Thank you for all your kindness. I will never forget you.' Lunchy tries to hug her but Gavaza fends her off. Then Lunchy goes with the officer and Gavaza sighs with relief. Now she can go back to her usual routine without having to babysit anyone. Hey, they mustn't bring any more political prisoners! They take too much advantage.

Muthal Naidoo, a retired teacher, is the co-founder of the Shah Theatre Academy in South Africa. She has been involved in theatre for a number of years as an actor, director and playwright. Most of her theatre work was done in Durban between 1977 and 1983 and her plays include *We 3 Kings, Ikhayalethu* (originally *Coming Home*), *Of No Account* and *Outside-In*, as well as a number of other short plays and revues.

Of No Account and *Coming Home* were nominated for the Critics' Circle Award in Durban. In 1983, her revue *The Master Plan* – a satire performed at UDF meetings in the Durban area – was banned.

The play *We 3 Kings* was published by the University of Durban-Westville in 1992 and in 2002 *Outside-In* was published in an anthology entitled *South African Indian Writings in English*. Last December, Muthal's book of short stories, *Jail Birds and Others,* was published by Botsotso Publishing.

Tindi in the Land
of the Dead

Ike Okonta

HE REACHED THE PLAGUED VILLAGE in the evening just as the light was beginning to fail. The motorcyclist who had brought him from A had dropped him off on the outskirts, refusing to go any farther. He had completed the journey on foot, his overnight bag slung over his shoulder, whistling a jazz tune to himself as he walked.

The first house he saw – a tiny hut, actually – was tucked away on the edge of the forest and you had to look really hard to see it was there. The hut was partially obscured by a big Iroko tree whose leafy lower branches formed an awning of sorts over the doorway. He went to the door and knocked. After a moment it opened and an old man stood in the doorway, peering short-sightedly at him in the waning light. He was a very old man with a head full of white hair. He had bushy eyebrows and they were white too and stood out sharply in the deep dark of his face. Tindi greeted him and asked for directions to the Youth Corps Farm.

'You have come to the land of the dead,' the old man said. 'I know. We heard. That is why I came. I am a journalist.'

'You have come to the land of the dead,' the old man said again, peering at him, trying to make out his face in the gathering gloom. 'Come,' he said suddenly, gesturing with his hand.

They went to the back of the hut. Then the old man stopped and pointed. Dusk had fallen now but Tindi could make out two fresh graves. Beyond the two shadowy mounds the forest began.

'My wife and my only son. They both died yesterday. Our people are still dying. The disease does not spare anyone. Men, women, children. They are all dying.' He stopped and frowned. 'But what do you people want again? Some of your journalist friends came here with the council chairman two weeks ago. They went round the village and drove away again after thirty minutes. That was the last we saw of them, except for the radio announcement two days later that a strange disease had broken out over Ikono village, but that it was nothing serious and would soon be controlled.' The old man laughed bitterly. 'An entire village is being wiped out by disease and the radio says it is nothing serious.'

'They say it is Yellow Fever?'

The old man shrugged. 'Who knows? That is what the doctor at the farm said, but one of the councillors who came with the chairman just laughed and said she was young and inexperienced. He said it couldn't possibly be Yellow Fever because it was public knowledge that the military government had wiped out such common diseases completely from the country.'

'And this young doctor, where can I find her?' Tindi asked.

'At the farm. She is the only one left. The other members of the Youth Corps have fled and the farm is now a death-camp for the sick and the dying.'

An air of desolation hung over the village, like a homestead whose head had gone off to war and never returned. Weed and garbage had taken over the winding lanes, and although the night was still young, the clusters of mud and cardboard shops in the main square were shut and boarded up. There was no sound of playing children, no bleat of goats being rounded up for the night, not even the occasional thump of pestle on mortar. Silence and gloom hung over the place.

As he crossed the square Tindi saw a man peering at him from a darkened doorway. He called to him but the face quickly withdrew and the door slammed shut. Tindi had a sudden feeling that he was dreaming and in his dream had wandered into a dead town. He tried to shrug off the shiver that was beginning to creep in on him. He hurried on.

It was the smell that hit him first, borne on the wings of a warm evening breeze that blew steadily from the direction of the farm. The unpleasant odour was strangely familiar but he could not immediately place it. Then it suddenly struck him that it was the smell of Little Sodom: its fetid, stagnant gutters, the stink of unwashed bodies crowded in a *molue*, the dank musty smell that hit you when you stepped into the corridor of one of the sprawling tenements. Strange, he thought, that the smell of Little Sodom was so much like the smell of death.

The camp was a large, crude bamboo affair over which was slung a green army tarpaulin, supplemented with palm fronds. Only the roof and windward side of the rude buildings were covered. The sick, over two hundred men, women and children, lay on dirty blankets spread on the hard baked mud of the floor, in six rows stretching from end to end. A thousand groans rose into the evening air and embraced him in a bizarre welcome. A few were sleeping, snoring and breathing stentoriously. But the majority were tossing and turning on their backs as though the blankets on which they lay were infested with bedbugs. A thin young man whose arms and legs and eyes had all gone a sickly yellow suddenly staggered to his feet, took two tottering steps toward Tindi and collapsed in a heap on the mud floor, his mouth working feverishly. A woman who had defecated on her blanket lay beside the fallen man, moaning softly, her gnarled dirty fingers clawing on the ground. Another held a squawling baby to her shriveled breasts. Mother and baby were covered with the yellow blotches. There were tangled limbs and old clothes and other domestic items all over the place; an overpowering stench of Dettol, vomit and unwashed bodies hung in the air. In the dull yellow light of the hurricane lamps the camp looked like a mad house whose occupants had been suddenly struck down by a nameless, vicious disease.

He walked up to the young woman who was writing at a table at the far end. When she stopped writing and raised her face he saw that she was really young. She wore a white laboratory coat over her dress; beads of perspiration stood on her dark-complexioned face, even though it was a cool evening.

'Good evening. I am Amina Halidu.'

Tindi explained who he was. They shook hands. 'I came to find out more about this strange disease.'

Amina closed her eyes for a moment. She looked tired, overworked, as though she had not slept for days. 'There is nothing strange about it,' she said opening her eyes again. 'It is Yellow Fever, only for some strange reason I have not been able to find out, nobody wants to believe me.'

'But the government officials said they have sent out blood samples taken from the villagers to Britain for analysis.'

'There is no need for that, and they know it. I pointed out the symptoms to the two doctors who came here with the council chairman.

A yellow tinge to the skin, sclera of the eyes caused by an increase in bile pigment, vomiting, haemorrhage and fever… Even a second year medical student would know it is Yellow Fever.'

A piercing scream cut through the din and sent Amina scampering to the other end. Tindi followed, picking his way gingerly through the tangle of limbs on the floor. A little boy of about four lay curled on a dirty brown blanket. He was naked and his body was covered with yellow splotches. His mother was sitting on the ground beside him. She was crying. She would let out a low animal cry, raise her palms to the sky as though asking heavens to come down and witness her tribulations, and then let out another cry, on and on. Another spasm gripped the boy and he yelled. This time it went on for what seemed to Tindi like eternity and then broke off abruptly in an ominous rattle.

Amina leaned forward and took his pulse.

'Can't you do something to ease his pain?' Tindi whispered.

'There is nothing I can do. I gave him the last injection this afternoon. We have run out of drugs.'

The boy's mother sprang to her feet, gripping Amina by the arm. Her eyes were wide open with fear. 'Save my son, Doctor! He is all I have left. His father died yesterday, that you know.' She burst into tears, gripping the doctor's stethoscope as though it contained the magic formula that would restore good health to her son.

Amina let her cry for a while, then she gently prised her hand open.

'The fever will pass, Nkechi. Your son will be well again. See, he is sleeping peacefully now.' The words were hardly out of her mouth when the boy began to toss again. He was sweating profusely now and his breathing came in short harsh gasps. The flesh had wasted from his chest and his ribs showed clearly as he fought to suck air into his lungs. Then he began to scream again.

Tindi turned away with a shudder. 'This is driving me crazy. Isn't there something I can do to help?'

Amina spreads out her hands in a gesture of helpnessness. 'What can one do without medicine, without food? The council chairman said he would send me medical supplies two weeks ago. I am still waiting. The little we found in the village dispensary has been used up. In a day or two our food and fresh water will run out too.'

Tindi looked at his watch. It was two minutes past nine. 'I'll go to A and get the supplies myself. If I leave immediately I should be able to see the chairman in his office in the morning, pick up whatever is needed and be back here in the afternoon.' He nodded enthusiastically. 'Yes, that's the thing to do. Make a list of the things you need.'

Amina looked at him doubtfully. 'Isn't it rather late? And besides, there is nobody to take you to A. The motorcycle taxis here in the village stopped working when the Yellow Fever broke out.'

'Isn't there one I can borrow?'

'There is the tailor's. They brought him here on it three days ago. He is dead now.' Then some of his enthusiasm seemed to infect her too and she stood up and hurried to her desk. She wrote out a short list and gave it to him.

Silently they walked to where the old Honda motorcycle leaned on a tree. Tindi looked at the old machine doubtfully. It looked like something straight out of the museum.

'Are you sure this thing can move?'

Amina smiled. 'It looks old but it is in working order. Tailor was very proud of it. He called it Old Reliability. We used to tease him that it was the oldest motorcycle in the world but he would laugh and retort that Old Reliabity was at least more faithful than his wife who ran away with a soldier. Tailor was a very funny man. He made the village laugh. Now he is dead.' The whole weight of what had happened seemed to descend on her and she lapsed into silence.

Tindi cracked the starter and true enough the ancient machine roared into life. He swung into the seat and revved the engine. Amina touched his shoulder. For a moment there was an awkward silence between them. Then he said, 'You are very brave.'

You are even braver, going to A all alone at this time of the night. And for our sake.'

Her hand was still on his shoulder. He looked at her face. He could make out its fine, even features in the dark. He raised his hand to touch her face and then stopped. 'I'll be back,' he said.

It was a journey of a thousand nights. Several times he thought he saw a seven-headed spirit pursuing him. On another instance an Iroko tree turned into Emekuku the giant and barred his way. But he did not swerve and crash into the undergrowth as the monster clearly wanted him to, but bore on and dazzled him with beam of the headlamp and he melted into tiny clumps of grass on the edge of road. After a while he broke out of the narrow forest path into the highway. Then Old Reliable broke down. He tinkered with the machine for a while, but when it refused to move, he threw it to the ground in frustration. It was well past midnight and nobody was about. He tried to flag down a speeding lorry but the driver looked at him, concluded he must be an armed robber, and increased speed. He stood on the edge of the road, waiting. He waited for a long time and when it became clear that no vehicle would stop for him, he brought out a wrapper from his bag and spread it on the grass and went to sleep. When he woke it was already full daylight. On the other side of the road a man was changing a flat tyre on an old mammy wagon laden with green plantain. He walked up and spoke to him and the man agreed to take him and the motorcycle to A for a fee.

Tindi rode with the driver in the front. He slept all the way. He dreamt he was back in Little Sodom and his landlord was chasing him all over the compound with a sharp machete. He woke up and wondered what it meant. The driver told him he cried in his sleep.

The council chairman was not in. His secretary told him he had gone on tour and would be away for three days. He asked for the supervisory councillor in charge of health and she pointed to a yellow door further down the corridor. He opened the door. The councillor was eating coconut and garri soaked in cold water. He hastily pushed the enamel plate into an open drawer and said angrily, 'You should have knocked. Why did you rush into my office just like that, eh?'

'I apologise, Councillor, but this is an urgent matter.'

The man waved a pudgy, beringed hand in the air. 'That is what they always say. Councillor this is very urgent, Councillor this is an emergency. What do you want me to do, divide myself in two? That is the trouble with this country. Everybody is in a hurry.' He straightened his tall cap and pulled a dusty file to him, making a show of being busy. There were several other files scattered all over the table and also on the floor. Tindi wondered how he kept track of the files and ever got any work done. Most of the files looked like they had not been opened for years.

The councillor began to open the file in front of him and then pushed it away with a sudden, violent flick of his hand. 'Minute on this, minute on that. No file go pay my children school fees?' He scratched a pimple on the tip of his nose and looked at Tindi. 'Anyway what can I do for you, Mr...?'

Tindi told him who he was and explained his mission. 'Oh, Ikono. The chairman himself was there two weeks ago. We are dealing with the situation.'

'That was two weeks ago. Half the village has since been wiped out. There is no food, no water, no medicine. They are dying like flies.'

The councillor was silent for a moment. Then he said, 'But you said you are a journalist. What is your own *wahalla* in the matter? Are you from Ikono?'

Tindi almost hit him on the jaw. 'We are talking about human beings, citizens of this country. Am I to understand that this council does not want to do anything to save the lives of five thousand endangered villagers?'

The councillor jumped up from his chair in alarm. 'I said nothing of the sort, Mister Journalist. If you publish that in your newspaper I will sue you for libel. I will sue you for slander. I will sue you for sedition. I will sue your editor, your managing director, your publisher – everybody!' He was shouting now, foaming at the mouth. 'It will be me against you, my family against your family, my village against your village–' Then he suddenly broke off and smiled a strange smile. 'But why are we shouting in this hot afternoon, eh? We are friends, aren't we? Sit down, Mister Journalist... sit down.' He pointed to a chair in an exaggerated, expansive gesture.

'I am not "Mister Journalist".'

'Okay, okay,' the councillor said in a conciliatory tone. 'What I am actually saying is that the council chairman is not on site and that it will be very difficult for us to do anything in his absence. But since this is obviously an emergency we shall see what we can do.' He clapped his hands together suddenly. 'Good! I have got it. I believe we have some emergency supplies in the store. It is nothing much but I am sure it will do until we mobilise properly.' He got to his feet. 'Look, why don't you come back tomorrow morning? Everything will be ready by then. We will provide a vehicle to take you and the supplies to Ikono.' He began to move around the office busily, picking up dusty files.

Tindi thanked him and left.

He spent the night in a cheap hotel. He did not sleep much. A record store across the street played Fuji music all night. He woke up in the morning with a pounding headache. He had a bath, skipped breakfast because his money was running low and went straight to the council headquarters. The councillor was writing a letter. He wore an embroidered yellow *agbada* and an even longer cap. He had trimmed his unruly moustache. He waved him to a chair and went on writing, a frown of concentration on his face. After a while he put down his pen and grunted in satisfaction.

'Yes, what can I do for you, young man?'

At first Tindi thought he did not recognise him. Patiently, he explained that he had come for the emergency supplies for the plagued village of

Ikono. There was a look of incomprehension on the councillor's face. 'I don't know what you are talking about', he said. 'Iko... Inoko? You say it is a village in this local government area? You must be mistaken. There is no such village in this council area.'

Tindi looked at him. He did not say anything. His headache was worse now.

The councillor turned to a big map of the local government area on the wall behind him. Tindi was sure he hadn't seen it the day before.

'Come see for yourself,' the councillor said, pointing to the villages one after the other with his index finger. 'Okwe, Idu, Oko, Amakom... You see, no Ikono.'

Tindi walked up and looked. A big square had been painted with green crayon on the spot where Ikono ought to have been on the map. 'There must be a mistake. What is this?' He asked, pointing to the green square.

'Oh, that. It is the new Integrated Wheat Farm Project. The site used to be a Youth Corps farm but we have relocated the members of the Youth Corps to make way for the new project.' The councillor rubbed his hands together. 'It is a very big project. World Bank sponsored. In a year or two the farm will be producing enough wheat to feed the whole country just like those mechanised farms in America. This military regime is a caring one. We will arrange for you journalists to visit the project at an appropriate time.'

Tindi's head was pounding now. He spoke with effort. 'This map was not here yesterday. Do you want to tell me what is happening?'

The councillor met his gaze without blinking. 'I don't know what you are talking about. I told you. Ikono does not exist. Not in this council area. In any case it is public knowledge that the present regime wiped out Typhoid, Yellow Fever and such diseases from this country years ago. As the supervisory councillor in charge of health in these parts, I am in a position to know.'

Tindi went to the street. He tried to gather his thoughts together. A brass band was playing in his head. There was something dark and ominous about the music. And then it suddenly struck him with a frightening, inexplicable certainty that something terrible had happened in Ikono. He broke into a run. The road-side mechanic whom he had given Old Reliable to repair was not there. Even the wooden sign which proclaimed to the world that he was 'A Wizard of Motorcycles' had been removed from the mango tree on which it hung the day before. He asked the shoe-mender across the road and he looked at him with alarm in his eyes and mumbled that he did not know about any motorcycle repairer.

Tindi stood in the street. He tried to think. He was sure he was dreaming. He took a taxi to the motor-park. It was afternoon now. It was very hot. There was dust everywhere. A crowd had gathered around a snake-charmer. A man suddenly screamed that his penis had been stolen. The crowd scattered.

He recognised the man who had taken him to Ikono the first time. 'I want you to take me back to Ikono. I will pay you fifty Naira if we leave immediately.' It was double the fare.

The man looked at him blankly. 'Ikono, where is that? I have never been there.'

'Eighty Naira.'

The motorcyclist licked his lips. Tindi saw the strange mixture of fear and greed in his eyes.

'One hundred Naira.' He brought out his wallet and extracted two fifty Naira notes.

The man stared at the money and then tore his eyes away.

'I told you!' He said violently. 'I don't know what you are talking about.' He fled into the crowd.

It took Tindi two hours to realise that all the taxi drivers in the motor-park had suffered a sudden attack of amnesia. They looked at him strangely when he mentioned Ikono and one or two even said aloud that they thought he was mad. It was late afternoon now although it was still very hot. He went into a *buka* to eat. It was hot in the *buka* and all the tables were dirty. A thin veil of dust hung over everything. The ceiling fan did not work. He ate with one hand and shooed away the flies with the other. A tall thin man sat on the other side of the table. He was not eating. He kept staring at his food. His blood-shot eyes had a ravenous look in them. When their eyes met the tall thin man looked away hastily.

Tindi pushed his food to him and called for another plate of food. The man did not thank him or anything. He ate quickly and hungrily. When he finished the food he crooked his index finger and scraped the last of the soup from the plate, belched loudly and wiped his greasy fingers on the seat of his trousers. Then he looked around him and, satisfying himself that they were alone in the *buka*, except for the proprietress who was counting and recounting a wad of dirty Naira notes, leaned toward Tindi in a conspiratorial manner.

'The last man who wanted to be driven to Ikono was taken away by soldiers in a Land Rover.' He got up and walked away before Tindi could ask him any question.

He was about to leave when a man who wore dark glasses and a wide straw hat walked in and greeted him with familiarity. He sat down opposite him and ordered two bottles of beer. He invited Tindi to join him. Tindi thanked him but explained that he was in a hurry. Another day, perhaps. But the man in dark glasses insisted and opened the two bottles. Tindi stood up and went into the street. He was not quite certain, but he felt people were staring at him strangely. He felt a sudden desire to run, but he shrugged off the impulse and walked out of the motor-park leisurely. When he had gone a few paces down the road he suddenly looked back. The man in dark glasses was following him. Dust was gathering now and there were many people in the street. He lengthened his stride. He felt rather than saw Dark Glasses increase his pace too. He came to a side-street and, without pausing to think, plunged down it. He heard a shout behind him. He pressed himself to a darkened doorway and saw Dark Glasses thunder past. He went back to the main road and hitched a ride to the expressway. A trailer driver going north offered him a lift. He jumped down at Ikono junction. He heard the distant growl of thunder. Rain clouds were gathering.

Tindi walked all the way. The rain was falling in torrents. He was cold and tired and did not notice the wide tyre marks and the grass that had been flattened on both sides of narrow path. He wished the rain would stop. A cock crowed suddenly in the dark, startling him.

The noise reached him faintly at first. Then it turned into a roar as he neared the village; bulldozers slamming into trees, loud voices shouting commands, an occasional sharp report, as of a rifle. He broke into a run. Panting, he knocked on the old man's door. When he did not hear any reply he pushed the door open. The bed was empty. Had he finally gone to join his wife and only son? But the noise in the village – what did it all mean?

He heard a noise behind him. It was the old man. He looked as though he had just come from the land of the dead. He was drenched and shivering. Tindi started towards him, but he put a finger to his lips.

'I have been waiting for you. Do you hear that noise? He made a vague gesture toward the village. Tindi thought he could hear his heart pounding.

'Soldiers have wiped out the village. They came yesterday at dawn. They came in ten Land Rovers and dragged everybody out. They took them to the square. Two soldiers were kneeling behind a machine gun. Then they began to fire. They did not stop until everybody was dead.' Then his voice broke. 'But why did they do it?'

Tindi looked at the old man crying in the rain and suddenly everything became clear to him: the new map in the councillor's office, the disappearance of the motorcycle repairer, the strange behaviour of the taxi drivers, the man in the dark glasses. He finally found the voice to ask the question. 'And the doctor?… Amina?'

'She was the first to go. The soldiers raped her in turns, then one of them cut her belly open with a knife. She tried to crawl into the bush. Her intestines were all hanging out. There was blood everywhere. They laughed and dragged her out. Then their officer put an end to the game and blew her brains out.'

There was a sudden shout. Then the sound of pounding booths. 'Come, I fear Obinna Nwokocha and the others have returned from their hunting trip and walked into an ambush. I went in search of them to warn them to stay away but I didn't know to which part of the forest they went.'

Tindi followed him down a winding path. He felt numb all over. *It is Yellow Fever, only for some strange reason I have not been able to find out, nobody wants to believe me.* He fought down the tears. They kept to the forest, skirting the perimeters of the village until they came to the square, still keeping to the trees. All the houses and the mud and cardboard shops had been levelled to the ground. In their place was cleared land, stretching as far as the eye could see. Even as they stood there, looking and shivering in the rain, a tractor uprooted the sacred Iroko tree and began to quarter it up into bits. Five soldiers lounged on the side of a Land Rover, smoking and chatting. They wore raincoats.

Four soldiers emerged from a camouflage tent pushing three men in front of them. The five who were smoking went and joined them. One of them was clutching a submachine gun. Its barrel shone in the beam of the tractor's headlamp. The three men were lined up behind the fallen Iroko tree. They did not say anything. Their expressionless faces glistened in the falling rain. The soldier with the submachine gun detached himself from the others and levelled it at the three men. He opened fire. Tindi started forward. The old man held him back. 'Don't be foolish.' The three men fell one after the other, without a sound. In the dull light of the tractor headlamps it looked so unreal.

The old man said, 'You have seen it with your own eyes. You must go now.' He brought out a long hunting knife from the folds of his wrapper. Before Tindi could do anything to stop him the old man sprang into the square with a shout and made straight for the man with the submachine gun. But he was an old man and was not quick enough. The soldier turned his gun toward the dark lunging figure and cut him down.

Tindi turned and plunged into the forest. The rain was still falling.

Ike Okonta is a post-doctoral fellow at the Institute of International Studies, Berkeley, University of California. A journalist and campaigner, Ike is involved with human rights, democratisation and citizenship in the oil-producing communities of the Niger River delta.

From 1991-1994, Ike worked as campaign adviser to the late Ken Saro-Wiwa, as part of the Movement for the Survival of Ogoni People. He has also been editor of *Democracy & Development*, the journal of the Centre for Democracy and Development in London, and has acted as co-ordinator of the Centre's Niger Delta Initiative.

His non-fiction publications include *Where Vultures Feast: Shell, Human Rights, and Oil in the Niger Delta* (co-author), and *When Citizens Revolt: Nigerian Elites, Big Oil, and the Ogoni Struggle for Self-determination* (forthcoming).

Celtel Caine Prize African Writers'
Workshop Stories 2006

The Consequences of Loving Mona

Sulaiman Addonia

A small village, Eritrea, late 1960s

1: The Last Dance

'Omer, you know you are my first love. But I can't go on loving you. I am a thirty-year-old woman, and you are thirteen. I can't. Not in this world.'

'Please let's run away, Mona.'

'But where to? Maybe we should just let it go. It is hard for us to break the rules set by society. They will not allow us.'

'Mona, you were twelve years old when your father made you marry a man of forty. Why does my age matter to you?'

She didn't say anything. She looked at me and then covered her face with her hands. Silence followed.

Then, 'Come with me, Omer, I want to show you something. I want to share with you a dance I learnt from Sonia, who was once married to an Italian soldier. You will love it.'

We stood in the middle of her hut facing each other. We were the same height. We were both naked. She caressed my face with her long black fingers. The gentleness of the touches made me release a moan. My body relaxed. I let go of any other thoughts in my mind. I closed my eyes.

'Omer? Omer? Open your eyes; this dance works better if you look at me.'

As I opened my eyes, she held my waist, pulled me towards her, looked at my face and blew my hair with her breath. She put both of her hands on the lower parts of my buttocks, squeezed them, and pushed her body against mine. I turned into jelly. We were glued together. With her head slightly leaning backwards, she pushed me slowly away. She looked at me seductively while approaching me with her mouth open and both her hands resting on her hips.

I gasped.

Suddenly, she ran away from me and sat on her bed. She sighed. She cried. She mumbled some words.

The rain started to pour down mercilessly. Rain-streaks cracked the mud hut and the wind pumped warm and humid air around the hut. The grass roof of the hut shook violently. The wind forced the thatches apart a little, and drops of rain came down in blotchy streaks on the inside of the roof. The warm wind enveloped me with its constant, disturbing and hissing noise, leaving a hollow feeling inside the hut, and inside me.

2: Present – The Moment of Confession

'Almas, when I gently and slowly pierced your mother's heart with a knife, it was the happiest day of my life. Mona smiled as she bled. I held her tight and kissed her – the most passionate kiss I had ever given her.'

As I say this, Almas's face is already brewing tears. I know Almas really well. Just like the sky's rain, her tears come after a few ripples on her face. At first, her face appears so calm, but get a closer look and you will see changes taking place. Her nose, which is small and looks like it is imprisoned between the high walls of her cheek bones, changes colour; her lips, otherwise so fine like blades ready to cut the veins of your heart with her beautiful words, relax and become moist. But it is inside her eyes where her resemblance to the sky takes shape. Like the morning sky of a fine day, her eyes are ready to brighten up your spirit. Then when you say something emotional, drops of water flood the whites around her iris and in no time the tears come rolling. I see the skin of her face as nothing but a mask hiding her depths. And I enjoy overwhelming her emotions because only then am I able to see the real feelings of this woman. This woman who whenever she breathes, talks, walks, dances, reminds me of her mother, my lover, my sweetheart, the woman that I used to call my Mona.

It is early morning and I brought Almas to this spot in the forest, where I buried her mother's body many years ago.

'My dearest Almas, I can't thank you enough for coming here to listen to me.'

I stop for a moment. I give her the knife and she holds it with her right hand, pointing it towards me.

Almas and I take a minute to adjust our bodies to what will follow. While she closes her eyes, gearing her ears, soul and whole being to listen to me, I retreat deep inside me and search for words.

Almas suddenly disappears from my view. A misty screen rises and envelops her whole body from her feet, lovingly tucked in red, flat-heeled shoes, to her hair, black and long. I lose track of Almas. My eyes cut through the mist, and there she is standing with both her hands holding the knife tightly.

I take a deep breath and begin to tell her the story of Mona and me.

3: The First Meeting

When I first saw Mona in the market one Wednesday morning, I remember asking myself, 'Who is this woman?' Our village was a lot smaller then and it is not an exaggeration to say that I knew most if not all the inhabitants. 'She must be one of those women who come to our market from the surrounding villages,' I thought to myself. From the way she walked around the market, her strength was there for every one to see. Her hair was thick, black and very long; her hips were wide and firm. When I looked at her from behind she resembled a lioness walking. Elegantly she would move around stamping her presence.

I fell in love with her. I followed her around the market. I inhaled the traces of the perfume she left behind as she strolled from the grocery to the clothes shop, to Afrem's shop, who sold sandals imported from Sudan, and to other stalls.

When she finished her shopping, I shadowed her, stealthily, all the way back to the bus stop, which was behind a yellow building occupying the edge of the Market Street. It was a long walk, like fifteen minutes. When she reached the tall yellow building, which once belonged to an Italian governor of the region, Mr Mileto, she turned left. Before I took the turn, I stopped and took a quick look at myself in the large wall-framed mirror placed outside Mileto's building at the request of his vain wife. It was one of the many landmarks the Italians left behind before they departed in a hurry after World War II. As soon as I saw the reflection of my long skinny legs, my disproportionate features that made me look older than I was, I thought of giving up chasing the woman.

'But I am not a boy who quits,' I told myself.

After taking the left turn from Mileto's building, Mona walked five minutes further before she arrived at the stop. As the bus, with Mona sitting at the back, sped away on the arid and bumpy road, the same road

71

on which my parents were killed when I was four years old, I hoped she would return.

She did.

And it was during her third trip to our village's market that it all started.

As she always did, Mona walked around the market and after buying from the many shops and stalls, she started her walk to the bus stop.

But when she got to the yellow Italian building, she didn't turn left as she previously did. Instead, she took the right turn and walked up the slightly hilly road, famous for having three bicycle shops.

I started asking myself some questions. Where was she going? Did she finally notice me? Was she running from me, thinking that I was a mad person?

I ignored my thoughts and walked faster. I turned right and I bumped into her straightaway.

I wanted to run back, but my feet felt heavy, as if they had been rooted in the hill for over a century. My legs were shaking badly. Somehow, I regained my confidence. I wanted to tell her that she was like the moon, but I learnt from an older friend in the village that women don't like sharing compliments even with the moon. *'Tell them something unique, something exclusive.'* I couldn't think of anything.

She leaned towards me, and whispered, 'I know you have been following me. I like it. I have never had any attention before. Come with me.'

'Where are we going?'

'Somewhere by the river.'

4: The Kitchen Knife

The knife you are holding right now – the one with which I stabbed your mother's heart – was the same one she used to cut the onions, meat, tomatoes, vegetables that fed you and your father. It was the knife that your father bought her as a gift to make him his favourite chicken stew. It was also the same knife you used when you were learning to cook. As you know, it was nine inches long and four inches wide. But your mother's heart was the biggest in the world and there was not a knife on this planet that it couldn't accommodate.

5: Walking to Somewhere by the River

'You know I am old enough to be your mother?'

'My mother died when I was four years old, it is hard for me to say how it feels to have a mother. I have no siblings either. When I saw you in the street I didn't think of you as my mother. I thought of you as a woman that made my heart leap.'

'How did you learn to talk like this?'

'From the streets. I learnt from listening to people, observing things, thinking about things. Since my parents died, I've had a lot of time to do all of these.'

I walked at her pace. It was as if I was leashed to her by an imaginary rope of seduction. She was tossing up the stones with her high-heeled Italian-made shoes. Under the drizzling rain that was leaving marks over her long brown jacket covering her dazzling body, Mona turned her head towards me and gave me a smile. A strong wind blew through her long, thick black hair, which she collected and tucked under her collar.

We reached a steep mountain, which I knew had a cave. We started to climb. I toiled on behind her, making painfully slow progress.

I was breathless. 'How do you know this place?' I asked her as we sat on large rocks outside the cave overlooking the river.

'I was born in this village. But I now live with my husband in another smaller village, on the way to Asmara. He drives a bus from Asmara to the Port of Moswa.'

This spot in the mountain became our Mecca, our Jerusalem; it was a place we returned to all the time. All we did was talk, tell each other stories, anecdotes, recollections of our hopes, and dreams.

Then one day she asked me, 'Why don't you move in with me?'

I didn't know what to say. 'What?… What about your husband?'

'I will take care of you and you can leave this miserable orphanage. And we can live as lovers.'

'Yes, but WHAT about your husband?'

'Don't worry, I have a plan and it will work, but only if you do what I tell you. Besides, it is time for me to live dangerously.'

6: Life Without Parents

Immediately after my neighbour buried my parents, he took me to the village orphanage, which was run by Sister Mary from Florence.

As soon as he handed me to her like a butcher handing a piece of meat to his customer, he turned to me and said, 'From now on you are your own parents. Look after yourself, son.'

And he was gone.

At the orphanage, I was fed reasonably well and I was sent to school. But I felt sad and lonely. My search for happiness took me away from the orphanage far more often than Sister Mary had wanted. But she understood why I did it so she let it be. You see, I didn't want to be with orphan children. Being amongst them, I felt, even at that young age, that it was a constant reminder of my loss and of death, which had stolen our parents.

My withdrawal from the orphanage was gradual. Over the years, I found happier times walking around the village, strolling alongside the river, dipping into the mysterious nearby forest, but most of the time just going to the market where people went to buy food, new clothes and shoes, and to greet each other, talk with each other. It showed me another side to life − a happier life.

Looking back, I think my neighbour did me a great favour by putting me in the orphanage. I became like he'd told me to. I learnt about life by myself through trial and error. Mentally I grew up quickly. I became responsible from a very early age.

I won't bother you with details about my philosophy of life since this has nothing to do with why I killed your mother. But what's worth bearing in mind is that when she met me, although I was thirteen, I knew what I was doing and where I was going.

7: First Job

I found my first job when I was eight years old. It was guiding a blind man. It was the result of a chance meeting. As I strolled to the market one day, I saw a middle-aged man struggling to walk. The stick he had didn't seem a useful tool in the uneven ground full of holes, rough stones and thorny bushes. I approached him and asked him if I could help take him to his destination.

'I don't think you would be able to, son,' he replied laughing.

'Why not?'

'Because I don't think you would want to go to where I am going.'

'I have plenty of spare time. So, I don't mind going a bit far.'

'I am going to a place across the market and then down the valley, and from there to the huts on the hill behind the check point. Do you want to take me there?' He laughed.

'You are going to the prostitute hill?'

'Yes.'

I paused and started thinking.

'So?' he asked.

I hesitated further.

'Let me continue on my way. There is no shame in struggling for love.'

He chuckled and walked on.

'Wait,' I said as I followed him. 'I will take you.'

'Are you sure?'

'Yes.'

'How old are you, son?'

'Eight.'

'You have a deep voice for an eight-year-old. Anyway, you are too young to go to these kinds of places. And I don't want to suffer beatings at the hands of your parents.'

'I am an orphan. I can do what I want.'

'Mmm, it is said that parents are the eyes of a child. Welcome on board to the blind quarters, son. In that case, you may guide me.'

'Can I ask you a question?'

'Yes, but not so many. I like to think on my way to the hill.'

'Doesn't your wife get upset that you are going to…'

'She left me. I don't blame her. People like perfection.'

'But…'

'Don't worry, you will understand these things when you grow up.'

We walked on silently.

The trip turned into a weekly affair. And after a few weeks, he started paying me a few shillings. He was very precise with his timing, a trademark, he said, he learnt from the Italians. The call for the evening prayer was his cue to leave his hut and head to the prostitute hill. He always liked to be with his favourite prostitute, who occupied one of the huts at the top of the hill. Her name was Mehret. She looked a bit older than him. The first time she saw me bringing Kamal to her hut, she smiled at me and asked Kamal, 'And who is this young boy?'

'This is my friend Omer. Look at this face,' Kamal said addressing Mehret but leaning forward and touching my face with his hand, 'and make sure you remember it.'

'I will and I…'

'Wait, Mehret. Omer, you must know that the most beautiful combination in life is when you mix love with experience. Are you listening to me, Omer? Go for experience, son. Nothing more, nothing less. Nothing is better than sweet love delivered with the sweetest of anecdotes. Mehret, I feel this boy is a special one, when he is the right age I want you to teach him everything about love.'

'When he is the right age, I will be old and less attractive,' she replied laughing.

'Your beauty is like—' he paused, extended his hand and searched for her. She took his hand and wrapped her body with his arms. She rested her chin on his chest and looked at his face. He was one of those blind people, who if it wasn't for his tentative steps even with a stick in his hand, gaze fixed straight ahead, head tilted slightly, no one would have assumed he was a blind man. His eyes were as normal as yours and mine, but their light had long gone and disappeared after a strange illness had befallen him one night. He woke up a blind man.

She blew her breath on his face and stretched her head to kiss his chin. He bowed his head towards her. Had he been able to see, he would have seen a woman with a wide face, shoulder length black hair, and who was wearing a short white skirt and a tight long-sleeve blue shirt. She swiftly changed her face position and now rested the side of her face on his chest; as if she wanted to listen to his heartbeat.

And she closed her eyes.

'Let's go inside,' she whispered moments later.

I sat outside the hut on a stool. Oil lamps were softly flickering in the near distance, a few men hurried down the slope and others strode up, little ants crawled on my leg. Then I heard Mehret and Kamal's moans. It was synchronised and felt like a soft music that went on and on.

8: Mona's Plan

'Omer, listen to me carefully.'

'OK.'

'When I left this village, I swore never to return. Over the years, my hatred of the village kept accumulating as my life with my husband yielded nothing but heartache. Then one day I decided to return. That was the time you first saw me and started following me. Don't ask me why I returned. Because I don't know why. It was just one of those things.

Anyway, you probably didn't notice but I stole a glance at you when you were sitting in the market having tea with Kamal. That same day, I asked Afrem, whilst I was buying a sandal from his shop, about Kamal. He talked at great length about him, his love of a prostitute and how he was grooming you to be a woman's lover. I laughed when he said that. Afrem also mentioned that you had been working for Kamal on an on-and-off basis over many years. I didn't think anything of this then. I just said that you must be a good boy.

I know Kamal from my childhood. He used to be the most poetic man I had ever encountered. As you know, for those who don't know him, or don't see him walking, Kamal doesn't look like a blind man.

And my plan for you to move in with me involves you acting as a blind boy. I am convinced this won't be difficult for you. Can you ask Kamal for one of his sticks?'

'Yes, yes.' I was very intrigued and captivated. It was like listening to an Italian army general in one of Kamal's stories.

'OK. Here is what we will do:

1. Today, I will go back home and I will tell my husband about you. I will say that I came across you by chance while you were crying in the street, and that after I had spoken to you, you told me about your difficult life in the orphanage. I will beg him to let me be your mother figure. My husband will believe that. Firstly, because he is one of those people who believe anything they are told. Secondly, because he is kind towards everyone except my daughter and me. He treats strangers as if they were his path to heaven. I wish he were nice to us too.

2. I will ask my husband to drive us to his favourite so-called doctor, a reclusive learned man somewhere behind the mountains, close to Asmara, whose access to knowledge is through his religion. The man doesn't have medical means to investigate if you are blind or not. And so you must convince him. He will believe what he sees. His blessing though will be a good reference, because my husband believes whatever this man says.

3. You must memorise the plan of our hut. All our belongings are lined up against the wall, and the space left in the middle is ideal. We have three beds. One for my husband, one for me, and the third belonged to my daughter before she married and moved out with her husband to a town on the border with Ethiopia. My husband's and my bed face each other. His is to the left of the hut, mine to the right, and yours will be right opposite our hut's door. That is why, you must remember to tilt your head to the left, so that you can always look at me when I am on my bed. And because my husband will think you are blind and can't see a thing, I will make sure, even in his presence, that whenever I change my clothes, dry myself after a shower, I will do so close to my bed. I want you to kill me with your beautiful eyes and their sharp stares.'

9: Happy Times, Sad Times

From the moment your father left to work, we became like one in every sense. It was like we had interwoven our bodies to each other. We slept in the same bed naked, we exchanged gazes, sometimes we sat with our legs crossed, and sometimes I rested my head between her breasts, or her head on my chest. We kissed. We drew shapes of flowers, small butterflies on each other's bodies with pens. But most of the time, we just talked and talked. We stayed in bed all day until before your father returned from work. She did all her housekeeping in the evenings when he was around. 'I want to spend every single minute of my time with you my love,' she used to tell me.

Then sad times... these only arrived upon us at times when your father had a day off work. Like one Sunday when she cried in my arms after she and your father had an encounter under my gazing eyes.

That Sunday, as usual, he woke up from bed and had breakfast made of goat milk, honey and some bread, before he went back to bed. He was nice to me. Always rubbing my head, bringing me sweets, buying me new clothes, asking me how I was, telling me not to worry and that I was like his son. But sometimes he would survey my face with a look full of hate.

After he had his breakfast, he said to Mona, 'I am tired. I need as much sleep as I can today.'

That day, as I always did when her husband was inside the hut, I sat on my bed with my head tilting slightly to the left. My stick was next to me. Mona was sitting on her bed.

Then he woke up and came over to Mona's bed.

He shoved her over with his hand.

He mumbled some words. I knew what they were, because Mona told me.

'Mona, I need sex.'

'OK, but don't make noise,' she said as she stretched her tall, lean and elegant body, full length.

'I wish he was deaf as well.' He threw himself over her. She disappeared underneath him.

All I was seeing was his bald head, with his face buried in the pillow, pushing back and forth, forth and back.

My heart urged me to do it; to beat him to death with my stick. I now regret that I didn't.

A few minutes later, he lifted his head from the pillow. His sweating face appeared tense for long seconds and then he breathed. He sighed. His eyes opened up and then he stared in my direction, as if he was in doubt. Our eyes met momentarily before he pushed himself up and walked to his bed.

'I need some sleep.'

Once on his bed, he started snoring.

Mona looked dishevelled. It was as if he erased her beauty with his hairy chest. I bowed my head. She then went outside. I don't know what she did, but she came back looking fresh and as beautiful as ever. She sat on her bed facing me.

I started to examine her face. My eyes were like a camera without flash taking her photo in complete silence. Her face was like a magnet, I never wanted to stop looking at it. Her long thin face was black, as if it was dipped in coal powder; and her cheekbones were like small hills, covered by a smooth skin. Her nose was straight and long. When she gazed at me, her kohl-darkened eyes were even darker than her skin, and when she blinked, her eyelashes were so thick and long that they spread gently like the feathers of a young peacock. Her upper lip was a bit smaller than the bottom lip, both lighter in colour than her skin, and with a line of soft pink protruding in between.

Then she stood up abruptly and went outside the hut and came back with a long thick and white blanket-like garment.

From under her bed she took out an incense-holder topped with incense and other spices, and started to burn them with charcoal.

Her husband started to cough.

'What are you doing?' he screamed with his eyes closed.

'I am doing what your doctor told me to do. Didn't he say to us that burnt incense would be good for Omer's health?'

'Oh, God.' He rolled over and covered his entire body with his blanket.

He started snoring again.

She went outside and came back with two stools. She put them next to each other. We both sat facing each other. She covered us both with the white garment like a tent placing the incense between us.

'I love you,' she whispered to me. She glowed in the dark and her breath seeped inside me, stirring my emotions even more. Smoke was rising from the incense-holder carrying beautiful aromas that rose and seeped from the pores of the garment. Sweat was streaming from both of our faces.

Again, 'Omer, I love you.' She kissed me passionately. I felt her wet hair and I inhaled her.

'I love you too.'

There was a long pause. Then out of nowhere, she reached for my hand and pulled it to her face. I ran the tip of my fingers across it and down to her swan-like neck. I stopped. I retraced back to her eyes.

'Are you crying?'

She didn't answer me.

'Mona, why are you crying? This can't be just the sweat.'

She squeezed my hand and then guided it to her breasts, thighs, before she stopped between her thighs. 'Because I am hurt here.'

10: The Long Silences

For many days after that Sunday, she didn't want to talk. 'Let's just look at each other,' she told me.

I stared at her so much that all I saw in this world was her face, her body. Nothing else filled my eyes but Mona. Everything else in the world looked blurred.

11: The Dreams

During those silent days and nights, I started to dream about her. In my dreams I kept going back to that Sunday when she cried in my arms. In my dream her husband didn't exist any more after he left her bed having brutalised her and went over to his bed to snore. Instead she came to my bed and slept with me all night long. I held her tightly with my warm body dissolving her Frankincense gum tree-like scent which was so adorable to inhale.

Then, still in my dream, I wrote her a small poem:

You are like a star

No, you are like a thousand stars

No, no, you are one star – but when you leap from the earth to the far, far sky you shine like a million stars

12: Last Breath

'Omer? Omer?…' she sighed heavily.

'Omer, the entire knife must be inside me; it hurts.'

I think… I think my heart will stop beating soon. Please kiss me and glue your lips to mine. I want you to have my last breath.'

13: Present – My Tears

Suddenly it all becomes too much. I break down in tears. I howl. I scream.

'Oh Almas, you don't know how much I miss her. Every day of the last ten years I spent in prison, Mona came to me in every single night of them in my sleep. She asked when was I going to join her? She said she needed me. Almas, she wants me in her world. She needs me. I want her too. I need her. I can't live without her. I am now free to go. When I gave myself up to the police after I killed Mona, because I couldn't bear living without her in the open, you were the only one who visited me regularly. You always wanted to hear the truth about your mother, the truth that I have been keeping inside me until now…' The tip of the knife Almas is holding with her right hand pinches my skin, the part under which my heart awaits the knife impatiently. I double myself. I bow my head. Almas caresses my face with her left hand. She wipes my tears. I continue to tell the story.

14: Mona Decides to Die – What is Life?

'When you are born from your mother's womb into the arms of life, when life slowly begins to make sense, because colours start to make sense, when you grow out of crying and you replace it with laughter, when you stare at your parents straight in the eyes and you ask them all sorts of questions, when you take your first crawl, first walk, first run, when you start to speak your first letter, first phrase, first sentence, when you walk out of your compound into the outside world and all you see is a long line ahead of you, a line full of unexplained and challenging things, when you go to school on your first day with a funny feeling in your tummy, but you come back waiting restlessly to go back again on the next day, when you work hard and get high grades and all the teachers talk about are the possibilities ahead of you, then you realise that the road from your small village to the capital Asmara seems possible because the high mountains in between are movable. When all of these happen to you, you start wearing life as a beautiful jacket around your body with its distinct smell of eternity, hopes, and dreams. But then your life is halted. Because your father tells you that the time has come for you to stop studying. "My daughter," he would say, "you are going to marry soon, so what's the use in spending precious resources on you. We have little money and it would be best if we spend it on your brother's education."

'Soon after this happens, you are married and you become an attachment to someone else, someone named *your husband*. You begin to live his dreams, help him to achieve his hopes, and fulfil his desires. You live someone else's life.

'And what is the worth of life if it is not my own?

'What is the point of this world, if it belongs to someone else?'

Silence. A long silence.

Then: 'Omer, if you really love me like you say you do, then can you help me?'

'Help you with what?'

'With my decision.'

'What decision?'

'I want to leave this world.'

'You mean you want us to run together to another country?'

'No, I want to go on my own.'

'But what about me? You know, I love you. You know I can't live without you. I want to come with you.'

'You belong in this world.'

We were sitting in the hut. I had never seen her so serious. Her eyes were cold, her lips dry, and pain was appearing on her face with every stare she gave me and with every word she uttered. That moment, I saw her slowly drowning in agony; and the more she talked to me, the more her face was overwhelmed. Then, she was completely under the sea of her sorrows. I listened to what she said with a heavy heart.

'I've hated my husband since the day I married him. He has been killing me slowly ever since I came to his hut, because that day was the day I stopped living my dream and started to live his. I can still live with him and continue to die slowly, but I'd rather die at the hands of a man that I love and who loves me in return.'

She then buried her head in her hands.

I ran outside the hut and I knelt, my hands facing the sky. It was raining hard.

It was the first time that I had ever knelt to God. 'Please God help me, I don't want her to leave me. Please God, make her change her mind. Please God. God.' I punched the wet ground with my fist. I sat with my knees folded. The heavy rain hit the arid soil. The noise reverberated throughout our round-shaped compound. It made the sound of ten drums drummed at once. After sounding raucous when it first started, the medley of persistent rain created a coherent sharp and bombastic sound.

The gushes of rain pushed wide and long deep lines in the soil. Filled with water these lines were like little streams that washed away some of the little things lying around in the yard fast down the light slope of the compound and into a bigger stream. The little ants, the yellow scorpions, and the small caterpillars pushed from the thin tree branches by the strong wind struggled to swim out of the thin streams. I watched them as they tried to struggle their way out from the little streams.

I cried. My heart ached, and felt so tender, that I put both of my hands on top of it to recede the pain.

'I am sorry.' I looked up and it was Mona. Even under the hard rain, I can see her tears rolling down her face. I held her knees as tightly as I can.

'Please don't let me do that to you. I love you.'

'Come sweetheart, let's go inside.'

When I went inside, she undressed me and herself. Over her shoulder, I could see the kitchen knife resting on her bed. She talked to me for a bit and then, 'Come with me, Omer, I want to show you something. I want to share with you a dance I learnt from Sonia, who was once married to an Italian soldier. You will love it.'

We danced. It was our last dance.

We then dressed and went to the forest, where I killed Mona, your mother and my sweetheart.

15: Present –

I lie full length on the grass of the forest. Almas stands over me. Tears roll down her face.

I smile.

'I am ready, Almas. I am ready.'

Sulaiman Addonia is half Ethiopian, half Eritrean, and lived in Sudan and Saudi Arabia before moving to the UK in 1990. He lives in London and he is currently writing his first novel. His publications include a short story, 'A Night In Dalston' (Kwani?); 'Only Up From Here' (a short story for a forthcoming anthology to be published by Frances Lincoln); an essay on a book of a collection of literature by exiled writers (Five Leaves Publications); as well as work for *Sable, Underground Focus*, and the *New Statesman* magazines, and *KIT Theatre Special*. Mr Addonia is a columnist for *Bulb* magazine.

The View From the Lake

Segun Afolabi

IT HAD SOMETHING TO DO WITH JIMMY'S BOY, Brenda said. 'Jimmy's doing,' was exactly what she had mumbled. A tree trunk lay across the path and she stopped and considered walking around it, then pushed against it with a booted foot.

'What do you mean "doing"?' her husband puffed. Brian: short, far-sighted, rivulets trickling down thick sideburns in the heat. 'You think Jimmy Junior could be mixed up in something like that?' He steered Brenda by the elbow as she balanced on the log. She was trying to rock it, daring it to topple her, but it wouldn't budge. He held her until she was safely on the other side. He walked back several paces and turned and ran, clearing the trunk by several inches. When he landed his rucksack bounced and something clinked or broke. He couldn't tell. He wondered whether Brenda had noticed.

'Well… I don't know,' Brenda said as he caught up with her. 'I don't know whether it was him or one of the others. Maybe it was all of them. I just have this feeling, that's all. A gut feeling.'

'You think?' He guessed she hadn't noticed.

'Yes… I think so.' Brenda stopped, glanced ahead, then behind, a hand on her hat. 'Brian, is this the right way? It doesn't look like much. Are you sure we're going in the right direction?'

Brian gazed up at the wall of forest around them and ahead at the feeble path, which almost instantly disappeared around the next bend. He took out a square of paper and unfolded it and squinted, then removed his rucksack and rooted around for his specs. He stared at the map again and turned it right-side-up. 'It says we're to follow this path… here… we get to this clearing... cross over, carry on to the other side. There'll be someone waiting for us there.' He glanced at Brenda. 'Just as long as we don't leave the path, we'll be okay. Don't worry.'

Brenda peered ahead again and then to where they had come from. 'I don't know, Bri,' she said. 'We could go back. We get lost, who's to find us?'

Brian removed his glasses and wiped his eyes, dabbed at his face with the back of his hand. He shoved his glasses into his shirt pocket, folded the map and placed it there too. He rubbed his bunions together and glanced down; a beetle the size of a postage stamp was working its way across his sandal. He watched it struggle to dismount and wobble into the undergrowth.

'What?' Brenda said.

'Wha... Wha-do-you-mean?' Brian looked up, startled.

'Brian, do you ever listen to a word I say?'

'What – you wanna go back, we can go back.' He held up his hands. 'Okay with me.'

She glared at him, then turned and marched ahead. Brian waited a moment and smiled. He looked down and observed the beetle scurrying back towards his foot.

'You coming?' Brenda called. She had disappeared into the forest and her voice seemed to carry from far away.

'Coming,' he yodelled. He began to walk, then jogged a little until he had reached her. 'Slow down, B. We've got some time.'

Brenda didn't reply. Just carried on walking at the same quick pace, pretending her husband wasn't there. When he fell behind he noticed she would slow down until he caught up with her, so he began to lag deliberately.

'Okay – give me one good reason you think it's Jimmy Junior,' he said. 'Just one.'

For a while Brenda remained silent, trudging onwards. Then without turning round she said, 'Well, for one he's not long out of jail. And two, he's done this sort of thing before – remember the Klosterman's? Cleaned out, like they turned the house upside down. Shook it out. Even the bathroom paper holders. Need any more reasons?'

Brian sighed. 'The Klosterman business is why he was in jail in the first place. He fell in with a bad bunch. He's okay now. He was okay before; he just had some bad luck, that's all. Who buys silver bathroom paper holders anyway?'

'Well – that's sort of not interesting to me; that's not the point.' Brenda stopped and studied him. 'You don't face facts, Brian. That's your trouble.

Open your eyes more often, smell the coffee. You… you…' She tried to think of something else, but nothing came. She turned and began speed walking again.

They trekked in silence until the trees began to thin and spill into a semicircle of grass and scrub. Brenda closed her eyes, lifted her face to the sun.

'Now, if I'm right we cross to the other side,' Brian said. He looked at the folded map. 'Should be someone waiting for us, called Mee… Meezee. Something like that.'

'I can't see anyone,' Brenda said.

Brian shielded his eyes with the map and surveyed the perimeter. 'Humph. Well, I'll be. They said he'd be here at ten precisely.'

'Well he's not.'

'I can see that.' Brian glanced at his watch and scanned the clearing again. 'We'll have to wait a while then. This is a good spot. It shouldn't be too long.'

Brenda scouted the area for a thick swathe of grass, then sank down, her rucksack still strapped to her back.

'You wanna take that off?' her husband asked.

'No… I'm okay,' she replied.

He looked down at her, then up into the trees. He thought he saw a movement, but the leaves were still. 'You wanna go back? We can go back if you like. We don't have to do this.'

'I don't know, Brian… I'm beat. Let's just stay here a while.'

He looked at her, then quickly turned away. It was her idea, after all, or both of theirs. Who had thought of it first? He couldn't remember.

A breeze circled the clearing, brushing the tips of the yellow acacia trees, avoiding Brian, who had removed his hat and now wiped his face and smooth pate with it. He put it back on and plumped down beside Brenda. They didn't speak, only glanced into opposing bushes.

'Sure is quiet,' he said after a moment.

Brenda sighed and remained silent and Brian rubbed his nose, feeling the kink where it had been broken twenty-five years ago playing soccer in front of Brenda, not married then, before Deborah was born. And here they were waiting for someone they had never met, only a name on a piece of paper; four letters. How do you get to this? he thought.

A branch swayed and thrashed a little and they looked up, but saw no sign of life. Silence descended again and a minute later, without moving her head, Brenda whispered, 'There's someone watching us.'

'Where?' Brian whispered back, snapping his head round, following Brenda's gaze.

'I don't know,' she replied. 'It keeps moving. It was there at first, by that tree.' She pointed. 'Bri, I think something's happening. Maybe it's them.'

'Sshh. Listen,' Brian got up on his knees and craned his neck.

They both held still and the sounds came gradually to them: the tweet and whistle of birds and the splash of leaves in the breeze and then intermittent cracking as if something had broken or was breaking by degrees. A bird honked and Brenda flinched towards Brian, then pushed him away as if he had been at fault.

'There's your prowler,' Brian laughed. He stood up and stretched and began to circle the clearing, still chuckling.

Brenda could see it now; Brian telling the neighbours all about it, the bird's cry. 'Lungs like a pterodactyl!' he would exclaim. 'Just about jumped out of her skin!' Judy Pinkerton would snatch a hand to her mouth. Her husband Mike would screech into her ear, attempt to scare her. Everyone would laugh. Even Brenda. That predictable.

'We've waited long enough,' she said, struggling to her feet. 'No one's coming. I should have guessed. I can't believe he brought her here.' She waved emptily at the forest around them. 'I don't get any of it.' She grabbed the straps of her rucksack and faced her husband. 'You should have said something, made him stay away from her. You always told me to let them be. But he's no good – never was, never will be – you know that.' She nodded to herself as if agreeing with some internal logic. 'And he's alive, doing God knows what.' She placed a fist against her hip. 'Well, the boy can go hang as far as I'm concerned.'

'Brenda, don't,' Brian said. 'Don't say that. Not now.'

'Not now? When, Brian? When? I'm *so* tired of going round in circles in my head: if we had put our foot down with them; if he hadn't taken her on that trip; if we hadn't moved to Cleveland; if you'd got that job with CalTech instead. You know? Something might have changed things. I keep thinking – one little thing would have made a difference and just by thinking it, maybe it still will. You know? Do you get that too?'

'Sshh,' Brian said. 'Don't B. Don't. Deep breaths. Slowly now.' He got up, removed her rucksack and held her until she was calm again.

They sat without speaking for several minutes until Brenda turned to her husband. 'I'm sorry, Bri. I can't stop thinking. I guess I don't think about you enough, what you're going through. Huh? Maybe we shouldn't have come.'

Brian peered at his wife and shrugged. 'We're here now.' He looked away, glanced at his watch. 'I think you're right, though – no one's coming.'

Brenda snorted but made no reply. The same bird's screech tore through the trees once more, but neither of them reacted. The cry returned again and again as if to taunt them, then seemed to give up, defeated. A whiff of burning, aromatic and sweet, sifted through the air and Brenda tilted her face to catch the scent.

Brian said, 'I asked him – Jimmy's kid – about what happened.' He let it hang there. Take it or leave it, he thought. She remained silent and he swung his head towards her. 'He came to the office.'

'When was this?'

'A while back. In November. Before Thanksgiving. He came to the office; he just wanted to talk. We talked…'

'And you talked to him?' Her voice seemed suddenly loud, too big for this place. 'You let that… that thing into your office? And you talked! You didn't tell me?'

'Brenda!'

'Don't you… how could you! We come here, all this way and you tell me this… now?' She looked at him, then at the ground and seemed about to speak, but nothing came. Only a kind of choked disbelief. She was up, rucksack in hand, racing towards the path they had arrived on.

Brian sighed and gave the clearing a final cursory inspection, then heaved his rucksack onto his back and jogged after his wife.

'Wait up!' he called. 'Brenda, wait.' He kept her in sight until she was out of breath and she was forced to slow to a walking pace, then trailed five metres behind her. Her straw hat had blown off and it bounced against her rucksack, kept in place by a string bow. She had worn them when they had begun dating, on picnics, and then someone had said something once and she had never worn one again. Until now. He tried to picture the faces, remember the names from college, but he couldn't imagine who would have injured her pride at the time.

She came to a standstill and he almost bumped into her.

'Is this the way? We've been walking a while. It seems to be taking longer this time.'

'We get to the tree trunk and then it's straightforward from there.' He took out the map and studied it again, drawing a finger from where they had begun, back to the clearing. He frowned, then squinted at the forest around them. 'Maybe we went the wrong way; I don't remember this. We should maybe go back.'

Brenda peered at where they had come from and grimaced. 'But we might get lost. If we walk a little further – just to the top there… we could come back if it's a dead end.'

'We're lost already,' Brian said, taking a swig from his bottle. 'Here, drink some water.' He looked back, then forward. 'Okay, let's go.'

They trudged slowly upwards, and when Brian slipped on the rocky surface, Brenda said, 'Careful,' but she didn't turn round.

At the top the land levelled and a bald area the length of a football field gave out onto bushes and renewed forest. Someone was waving at the far end.

'Who's that?' Brenda asked.

The couple squinted and waved back hesitantly. A large angular bird alighted in the middle of the field, and Brenda screamed. It seemed to seize something and dance upon it, then prance, crowned and thrusting, to the edge of the clearing.

'What the fuck?' Brian said.

They scurried to the other end, towards the waving figure.

'You miss your way,' the figure called, a man they saw now, leaning against a grey-black rock. As they approached he appeared to grow older, and strangely, smaller.

'Oh – *you're* Mister Meezee?' Brian asked, reading from a corner of the map. He turned to Brenda. 'He's the guy – the one we're supposed to meet.'

'Yes – I am Mzee Samuel,' the old man smiled. 'Since ten o'clock, I am waiting.' He giggled as if the inconvenience had been the punch line to a joke.

Brenda glanced at her watch, then shrugged at her husband.

'I'm *so* sorry – we must have got lost somehow,' Brian said. He wiped his face with his hat again. 'It looked straightforward on the map... I don't know where we went wrong.'

The old man laughed in dismissal and said, 'You are ready?'

'I guess so. Honey, you ready?' Brian turned to his wife who only stared back at him, bewildered. She seemed suddenly frail and frightened. 'Brenda?'

'Huh?'

'You okay?'

She nodded.

'It's now or never, B,' he said.

Brenda nodded again. 'I know, Bri. I just need to think for a minute. There I go again – thinking. Come on, then.'

'Okay, we can go,' the old man said. He reached out for a broken branch leaning against his side and pushed away from the rock. He seemed to sway for a moment before pitching forward, settling into a lopsided shuffle.

Brenda glanced at her husband and they held back for several seconds, watching, before following him.

'You see the bird?' the old man asked, pointing his stick at the now empty field. 'Secretary bird. You see it?'

'Yes, we saw it,' Brenda replied. 'Very big. It scared me.'

The old man giggled again and ducked into the bushes, onto a path invisible from the clearing. He made a gesture of thwacking at tendrils either side of them, but the track had widened so that Brian and Brenda could walk side by side.

They followed the lip of the hill for several minutes, dipping in and out of the sun, then descended into forest again. The old man kept indicating with the broken branch: 'Waterbuck,' he said. 'You see?' and, 'Hyena's cave... You see the monkey, there? Another one... You see the baby?' All the time pointing with the stick, leaning on it for support, waving it again.

Brian unfolded the map and saw where they had veered in the wrong direction, almost half a kilometre from the rendezvous. 'I can't believe we got so lost,' he muttered, shaking his head.

The old man pointed to a pile of excrement. 'Buffalo,' he explained.

Brian and Brenda cooed in approval.

'What did he say,' Brenda asked, 'when you talked to him?'

'What? Oh, that... I don't know, Brenda.' Brian held onto a hanging branch as he negotiated the descent, then considered the possibility of snakes and let go. 'Well, he said he was sorry. He cried... I didn't know what to do, sitting there in the office. We went for a walk, ended up in a bar round the block. He was all choked up. He thought everything was his fault – that he couldn't do anything. Couldn't stop them. But it's not Jimmy's fault and I told him so. He brought her here, but it's not his fault, B. I think you know that.'

Brenda stopped, inhaled and exhaled slowly, then pointed. 'I guess we're here.' Through a gap in the trees they could make out a bright expanse of water and the reflection of the surrounding forest.

'You see the water?' the old man said. 'It is not far now. We can walk this way.' He guided them around the perimeter until they emerged onto a lawn peppered with dwarf thorn trees and a sky-blue rowing boat, turned upside down, oars splayed on either side. A bell-shaped lake shimmered in front of them, strewn with flamingos on opposite shores.

91

Brenda nodded and took in the lake and the forest, the clear sky. 'I see,' she said to herself.

The old man held his stick in one hand and began to lever the boat.

'Let me,' Brian called, running to help manoeuvre the craft until it was righted. He noticed how light it was, and ancient. 'This is strong enough?' he asked.

'Oh, yes,' the old man laughed. 'Yes – very, very strong. It can carry many people, all over.' He waved as if referring to the entire country.

Brenda and the old man pushed while Brian pulled the boat into the water. They placed the rucksacks first, then Brenda clambered in as the two men held the boat. They pushed it further out and the men climbed in, the old man taking up the centre plank, struggling to position the oars. The boat wobbled for a moment until he began to row, drawing closer to the centre of the lake.

Birdsong surfaced and vanished all around them.

It came slowly at first, then a great patter of feet beat the water and the flamingos took flight, soaring away from the opposite shore as the boat drifted towards them. The birds, black and fuchsia pink against the forest, stretched out their wings and circled them. They flew around the lake a second time, then with a final swoop they glided to the far shore.

The old man asked, 'You are ready?'

The coupled looked at each other, at the water, back to the old man as if he held all the answers.

'I don't know,' Brenda said. 'Is this the middle?' She looked from shore to shore as if making exact mental measurements.

'Here is the middle,' the old man laughed. He stopped rowing and drew in the oars. The silence was immediate.

Brian began to undo the straps of his rucksack. He removed a T-shirt and then a plastic bag, and from there a metal canister wrapped in another shirt. He replaced the shirts and the bag and looked at the object in his hands. His face creased suddenly and his shoulders shook. A matter of seconds. He wiped his eyes with the back of his hand. 'You know, B. I don't think this is such a good idea,' he said. 'We can't leave her here like this. Alone. I can't do it. I can't.'

Brenda nodded. She saw him then, drawn and hollowed out, something expunged from the old Brian. She hadn't noticed until now. She reached out and the old man eased the container from Brian's fingers and passed it to Brenda. She unscrewed it and poured the ashes in slowly, watching how some parts floated, other parts sank straight away. She shook the canister until it was empty, then rinsed and covered it again. She looked across at Brian. 'There's that,' she said, but he only stared into the water lapping at the side of the boat.

The old man looked at Brenda, then turned to Brian. 'We are ready?' he asked. 'We can go?' He held onto the oars.

'Maybe one more minute,' Brenda said. 'Then we go back.' She smiled.

The old man smiled back at her and they waited in silence.

Segun Afolabi was born in Kaduna, Nigeria and grew up in various countries, including the Congo, Canada, East Germany and Indonesia.

Afolabi has been writing for over ten years and has had stories published in *Wasafiri, London Magazine, Edinburgh Review, Pretext* and others. A collection of short stories provisionally titled *A Life Elsewhere* is due out in spring 2006, and a novel, *Goodbye Lucille,* will be published in spring 2007. Both will be published by Jonathan Cape.

A graduate from University College, Cardiff, Afolabi has previously worked as an assistant content producer and sub-editor for the BBC.

The Biology of Women

Dayo Forster

'You work too hard,' she says, 'you have to learn to let go, turn the mobile off, relax.' She is in a lounger and he is standing. She stretches her arms above her head, forcing him to look at her, look at the line of her body – sleek, curvy, pampered and expensive. They are on the verandah of a purpose-built villa in a luxury retreat. There is a wide-angled view of Mount Kenya, its edges blurred against the sky. She turns sideways and curls her knees upwards, 'That's what all the books say. Successful men need to know how to de-stress.' He turns his back to her, shoulders taut.

Olufemi strides to and fro on the lawn, phone close to his ear, eyes cast downwards at the wet grass rinsing the toecaps of his Merrell walkers. 'I don't want everything to fall apart as soon as I leave the office. For God's sake, I've only been out of there for a day.' He kicks at a little mound of deer droppings, the round pellets scattering, fanning out on the grass in homage. 'Deal with what you can on your own, leave the rest for when I get back. Tell her I shall ring her after my holiday.' His voice carries across to Muthoni, who is still in the lounger, now leafing through *True Love* magazine and shaking her head at the folly of an eighteen-year-old girl who has gotten pregnant in a doomed love affair with her father's best friend. 'Oh life,' she says as Olufemi's feet scuff the steps up to the verandah, 'you can never tell can you?'

'Hmm,' replies Olufemi, as he passes through into the villa, to the bathroom at the end. He loiters at the mirror, stares into his reflected eyes, and wonders why he feels so strange.

'Heading for a quick walk.' He doesn't invite Muthoni to join him, he walks past her and strides off towards the woods behind the last villa. The path runs under large heavy-trunked trees which wave glossy leaves at each other. There are birds everywhere. Unimportant peckers in speckled brown uniforms chirp and hop about. A pair of red-billed hornbills caw and land heavily into a yellow acacia, announcing their importance in the bird world. Nature is supposed to relax. Instead Olufemi finds a sturdy stick, a branch with jagged ends, which he breaks and shapes into a fork ended weapon. He thwaps at the base of the nearest tree, scraping into its bark.

There's a rustle in the bushes. He stops. A warthog, tusks curling down and up, stops to stare back. It trots off, the bristles on the end of its tail tapping at the air as it disappears into a tangle of vines and thin branches. Two baby warthogs dash past to join their mother, their tails up in imitation or in obedience to what's in their genes.

He walks on. There is green everywhere. Walls of green pushing, shoving, thrusting, living. He swings his forked stick about, sometimes whisking through the odd leaf or making a branch shudder, more often than not simply parting the air then thudding into the ground, ahead of his next footfall.

At a clearing ahead, the bush parts around a large tree with branches that start just above head height, creating a canopy underneath. He walks towards it, glimpsing wisps of unevenly blue sky overhead. At first, he wonders what it is, why a cobweb would feel so cold, yet so silky. He can feel it on the back of his head, a bulge dropping onto his shoulders, cool. He turns around, to face the way he's just come, and steps forward. It touches his nose then the cold covers his face, extending past his chin onto his neckline.

In the middle of a dusty laterite road, dressed in a pair of dark blue shorts and a blue and white checked shirt, a boy scuffs the dirt. Strings of white thread and little bumps of rolled-up material show their age at his neckline. He has a large black bag half slung on his shoulder, half carried on his back. He walks into a compound with scattered fires in front of doorways. The rooms are in three dashes of buildings. Concreted bases, with corrugated tin sides and roofs. Sweltering hot in the daytime and cold when rain drips through the holes manufactured by the many nails hammered into the roof beams. The ground is soggy and wet. The boy loses his footing and slips in the mud, falling onto his bottom and covering the base of his bag and shorts in a thick layer of oozy black. Heads lift from around fires, calling out. The nearest hand helps him up and he trudges on towards the first door in the middle block of houses. Towards a fire, and a woman stirring into a potful of something, a pot balanced on three stones with hot embered wood between them.

Her feet are in black slippers made from used car tyres. They are too small for her and her heels bulge out, thick cracked skin edged with mud.

There is a crackle of black and white, like the end of a roll of old film. The image repeats. *In the middle of a dusty laterite road, dressed in a pair of dark blue shorts and a blue and white checked shirt, a boy scuffs the dirt.*

Olufemi takes a step forward. The image stops playing. Another step and he enters into a new space of cold.

A mother sits in a dark room crowded with shadow. She bends over as she pushes embroidery thread through calico cloth, creating an intricate pattern of blues, greens and purples. She pushes at her glasses, one handle bundled into the frame with tape. There is a blue metal kerosene lamp on top of a school edition of the Oxford Dictionary lying on a small wooden table with spindly legs. A boy perches on a stool. Two pieces of paper are on the desk. One has writing on it, several words crossed out and corrected. He uses a blue biro and starts to copy, line by line, filling up the blank lined sheet. His address on the top right corner: c/o The Headmaster, Ikeji Secondary School, Ikeji Village. 'Dear Father,' it begins, 'I have heard it said that you are a fair man and that you reward hard work. I am soon to complete my secondary studies and my teachers have been pleased with my schoolwork. I would like to attend Ibadan University but my mother cannot afford to pay for my tuition.'

The scatter of black and white marks the beginning, playing over again: *A mother sits in a dark room crowded with shadow.*

Olufemi makes his way back to the villa, this time holding the stick loosely in his hand, letting it trail a mirrored line with its forked end, back down the path. The line bumps over the odd tree trunk that sticks up into the path, it pushes pebbles aside, and scrapes itself over a large boulder, which half-protrudes from the ground. The trail disappears when he reaches the lawn, and makes his way back towards his girlfriend.

Olufemi pulls up a canvas-backed safari chair and sinks into it. He stares into the far distance, not caring whether the wind whips his words away or not, 'That's why they're called retroviruses. They retrofit themselves into junk DNA – they start making copies of themselves everywhere and stitch themselves into their victim. The clever little buggers have evolved into efficient colonisers.'

His fingers drum a staccato on the wood frame. He continues, 'To get that, I need a company that works. That has cash to work. Cash to make drugs that stop the replication. To block the viruses so they can't just rampage through bodies. My company does that – and it's important work.'

Muthoni never understands these occasional sermons on science and its power. Her eyes bounce onto his face, uncomprehending. She waits for silence to insist she's given his words adequate weight. She's pleased with the beginnings of a conversation, any conversation is better than the density of his silence, much like the fog she saw early this morning, clasping the foothills of the mountain.

'Everyone thinks you're important,' murmurs Muthoni from the lounger. 'You and Kamau have done great things at Vanguard. The newspapers say so. You are a success.'

She pauses. Then adds in a snippet of something of import to herself. 'There's a new shop opened at the Junction – a lifestyle shop. They don't sell just clothes, but also kitchenware and bedlinen. Some cookbooks too. I'd like to have a look when we get back.' She holds up the magazine, folded into an air-filled roll along its seam, 'That's lovely, isn't it?'

That is an arrangement of 'organically shaped' vases, unstructured forms, bulging in cream ceramic, with unevenly shaped mouths, squatting in a tableau of desirable stylishness. 'The birds of paradise look fantastic,' Muthoni continues, 'as if the vases were made just for them. They'd be dramatic in our living room, wouldn't they?' Olufemi wants to say, '*My* living room, yours is in the guest cottage attached to your parents' house.' He nods and says nothing in reply.

Olufemi considers the woman beside him. He's only ever wanted two things from a girlfriend. The first is beauty and a commitment to staying beautiful. He wants women who rub scented moisturiser into their skin, not thick *orie,* homemade from sesame seeds over a wood fire and earthy smelling. He doesn't want hard, thickened fingers on a woman lying next to him or thick-soled feet with dirt-rimmed cracks. The second thing he's always desired has been toughness. He prefers women who are obvious about what they want, prepared to strut and shove as necessary. The ones who get themselves places. Like Muthoni, who uses her beauty with the scraps of intelligence she possesses to make something of herself. Not sit around being soft. Boring perhaps, but never *soft.* She's not someone who would live in a tin shack struggling to send her child to school; raising a child whose rich father rides in fancy cars and strides around city skyscrapers in suits.

'Shall we go up for dinner tonight?' she asks.

'Don't feel like it. Can I have a cheese sandwich or something here, in the room?'

'As long as you promise I can have some company tomorrow.'

'Sure, we can eat up there.'

'I'll see to it then. What would you like to drink? A beer?'

'Great.'

She clatters down the steps in her multi-coloured flip-flops, the ends tapping a rhythm on her heels as she makes her way across the lawn, stepping onto each flagstone. Her hips propel her forward and they sway from side to side, her shoulders back, arms swinging. She does not have a care in the world. And she need not have a care. She knows her worth. She is a desirable companion. Her hand on a man's elbow confers his arrival. She knows how to glitter. How to live rich. She's always known how.

In the twenty minutes of head space she leaves him with, Olufemi stares down at his shoes. They're soft, brown and keep his feet protected from hard, sun-baked earth that eats crevices into your skin, embedding jiggers, trekking dirt in as if it had every right. Ants are busy ferrying grains of sugar in chunky black lines going away from the table. He reaches out a casual foot and stamps on them, squashing them and twisting his foot into the floor. His foot stays, near the ants' broken track, daring them to come bite him.

She returns soon enough. 'Guess what I found out? We can go on a sundowner game drive tomorrow evening. I booked one. It'll get us out to see nature in the wild. Oh look at all those ants, careful – they might bite!'

She hurries into the villa and comes out with a can of Doom spray. 'Watch out.' She squirts the insecticide over his shoe, over the rest of the ants, over the invisible crystals of sugar they are still searching for. They curl into half-formed punctuation marks.

Through a dinner that Olufemi finishes in four bites per toasted sandwich, washed down with swigs of beer, Muthoni chatters. Her dinner is more substantial: grilled chicken, *irio* and a green salad.

'I got the kitchen staff to make me some *irio* – felt like it tonight. Would you like a taste?'

He gets a forkful and slowly chews on hard maize kernels before swallowing them in a mash of potato and peas.

'Delicious.'

'Would you believe, only two other people are staying here? It's like having our own special hideaway. This was such a good idea wasn't it?'

At night, Olufemi puts his head under the pillow, hands on top of either side. Sleep sweeps across him, drifting into his eyes, snatching his limbs, harvesting his thoughts. It replaces them with what it wills.

A teacher stands in an open air classroom with thirty little dark heads. Sums are written out on the big board at the front. A little boy sits at a desk, his face holding concentration in every pore, tight with focus on the slateboard across his knee, a piece of white chalk in his hand.

Dim, greyed memories. Fires under cooking pots, mud on blue shorts. Scratching chalk on a squeak of rectangular plywood, painted black.

The next morning, there is a breakfast of sliced fruit, crisp-crusted bread rolls and two aluminium flasks. Muthoni is at the table, leafing through a copy of *Cosmo Kenya*. 'Morning: coffee is in the flask marked C and tea in that one,' she points at each flask in turn. 'What do you feel like having?'

'Coffee.' Olufemi thinks the *please* but does not mouth it. She pours and pushes the cup and saucer across the table towards him.

'You were flinging yourself about all night. I got up in the end and dozed in the armchair. That's why I got breakfast in so early.'

'Was I?'

'Could not make much of what you said. At one point, you shouted – "He gave me the money," but that's all I managed to figure out. I was half-asleep myself.'

'A lot on my mind at the moment.'

'Well, it must help to eat something. Have some marmalade with your bread.'

The long, green Toyota Landcruiser idles by the front entrance. A chubby cheeked man in khakis and safari boots waits alongside. When Olufemi and Muthoni approach, he says, 'Good afternoon. I am Ezra, your guide for the afternoon.'

He holds open a back door. Muthoni smiles at him and clambers in. Olufemi follows. The roof hatch is open. Ezra gets behind the wheel and leans over to reach for two lap blankets on the front passenger seat. He turns around to hand them over to the back, saying, 'These should keep you warm when we get moving. I shall be taking you to the top of Leopard Rock today.'

The clutch and handbrake disengage; the gear moves into first. The car rumbles across a cattle grid, past the watchmen near the guard house, as they lean on their sticks. Muthoni slides across the back seat towards the middle, past the middle, her legs angled away, her body trying to rendezvous with his. He is expected to do likewise, move across the seat towards her, stretch out an arm to curve her in, against his shoulder.

'We have many things in the game reserve. If you are lucky today, you'll get to see the leopard. If not, we'll see zebra, giraffe, some antelope,' says Ezra.

Olufemi stands up, 'Look,' he says, 'wildebeest.'

The pair at the side of the road turn their bearded faces towards the car. One lifts a leg and paws at the ground, then moves away to lower its head at the nearest mound of grass.

The Landcruiser creates a cloud of dust as it climbs up a hill, winding its way past large boulders and yellow acacia gleaming in the late afternoon sun. There is a view of a plain, with stubborn knobs of brown grass sticking through a scatter of loose stones. Hardy scrub inches down the slope towards the plain. In the far distance, a thin sliver of river; beyond, a blue haze blends the mountain into sky.

'Here we are.' Ezra takes out an ice box, two safari chairs and a folding table. He finds a flat spot on which to set out the chairs, angled close to each other. He puts the table in front and, opening the ice box, extracts a red Masai checked cloth, which he spreads out.

'Please sit,' Ezra says.

Next come two bowls of nuts and crisp fried chevda. A flask of chilled cocktail. Ezra pours the drink into two glasses – thick, green and heavy-bottomed. He adds in some dark brown syrup and sticks in two fat bamboo stirrers.

'A *dawa*,' he says. 'A cocktail I make – my specialty. I shall leave you alone to enjoy the sunset. I will be back in half an hour or so.' He starts the car and goes down the hill, leaving them in a quiet that claims the place of the disappearing engine.

Muthoni looks at Olufemi. Olufemi looks out at the view of the plain.

'Nice isn't it?'

'Yes.' He gulps at his drink. Muthoni sips hers.

'Looks dark over there, doesn't it?'

'Sure does.'

'Think it might rain?'

'Maybe not.'

The shadow underneath the clouds darkens and the wind blows them closer.

'I can feel a drop on my nose,' squeals Muthoni, her drink jerking onto her safari brown trousers.

'So can I.'

They stand up. There is a darkened oval of wet on Muthoni's thigh.

'I hope Ezra comes soon,' she says.

Raindrops plop into their abandoned drinks, make indents in their *dawa*s, diluting their strength. The rain splodges circles on their canvas seats that then join together.

The noise of the engine comes closer. Ezra drives up and hops out, 'Sorry. We need the rain but I thought it would not reach us until night-time today. Please get in, I'll clear up.'

The weekend's over and their bags are packed in the boot.

'Shall I drive?' she says.

'Yes,' he replies.

Doors slam. Bodies adjust into their seats. 'Shall I put on a CD?'

'Sure,' she replies.

He slips in an audio book, something to edge out the silence, and avoid the risk of another conversation like they'd had at the sundowner – weak, empty, about nothing. He sleeps for most of the journey home.

He pulls out her bag, then his. The Cabro-paved driveway is dark wet grey. The leaves on the plants in the flower beds shiver in the breeze, freshly shampooed with rain. Olufemi and Muthoni walk quietly to the lift, then up to his apartment. He opens the door. She walks in ahead of him and into the kitchen. He hears the kettle grumble in bubbles.

He puts on some music, and sinks into an armchair, flinging his legs sideways over the arms, and leaning back against a cushion propped in a corner.

She brings him a cup of tea in a promotional mug printed for his company. The logo is a linked chromosome printed in blue. The company name, Vanguard Pharmaceuticals, ranges from a dark blue tint to a shade of green the marketers had called 'spring shoot green'. The slogan underneath proclaims: 'Beating back disease at the frontier of science'.

He reaches out for the mug and half-heartedly says thanks. She stays there, standing, a long-fingered hand on one hip.

'The weekend hasn't worked has it?' She sips at her mug.

'No,' Olufemi replies.

'What are we going to do?'

He's silent.

'I'll go to my parents for the night,' Muthoni says.

He nods.

She picks up her bag at the door and turns slightly, as if she's forgotten something. She puts her mug down and waits. He says nothing. She opens the door and is gone.

He puts his mobile on vibrate, and turns to nestle in the armchair. He waits into the dark, staring at nothing in particular until the lights in the car park come on and throw shaded lines through the curtains. The music plays on.

Kamau opens the door when Olufemi rings the bell.

'How are you, my man?'

'Getting along.'

Kamau peers out through the door, 'Where's Muthoni?'

Olufemi puts up both hands in defence.

'Bad?' says Kamau.

'Yes.'

'Finished?'

'Very probably,' replies Olufemi.

They walk through into the sitting room.

'Joyce will be through in a minute. She's finishing off something in the kitchen.'

The microwave pings. Joyce calls out, 'Get yourselves something to drink, but sit at the table. Food's almost ready.'

The table has been set for four. Joyce bustles in with a Pyrex bowl held between two floral oven mitts. Her face shines with effort.

'Nice to see you Olufemi, we were beginning to think you wouldn't turn up. Where's…' She does not see Kamau shake his head at her, so she finishes her question, '… Muthoni?'

'Gone home to her parents,' replies Olufemi.

Joyce thumps down the bowl and looks up, 'She's gone where?'

Kamau shakes his head again. This time she notices. 'Oh,' she says.

'Let me get the rest of the food.' She picks up the extra place setting, moves the trivets around the middle of the table before heading for the kitchen door. Her feet are in brown bunny-socks with ears at the ankle that flap up and down as she walks.

While the men discuss the qualifiers for the African Cup of Nations, Joyce walks to and fro, bringing in more hot dishes.

She sits opposite Kamau, her upper arms jiggling. 'Help yourselves, there's an awful lot of food so I hope you're hungry,' she says, as she uncovers a casserole using the kitchen towel in her hand. She sticks in a serving spoon.

Olufemi dishes out greens, chicken stew, chapatti and *ugali* onto his plate. The mounds of food on Kamau's and Joyce's plates are much higher.

'Tell me what's been happening in your life,' says Joyce.

'Not much. I'm working hard, and Muthoni has gone home.'

'You and Kamau are just as bad as each other, working long hours.'

'Not me,' Kamau says, 'I always get home for dinner.'

Joyce scrunches the kitchen towel into a ball and throws it at Kamau's head. He ducks.

'I've still got instincts,' Kamau says. They all laugh and settle into their food.

'The children's term ends soon,' says Joyce, 'and then I'll be back to being their full-time driver, taking them to and from their friends' houses.'

'How are they? I haven't seen them for a while,' says Olufemi.

'Doing well at school, but hating homework. We have fights every night, don't we?' she turns to Kamau.

'Yes, by the time I come home, there's always one child running up to me, begging me to read instead of their mother,' says Kamau.

The conversation meanders past Joyce's concerns: the Parent Teacher Association holding an international food night, a swimming gala, tae kwon do tournaments, and the cost of school uniforms.

'That was delicious,' says Kamau, patting his stomach and leaning backwards. 'Now, let me clear the table. Olufemi, why don't you sit with Joyce in the living room. We've been looking at photographs over the weekend.'

Joyce lowers herself onto the carpet with an 'aah', and sits sideways with an elbow on the seat of the nearest sofa. Photo albums of different sizes lie in a pile next to her. The side of her thigh looks enormous from where Olufemi stands, straining against beige tracksuit bottoms. Olufemi edges past her to perch instead on the velvet print armchair against the wall.

Joyce reaches out for the first album on the pile, 'Thought you might want to see some of you and Kamau when you were young.'

Kamau barks a laugh from the kitchen, 'When we were good looking, cute and poor she means.'

Joyce turns over a few pages, 'Look at this one.'

Two young men stand together in a carpeted room. One is slimly built, of average height; the other shorter, rounder. Their faces are in a sea of others, turned towards a sharp suited man with floppy hair, holding an empty wine glass in one hand and hitting it with a fork held in the other.

'This seems such a long time ago,' Olufemi says to Joyce. "May I see the album?"

He leafs through pictures of them in snow, in restaurants, playing football, in a park, having a Sunday barbecue.

'When you're done with that, look, here's one of the day you started Vanguard,' Joyce points to a photo in an album she holds out to Olufemi. He remembers.

There are smiles and laughter among those assembled. A few congratulatory thumps on the back as glasses are raised. Several newspapers are scattered around the room − one on a chair, another on the mantelpiece, one on a coffee table. Each open to a page with headlines that include the phrase: Vanguard Pharmaceuticals. A stout-framed woman walks into the middle of the room. She claps her hands and points towards the laden dining table. People ease out of chairs and move as one. They form a circle around the table. She bows her head, clasps her hands together. Some follow suit. Others stand ramrod straight, eyes wide open.

Kamau walks in to stand next to them, looking down, 'Those were the days, hey? Have you shown him the wedding photos we found?'

The evening passes in a wave of exclamations and prodded memories of: Who? When? What? Where?

After work the next day Olufemi walks into an apartment that immediately seems cold and empty. He hangs his suit jacket on the back of a dining chair and loosens his tie. He starts to notice what things are gone when he heats up a tub of Chinese noodles in the kitchen − the cookbooks Muthoni used to leave on the window sill are no longer there. He walks into the living room and eases himself into an armchair, back straight, noodle cup held out level. The wilting lilies have gone. As have the vases they were in, which used to be arranged on the mantelpiece. In their place lies a single key.

After finishing his soup, depositing the container in the bin and the spoon in an empty sink, Olufemi goes to his bedroom. The side of the wardrobe he'd cleared for her is bare, as is the first drawer of the dressing table. In through to the bathroom − no makeup bag, no hand-washed underwear drying, no orange striped flipflops under the sink next to the set of scales she uses religiously each day.

He takes off his tie and unbuttons his shirt half-way before falling onto the bed, his lace-up brogues still on.

In the middle of the night, he hears the burring of his mobile phone, vibrating against the chair. With sleep-laden eyes, he reaches out for a pillow to block out the noise. The louder, more insistent tone of his landline phone makes him roll over and reach for the extension by the bed.

'Huh?' he says.

'Kamau's in hospital. He's been shot.' Joyce, garbled and confused, her voice drenched with sobs.

'Where is he?'

'Nairobi. They got him in the stomach.'

'I'll leave now.'

The drive to the hospital, through streets unclogged with *matatus*, is quick. Accidents and Emergency directs him to a corridor with some red-vinyl upholstered chairs. Strips of fluorescent light glare overhead. Joyce is in a huddle of four women, who all turn to look at him as he walks towards them, his shoes squeaking against the rubbery floor.

He bends in a squat in front of her, his hand reaching out to pat hers, folded together in her lap, clutching a white handkerchief that peeks out of her fist.

One of the women says to him, 'Come with me, I'll tell you what happened.'

Kamau had driven up at their gate that evening, at seven o'clock, barely dark. The watchman said a white car had pulled up behind Kamau's car, blocking it from the road. Three men jumped out, the first waving a handgun. They'd wanted Kamau out of his car. When he hesitated, one of the men reached in through the wound-down window, and opened the car door. They shot him in the stomach, then half-dragged him onto the flower beds in the driveway. The driver in the white car sped off and the other three got into Kamau's car, reversed, and followed.

They have extracted three bullets from Kamau's stomach, and stitched it together. He's needed a lot of blood. The doctors have been in theatre for the past four hours.

The operation, the blood, the medicines keep Kamau alive for another day.

Olufemi has never understood Joyce, and now he does not understand the grief that pours out of her, blotching her face, making her incapable of stringing sentences together. When he goes to see her at home, he finds her in a hushed living room, face bloated, wig askew. All sound has been sucked out of the house. It has been drained like a vacuum, leaving a deadness in its wake. The room is filled with grim-faced people, sitting still.

Kamau's widow and their three children move out of their house the day after he dies, unable to relive his death several times a day, knowing that they will never be able to do normal trips out again: to school and back, to the shops and home.

The insurance money is good. When they started the company, Kamau had ensured his dependents would be cared for in any eventuality. This had mattered less to Olufemi – who would he leave it to anyway?

In the *Daily Nation* that includes Kamau's obituary they add a two-page special in the business section. It lauds Vanguard Pharmaceuticals as a company which has profitably bust patents in its heroic ambition to provide cheap drugs. The article borrows from an earlier interview with the two of them, and shows a photograph of Kamau with Olufemi, standing together by their company logo at the office entrance. The caption says: 'Two of the most admired businessmen in Kenya.' In a country where Nigerians were all stamped as foreigners with an affinity and fondness for banking scams and drug running, this was high praise for Olufemi. The *Nation* says their company is the one most likely to produce a million pills a day in the fight against HIV/AIDS in Africa. The loss of Vanguard's CEO could derail their admirable beginning, the article concludes.

Muthoni phones him at work and leaves a message with his secretary: 'Phone me if there's anything I can do.' Olufemi is busy and stays busy. He doesn't call her back. He does his job, and he also steps into Kamau's shoes.

A month later, Olufemi calls Joyce to find her still incapable of holding a coherent conversation without descending into a puddle of sobs. He wants to scream at her down the phone: 'Husbands die! Pull yourself together. Life will take advantage of you otherwise.'

His work days stretch to cover sections of night. He sorts out business and marketing plans. He oversees quality control, staff training, factory plant repairs, distribution deadlocks. Reams of figures about production costs and sales income land on his desk. They show a burgeoning profit. Time plucks up the months and flings them behind his back.

The accountant comes to Olufemi's office to discuss their mid-year financials, 'The company sales have risen fifty per cent in the last six months and this is reflected in our profits. At this rate, share valuation will become a major issue at the end of our financial year. What are you planning to do about the shares you do not own?'

'Don't know yet, buy them back I expect, if Joyce wants to get rid of them.'

'May I suggest a bit of creativity? The company shares are grossly undervalued. Kamau was the majority shareholder and if his wife decides to turn nasty, well…'

The accountant comes forward with a sheaf of papers, with a printed Excel sheet on top. He places them on Olufemi's desk.

'Look, this is what I can do. I can arrange to set up several subsidiaries and pump cash into them. Then the subsidiaries will pre-pay significant amounts to suppliers. Only to people we know understand the need for discreet money transfers. We'll let them keep the interest – all they have to do is keep our cash in a bank and sit on it. The subsidiaries will all operate at a loss this year. The holding company will show a mild profit.'

He shuffles the papers and pulls out another spreadsheet that yells out 'Projections to year end' in bright red. 'When we are audited, our real profits will not show. This is what you should use to make an offer to buy shares. It will keep the price down. When the accounts have been audited and signed, we will ask the suppliers for the money back.'

When the accountant leaves, Olufemi leans back in his swivel chair and sticks his hands up behind his head, elbows folded. He notices a cobweb in a corner leg of his desk: the web glimmers with a ghostly grey. A bump of memory paints images with cinematic clarity in his mind, even though there are no trees today, no canopy of nature. The sound is off.

A young man enters an office with windows on two sides. An older man rises from a low leather sofa to greet him, first shaking him by the hand and then putting an arm round his shoulder, slapping it twice, then guiding him towards a view from the window. The older man points towards the port and the water beyond. The young man nods. The older man shoulder taps again then gestures to the sofa. At the desk, he picks up a long thin envelope which he brings towards the cluster of seats. Sitting next to the young man, he takes a flimsy airline ticket and a clump of green dollar notes out of the brown manilla envelope and hands them over. The young man mouths something and pushes the contents back into the envelope. The older man stands up. So does his companion. They shake hands again at the door. As the door closes behind him, the young man stops, lifts the envelope up to his nose, and sniffs it. He smiles.

Here's Olufemi's chance to act out his blood. Be like his father, who always acted on the principle of: *I can, therefore I take.* Isn't Joyce simply asking for it, begging to be walked over and trampled on? Hasn't the insurance money covered her immediate needs, as well as the children's school fees? She has sold Kamau's house on Riverside Drive and bought a smaller apartment in a compound with a swimming pool and large gates guarded by Warrior Security. There'd be change from that too. He's worked bloody hard getting the company through the past few months – should he not now hog the rewards?

Olufemi has the pile of papers his accountant has prepared on the low table between them. Joyce walked in five minutes ago wearing wide-legged jeans that manage to accommodate her bottom, which she's partially covered with a roomy white T-shirt. Now her hips spread across the leather armchair as she tucks one white-sneakered foot under the other. The plan for the meeting is to discuss Kamau's shares.

There's a strange fire in her face. The pinched grey look he remembers from a year ago is no longer there.

Joyce is chatty, 'Your secretary was telling me how busy you've been, and how hard you've been working.'

Olufemi stretches his face into a smile, which he only allows to flicker for a second.

She continues, 'I've been busy too, but in a different way. Do you know, the person who's helped me most in the past year hasn't been my sisters or my parents. It's been Muthoni.'

Olufemi isn't sure where she's leading, but says, nevertheless, 'I haven't seen her since she moved out.'

'I know. She told me. But we've seen a lot of her. She's either phoned or visited every week since Kamau died.'

She moves forward to reach for the papers on the table, 'Anyway, let's talk about these figures you wanted to show me.'

She flicks through some of the pages, 'This doesn't make much sense to me right now. I've been wondering how to deal with Kamau's business in a way that would respect all he achieved in partnership with you.' She pauses. 'The other day Muthoni said to me: "Look, Joyce, business is just common sense. If you have something good to sell and people want or need it, you'll make good money. It's as simple as that." Well, what I have decided is that I want to hang on to Kamau's shares. It's too early to sell. On my way here, I went into the University of Nairobi to register for their part-time MBA. They accept mature students like me, as long as we pay up.'

Joyce's smile radiates across her face, rounding out her cheeks, making her eyes sparkle. 'Over the next two years, I'm going to learn how to do what you do. Then I'll be able to use my new knowledge to understand figures like this.'

Olufemi stares at her and his hearing fades so he can no longer make out what she says. Yet her hands continue to speak as they move about. They wave with her words. They punctuate the air. At the end of her sentence, her fingers stand still, pausing. Then they fall into her lap. Olufemi swallows. His ears clear, but not enough to hear what Joyce says next, 'In the last year, what I have learnt is that strength comes in all kinds of ways. Kamau still lives in my children. He lives in this company. As long as I have this, and the children know this, he's alive.'

Dayo Forster is a Gambian writer living in Nairobi. Her work has been published by *Kwani*?

Travelling Cargo

Shalini Gidoomal

'INTO THE BOOT. IN! IN! IN!' shrieks the Pink Beach Hat, looping his pistol arm backwards like a shot-putter taking aim.

He releases. There's the sound of metal crunching onto high-curved bone.

Then the door slams, taking with it the final snatch of light.

Darkness.

I guess we're fortunate he used the blunt end of the gun.

We're tangled together in here, courtesy of an expert high-speed finger-shuffle that shifted our hands this way and that, locking them intertwined. Vinnie's panting hard. Or is it me?

'Be good. Be silent. Any noise from here and we shoot you.' A parting threat as the lid of the boot clunks closed. It's hard to be quiet. As we lie in the blackness, my eardrums fill with our breathy panic. We sound like a porn movie on digital-surround sound. I try to inhale sparingly, little sucks, get a little control. Vinnie's wheezing speeds up in turn.

'Calm down Vinnie, *Nyamasa*. Shut up, we need to be quiet,' I hiss-gulp.

But he continues to labour for breath, hyperventilating, small squeaks sliding in the space towards me, as the air catches in the back of his throat. I lift my left hand to reach for his mouth to muffle him. His arm – the one he's lying on – tries to come with it, a dead-weight lump caught under his body. Clever tactic this criss-cross handcuffing. I can only move with his co-operation and a lot of shuffling – not so easy in this confined space. Right now, Vinnie's too shocked to help. I yank harder, stretching my fingers towards his chin, grazing the tip with my nail.

At that moment we take off, engine revving into a high-pitched complaining screech, drowning out all noise. We're propelled into motion, the top of my back thumping into the corner of the boot as Vinnie is dragged helplessly into me. The car swerves again, and it's his turn to take the blow as we slide-bounce in the other direction. We're like a useless sack of potatoes, scudding from one end of the boot to the other. Each lap we make of the small space increases our momentum. I bang my head along the side. I'm glad I had the interior relined a few weeks ago. It's a minor comfort, cushioning the uncontrolled bumping of our body parts against metal.

When you learn to scuba-dive you learn about underwater vertigo. It comes on suddenly, this sensation. One second you're floating along in the big blue and the next you can't figure out which way is up or down. The head-churning disorientation is sufficiently dizzy-making for divers to tear off their masks and instinctively strike out wildly for the familiarity of the surface – even if they don't know which way that is. People die in this process. Being stuffed in the boot of the car is much the same. A few seconds of rolling around in the darkness and I'm lost. Are we driving backwards or forwards? Which-wards? There's silence from the directors up front, only the strain of the engine and the thud of our bodies flung this way and that. Are they still in there at the wheel? I convince myself we're alone, locked up, heading in reverse at high speed. We must be at the edge of a valley and they're going to let the car hurtle down – an out-of-control descent of a steep hillside, crashing to the bottom to blow up like in a crappy Hollywood action fest. Only, in this script, it's innocent cargo that's about to be toasted.

The heel of Vinnie's riding boot catches my ankle. I feel my brain collect my fear, convert it into unreasonable rage and hurl it at him. 'Oouch, clumsy fucker! Get it together and be careful!'

'Shiiiiitt…' he exclaims. I've head-butted his cheek, the newly-bruised one, as we slam into each other again. I try to move away. Not because I don't want to hurt him – I do right now – but we shouldn't touch, Vinnie and I. It's not that kind of relationship.

We'd only met a week ago at the Carnivore, at a naffly-named 'Sinners and Angels' night. I was drunk, hot with distress at the head honcho's sidelining of my very important work promotion. I wanted distraction and grabbed him to dance. Like a trapeze artist on a swing, I spun my body round the horizontal hip-high wooden barrier surrounding the concrete dance floor, hair flying, and then sweeping the ground, money escaping from my pocket. As a reward, he bought me many *dawas*, flashing his gold Diners Card. The first slushy SMS arrived early in the morning. I ignored it.

He got me in the afternoon, calling on my direct line at the agency, catching me just after a sticky meeting with my unimpressed boss who wanted to know why I missed last night's dinner to greet the newest recruit – the usurper of my promotion. Hungover, feeling maligned and under pressure I agreed when he asked to go to Tigoni to check out my horse – he wanted to take her on livery, share costs on her maintenance. He's not good in the saddle, but I needed subsidy in that area so I agreed. It would be subject to contract of course – and I sneaked in a clause insisting he take weekly riding lessons. My horse is precious to me after all, even if I can't afford to keep her any more, I don't want her spoiled.

'I can't believe you have the nerve to suggest I'm not a sufficient horseman,' he exclaimed, as he skimmed through the paper I thrust in his hand. He's kitted out like one – the full regalia, a new emerald-green velvet cap, breezy beige jodhpurs and, as a concession to his time at the University of Texas, a pair of brown two-tone, heavy-heeled, shin-length cowboy boots. I make him take off his spurs before we set off.

I get anxious when strangers ride my 'donkey', the nervy ex-racehorse that was thrust into my care a few years back. 'Don't pull,' I instruct as she thrusts her head up in the air. 'Don't kick' – this to vanishing horseshoes as they took off through the tangle of tea bushes – 'she'll break her leg on the roots,' I shouted after him.

'I'm not sure you care much about me,' he said when we dismounted. He paused, 'and I'm not sure I can take her on these terms.' He handed the contract back to me.

We'd left the stables in silence, my new leather saddle, hand-made and hand-carried back from India, upended on the back seat of the car. I focused hard on the road ahead, forgot the rearview mirror in my inner search for neutral conversation topics. It was a mistake coming here. We still hadn't exchanged a word when I saw the gun pointed at my window, when I heard Vinnie's *heh-heh* pant of fear next to me, when their car drew level, then slid closer to my door, pushing us towards the verge.

'*Twende*. Floor it; c'mon get us outta here.'

'Better to stop. My dad says let them take what they want… the gun's in my face Vinnie… not yours.'

I slither to a halt on the side of the road. The 'jackers park ahead and leap out of their car.

'Hit them! Drive past, you have a chance now.'

But my leg is trembling on the brake and I don't know if I can get it onto the accelerator. It's so heavy. Who said fear gives you wings? It's given me legs of lead. I've dreamt about this treacle feeling – trying to move and not being able to do it. I retort: 'Vinnie, what do you know – you've just got back to Kenya – it's better to wait, they could shoot us otherwise.'

He grabbed the wheel, leaning over me. '*Songa*. Let me do it.'

And then the 'jackers reach us. They shovel us into the back seat of the car, jabbing the gun into my arm, tossing my lovely new saddle into the ditch to make space.

'Look down. No eyes onto us. Just give us everything.'

They hoover the cash, disappearing it into their pockets, dropping my handbag carelessly at my feet. I want to ask for my precious address book. I can see the Africa Remix logo on its cover, peeping through the open zip of my bag. I try to sneak a sideways glance at Vinnie. I'm not sure he would approve of that kind of request.

'Look down!'

Eyes zipped back on my bag, I rip off my gold bracelet as instructed, give it over in this modern highwayman transaction. It was a 16th birthday present, and hasn't been off my wrist in the decade since my ma gave it to me. The elephant clasp nips through my skin as I tear it off. My hands are bigger than they used to be.

They push us out of the back seat. We stand awkwardly waiting on the verge, eyes downcast. I can't help notice that one of them is wearing heavy black leather patent boots – of the sort issued to the police force. Behind it, there's a scuffed pair of Nike trainers and a flash of pink, the Beach Hat, his rainbow embroidery proclaiming *Karibuni Kenya*. It is over, I hope.

Not so. Our descent into blackness begins. When Vinnie gets slugged for resisting, I vault into the boot – a clean quick movement that required no further instruction from any of the men. The Beach Hat's the one I fear most. His pupils roll sideways then upwards, opaque blobs cartwheeling in their red-lined orbit. He's very stoned.

'Aww, my bone, man.'

Vinnie tries to lift his hand to his face. I fumble away from him and onto my back to release my trapped arm. The cuffs clink at my wrist as they proceed over my body, allowing him to press his fingers to his sore cheek, bringing my shoulder and face closer to his. Our other pair of hands lie awkwardly crossed lower down on his thigh. There's a faint blood tang in the air mixed with his breath, which gives a history of yesterday's dinner; wine with palak masala, rice and chips with brown sauce.

'Shit, I think it's broken.'

I hear his head shift in my direction as he speaks and swivel to avoid eye contact. As I do I spot something bizarre.

'Look. Light!'

As I point, his hand comes off his dented cheek. I can clearly see a sliver of noon sky above us in the ceiling of the boot. Strange. I'm sure there's no discernible hole visible in the exoskeleton of the car. Is this some periscope illusion?

'Maybe these Japanese carmakers know their Africa-bound cast-offs might carry more than a spare wheel and luggage?' whispers Vinnie.

It's amusing, but I don't giggle. I don't want to make noise.

Through the peephole, flickers of cloud rush by. Occasionally tree branches flutter over the sky. It's always fleeting because we're moving so fast. I didn't know this tinny little machine could do such a clip. It's a white Nissan Sunny purchased specially to merge with the rest of Nairobi's homogenous Japanese car population.

'No. No. Mine's safer than being in a flash Wabenzi,' I said when Vinnie suggested taking his foxy red two-seater. 'It's specially anonymous for personal protection. Get in.'

I wonder whether his heavy metal Merc would have a peephole for passengers forced to travel cargo.

'We can call it the Japanese Window – small for slitty eyes,' adds Vinnie.

Funny, he was so earnest at the Carnivore. I felt like I had to do all the entertaining; the smiling, encouraging nods, the conversation leads. It was a hard slog at first, but a good diversion from my work-induced anger, which had only marginally been dulled by the too-much-drink. He danced lumpenly, a fixed smile on his face, head down as he concentrated on his footwork. I felt sorry for the guy – he was standing there all alone in this long white caftan number that was his angel get-up. He'd just come from some meeting, he said, new business partnerships being forged. I wasn't listening. I was there to forget about my work woes.

Still, I'm glad that he's making the effort now. His whisper lightens the atmosphere, but it also reshapes the interior. It is, after all, not a good situation we're in. I reckon I had about half a tank of fuel. That's a lot of driving around, even at this pace, and then what? I remember pictures I saw of a man, some villager from the look of it, caught by Idi Amin's army boys. It was a before-and-after sequence – the prisoner erect, even though he knew his fate as they yoked him to the tree. In the second shot he was gone, his body floppy after they'd pumped a few rounds of metal into him. He looked like an indolent piece of bent, ragged washing, folded carelessly in half. There were two soldiers chatting in the background of this photo, one blowing a plume of smoke nonchalantly into the far distance. So creepily casual. It's easier to hold this image in my head than think of alternative activities they might have in mind for me. Mustn't go there, or I could lose it. Hey, isn't it Uganda where they take these 'jacked cars to sell at a higher price? That's eight hours drive from here – as long as it takes to fly to the UK. I guess they'll have to use some of the money they nicked from us to fill up, if they take that option.

'Or the Nikon Shutter. At high speed.' Vinnie chuckles softly still staring at the skylight. 'The Nippon Shutter.'

I don't really care what he wants to call it actually. If only we could see more out of this slit. At least, where we are heading. Thank goodness our jacked mobile has found a straight stretch of tarmac. I don't remember a switchback road like the path we've just zig-zagged anywhere in the area. But then, I'm not at all sure where we are or how long we've been going. The hot blue sky doesn't give much of a clue, however hard I stare.

Vinnie stretches his hand up to the skylight, with mine reluctantly following. He touches it, blocking the light, taking us back into darkness. He shifts his legs, angling them awkwardly to one side as he reaches forward. I feel my right shoulder pulled along, my left pushed into his as he rolls into a crouched sit-up, his chin advancing to the area of the boot lock. I have to move – these handcuffs are grating hard into my skin. And I don't like this idea he's hatching. I clench my teeth, hiss savagely between them.

'Vinnie, what are you doing? Ask before you shift position. Look how we're attached.'

'I want to check the lock, maybe we can open it from inside.' His whisper gurgles in the back of his throat, as he strains to reach. I'm forced into a back-bend by his effort and I can't keep my face off his neck in this position. I repress the urge to lift my head, bite his ear, chew it off Tyson-like in my frustration.

'What! And hit the tarmac with no hands at this speed. Shall we use our heads to cushion the blow? And what do you think these arses will do then? Listen, these guys have *guns* Vinnie. Let's just play it safe. Please.'

His long fingers find an indent, a possible internal boot-opening chunk of metal, and he begins to fiddle, tweaking, pulling. Small tinny twangs emerge and echo round our prison. Enraged, terrified that our captors will hear us, I haul back on my hands, pressing my forehead down into his windpipe until he's forced off the lock.

116

'What did you do that for? C'mon girl. It's not easy being here for me either. At least let's test this lock option, see if we can release it. I want to be prepared in case we get another opportunity to get away.'

'Another one? Are you saying we had a chance before?'

'Well… My sister was six months pregnant when she was jumped at night on the road to her house. She put her foot down with her head below the wheel. Got away. Mind you, she was in a 4-by-4. We were scared she'd miscarry after; she kept puking that night.'

My father's tuition reverberates loudly in my head again. I'd reflexively behaved according to that in-drilled instruction. Stop, be co-operative. It's safer. But it didn't have the result he promised. I deflect, defensive: 'You freak me with your ideas Vinnie. Look at your cheekbone man. Mushed! It's too much flack to fling onto me. I could blame you for us being on that road in the first place. Does it help? Look we're in this situation now. We're tied, like it or not. Your actions affect mine – this is a two-way deal.'

We hit a bump. A big one.

Vinnie's head meets the ceiling with a glorious thwack. Great – might re-arrange some of his brain cells in a more reasonable fashion. The car turns sharply, slows down and the road takes on undulations, each side of the vehicle rising and falling in response to the stones and humps of the track. We're dawdling now, crawling along, and I can hear shushing against the axle of the car. God. We're off road – not just dirt track, but through long grass. It must be somewhere distant, if cows haven't reduced the vegetation to stubble in this February drought. I can hear two revving sounds, another car behind us. Their radio's set to a gospel station and the Jesus music enters our space like an unwelcome visitor. There's a shouted telephone conversation in a language I don't understand. Should I have floored it, made the effort at least to get away?

The Nissan halts. I hear the front fan begin its whirring grind to cool the overworked engine. We're not so lucky. Travelling cargo means we don't have such luxury. The stream of fresh air that in our helter-skelter pace had filled the car no longer flows through the boot. It's replaced by heat, stealing in around us, cloaking our bodies. Our confines become stifling, threatening to bury us alive, trapping the recriminations of our last whispered exchange.

What happens now? My trepidation morphs into terror. I don't want to share air with Vinnie. I don't want to be further mugged or thugged by The Boots or the Beach Hat. I can't even think about what they might want to do to me. I want something to cool the shape-shifting gremlins in my head. A cigarette – a kickboxing Sportsman. With a triple Jack Daniels. No coke.

There's a voice outside, coming closer. I reckon it belongs to The Boots – it's modulated, reasonable. The volume increases, and there's a *whump* of body on top of our cage. Then a drumming – a casual proprietary rat-tat-tat of fingers idly playing a ditty on our heads.

'Heh... *hii wawili... Raisi sana... Bado... kimbia.*'

A woman laughs in response to his comment. Even in my fear, I bridle at the thought of our capture being such a simple venture. The Boots's tone is so matter-of-fact. He's good at this – measured, menacing but polite – not crazed like his partner. I hope Vinnie didn't hear what he said. I daren't look at him. He and the 'jackers think the same. It's my fault we're here. So flipping compliant, me. The fingers continue tapping a tuneless drill, muffling the voices.

'*Lakini pesa... kidogo.*'

What! Not enough spoils! They got a car, cash, gold, plastic and us. What do these fuckers want? Are they going to punish us for our lack of generosity? For not carrying the contents of Central Bank in *shillingis* in the car? A grunt escapes my lips, as I resist the urge to bang on our ceiling and request a correction. My papa said to be submissive! You have it all – bar the saddle, which by the way, was very costly. This silent-by-necessity humiliation is worse than the earlier terror-tango of our high-speed tumble round the boot. There are bloody chickens in the background too, the squawks mangling the him-her conversation over us, preventing my search for clues as to our ultimate fate. It's so very hot in here. The sun beating down. I hate the woman for knowing, *knowing* we are trapped, and not reasoning with him to let us go. What kind of callous person is she? I wish her barrenness, and years of beatings. Did that last cackle of appreciation mean she's been given my bracelet?

I think they have something to eat. Smells of cooking head our way. Have they killed a chicken? *Choma'd* it like they're slowly doing to us in this boot? I hope they're not kicking back with the Beach Hat's favourite mood-altering substances as well. I feel sweat begin to trickle down the side of my cheek and round the back of my neck. It tickles but I haven't the energy to swipe it away. To move both our hands, to scuffle my body enough to undertake this seemingly simple manoeuvre. I rub my head against the bristle of the car mat instead.

We're there one hour, two hours. It's hard to tell. The air's exhausted now, sour from lack of circulation and the fetid aroma of our bodies. We take turns lying on our backs, Vinnie and I, swapping when pins and needles set in. It's the most comfortable compromise we can find. I'm shorter and my shoulder is under constant traction, pulled towards his body by our handcuffed hands. His legs are squished by the squat dimensions of the boot; occasionally he throws a thigh over mine to stretch it. It's an endurance game this, and our snatched whispers are the only diversion from the dull thud of silence.

'Sorry about my sister's example.'

'S'OK.'

'You want me to wipe your face?'

'Thanks.'

'It's such a beautiful face. Even in the dark.'

'God Vinnie. Let's hope the 'jackers don't think so.'

I am not even aware that I am sighing, that the last slug of breath exhaled as a sob. He rubs his hand along my waist, stroking as far as he can reach, my palm listlessly trailing his. My voice trembles as I whisper: 'Can you see the light? It's got that four o' clock glow to it, not bright any more.'

'Hey, we're only here so we don't report them to the police. They'll let us go.' His hot damp nose is close to my ear, breath fluttering inside my lobe.

I wish I could believe him.

'Didn't you see the footwear when they shut us in? I'm sure they're cop boots. And these handcuffs are not from Toys Bazaar. That guy, The Boots – I reckon I can guess his day job.'

'*Nikweli*. I thought the same. But better someone used to extortion than one who's not. When they finish whatever they're doing, they'll spring us. We're not useful to them. It's going to be cool.'

We turn sideways; Vinnie, behind me. He lifts his hand over my head in a rock and roll movement, almost cocooning us, cuffed wrists crossed over in front of my stomach. I know his arm must be squished by that move. But for a few moments I'm cosy; and I'm grateful.

'Sure they will,' I mumble. I just want to sleep. My head's perpetual low-grade thrum of dread has expended a lot of energy.

Vinnie's body moves in closer. I can feel the heat coming off him, the change in his heart rate as it gears up a notch. I stiffen, almost hold my breath in an effort to turn my back into a wall between us.

'Hey, this is, like, our time. Don't you think?' He presses my hands in his. 'You're right. We're tied together now.' He hums, 'Oh what a night…'

'This isn't the time for hammy old song lines. Please give it up.'

'OK then, Let's get real. Our evening…'

How can he bring this up now? In this situation! When we still don't know what our captors want to do with us – me really. I have to stop this.

'The heat and stress has got you now Vinnie. A few drinks and you moved onto Fantasy Island. Leave it be – how can you want to talk about such nonsense at this time?'

The pause punches into my back. He takes a long breath, leaving me in the vacuum.

'Oh. But babe, you said… you *said* it was a night to remember.'

Remember? Don't remind me. I'd gone to the off-license on the ground floor of Ufungamano House, close to my place of work. I'd grabbed a batch of Two Keys whisky sachets, little double-tot plastic packets, and plonked them on the counter, fuming.

The woman sitting behind it stared at me impassively. I wondered if my big indolent fuckwit of a boss shopped here too. He's brain addled for sure to not give me that rise. Talking instead about bringing in a new person from outside. The assistant took her time – ten minutes – to write the bill laboriously on a blotchy Textbook Centre receipt book, which she stamped in a purple flourish with the name of the shop. I grabbed my purchases, slung them into my bag, and stalked back up the stairs to work. I made a cup of coffee and poured a couple of sachets into it; took a big slug. It was comforting. Calming. Time wasting. I fixed another. Stronger this time. They're not getting any more benefit from my brain cells in this office today. And a little numbness would help me get through that tedious work-dinner tonight. The cheesy welcome to the new manager that I dreaded. All the same, I popped a piece of Juicy Fruit gum into my mouth to mask the smell. But an hour later, as the booze took hold, I made a defiant last-minute decision to abandon the evening office engagement, to head home, dress up, and then go out to get mothered.

That bit is clear.

Leaving Carni – that's embedded too, the gravel walk to his car, which wobbled my killer heels – I leaned on him, just a touch too many *dawas* maybe, along with my fortified coffees of the afternoon. Then his little two-seater number roaring onto Uhuru highway, the hem of my unravelling lace confection caught in the door, trailing on the tarmac. I hear Vinnie's voice butt in on my thoughts.

'And what about at your place? Things were so fine when we jived so smoothly on the drive?'

Does he mean the hazy sway in front of the amused eyes of the *askari*? The one that nearly tipped us into the cactus? It was still fun then, feckless even, but I don't respond. I don't want this sequence of events to be explored further. Vinnie swivels his limbs, twisting me over to the other side of the boot. Not out of arms length though. That's not possible in our situation.

He lobs his confusion over to me; 'I know you didn't reply to my SMS, but still. We had a great night. And you brought me to see the horse today. I can't understand why you turned so hostile…'

Footsteps. A door slams, then another. Engine on, and we're off again, the car picking up speed as it moves off the grass, swerving fast onto tarmac. The sweet relief of breeze rushes between us. I almost enjoy the crack of my back against the side of the boot as we resume our bumpy tour of the interior. It's a distraction. A penance.

Frankly the next chunk of that night is a bit blurry. I recollect the key jiggling in the wrought iron gate at the kitchen, me trying to stop it from clanging and waking up my housemates. I have a misty memory of wiggling my pretty way into the kitchen, while he fixed yet another cocktail, still enthralled with the turn of events, occasionally exclaiming 'cool man.' He wasn't really my type – too skinny, too serious, woodenly bringing the talk to work, while I blithely switched it to inquisitions of music taste and his Texan experience. I wanted diversion and I got it. I was, after all, trying to forget about office things, about my own disappointment. Vinnie didn't have such issues – he'd come back with his cowboy MA and slotted straight into work with the family firm – smart car, credit card and regular manicures thrown in, to judge by his nails.

I'm not usually a woman prone to memory lapse, but I wished the fog that covered the middle of the evening also covered the end. When I woke up alone, there was a moment of blissful befuddlement to be sure, but then the thud of hangover and reality set in.

When I slouched reluctantly downstairs to get some tea, there was confirmation of course. I found the remnants of my tattered 'devil's chocolate cake' costume sprayed on the sofa. Propped on the low glass coffee table were my perspex diamante stilettos, the left one half full of some stale screwdriver concoction that he'd mixed. Beside that, an empty box of *Rough Riders*, its rubbery contents scattered like confetti across the floor. Only that night's waywardness was no celebration. I remembered his feet on the table, smiling face turned up to me, caftan skewed, revealing a thin lower leg, then as I turned to change the music, heard him quick-spray his mouth with one of those breath fresheners.

I think it was then that I found the note from one of my housemates – my boss had called a number of times asking about my whereabouts. I'd scrunched it up in renewed rage, lobbed it out of the window and turned to Vinnie.

I blink to block out the rest of the memory and twist my head away from him, dodging as best as possible any further elaboration. I wish I could morph into a puff of air, wiggle out of the skylight, avoid this mess altogether. As I move, I see the light well-shows that it's nearly dark outside. I can't believe my heart has the stamina to keep hammering at this pace in my chest. I didn't know stress was such a long-distance runner. Just when you think it's all out of energy, it gathers strength for a final push, the sprint to the finish line. I'm having trouble holding back my fear – the dark thoughts, night thoughts – us still here in this bloody boot. Vinnie's come-on just now only served to speed up the panic. Why do these guys still have us here? What are they planning? What if they rape me? How many are there? I'd almost rather they do whatever filthy things they might want to, and get this agony of lingering over with. Oh God! We're stopping. I take that last thought back.

The wheels squeal as they leave a rubber layer on the road. The car door creaks on its hinge.

One step, two steps. Three. I hear fingers fumbling with the lock.

The lid is thrown open. Even though its daily trajectory is nearly over, the waning evening light lasers my eyeballs. I blink, blink again, shrink away from the glow and its murky message.

The tall frame of a person looms over us. He reaches down.

I think I'm going to throw up.

Click, click and I'm free. Of them, of him – on my own once more.

The Boots hands me back my bag. Complete with address book inside. Apologises for the inconvenience. I'm so startled, I almost say thank you. He gestures with his gun. 'The police station is that way, to the right at the bend. Now you run or I'll shoot you.'

I give full power to my legs; pump thump as my feet hit the ground, ignoring the wobble of cramp from long hours curled in a small space. I'm the six million dollar woman. I barely feel the thorny branch tear into the side of my arm, just tug to free myself, as I hear the shots. I career through more bush, swerving, skidding, dancing away from the thwumps and cracks, before I finally dive ditch-ward. Panting, thudding heart, face full of heat. With no idea of where I am still, the batteries in my bionic legs switch off, and in that moment of stillness, the floodgates open. I barely have time to rip off my trousers.

I take the longest pee, half squatted on the slope as darkness descends, the splashback flicking bits of dust up my legs. In the distance is a flickering light. I'd kill for a cigarette.

I hear a scrunch of leaves, whip up my thong as there's another release of liquid close by. A long shaky sigh of relief.

Vinnie.

The night closes in. So he got away then. And we ran in the same direction.

I look around cautiously, then step out in the open. In the fading light across the valley I make out the plump shapes of squat tea bushes. They've dumped us less than a mile from where they scooped us up. Either that, or in Uganda.

'We're free, see,' smiles Vinnie. His cheek looks a mess. There are blood stains along his face and part of his neck. He sees me looking and puts his hand up to gingerly touch it.

'*Hakuna matata*, it'll get fixed.'

We walk, both bolting bushward at the sweep of headlights from a car on the nearby road, jumpy that the 'jackers might change their mind and come back for us. The dusty trail leads up through the tea plantation. Vinnie slides his arm around me. I pretend to slip on the scrubby ground, shrug it off and move away from him.

As we tramp along in the still night, I struggle to shut out a flurry of new niggling thoughts, rising up unbidden, like restless ghosts. Vinnie was right in his assessment of the 'jackers. How did he know that? Maybe he's more savvy than I thought. His cheek looks bad, whatever he says. Am I treating him any better than the 'jackers did to us? I was so afraid of what they would do to me – use me like a plaything; easily discarded when it's served its purpose. In a flash of memory I remember shuttling Vinnie to the door that night after we finished, ignoring his 'hey, don't push babe.'

'I'll pay for a new saddle if you want,' his voice breaks my reverie, appeasing.

'There's no need, it's not your fault.'

'Yours neither,' he replies. 'You're blameless.'

I come closer again. He takes my hand. This time I don't resist. We continue in silence, eyes fixed on the beacon of wavering light up ahead. A promise of rescue.

Shalini Gidoomal is a freelance journalist, writer, businesswoman and inveterate traveller, born, and currently living, in Nairobi. She has worked extensively on various UK and international magazines and newspapers, including *The Independent, News of the World, FHM, GQ* and *Architectural Digest.* She profiled five Northern Irish photographers for the book *Parallel Realities,* and has worked locally for the *Standard* and Camerapix.

Treadmill Love

Billy Kahora

They met in the mirrors…

EXACTLY SIX MONTHS BEFORE MAXWELL KUNGU KAMANDE fell in love with the girl in the mirrors, he stirred from months of long sleep one late Limuru afternoon and decided he never wanted to see his immediate relations ever again. It was during the failed long rains of 2005 and he had spent the last six months lying in bed, drinking soup made of large bones, mouthing different farm animal sounds and masturbating himself to distraction. He got out of bed and all he had on was a tight, ugly blue knitted sweater that lacked ambition and stopped at his midriff. Wobbling to the curtain slit of light at the window, he almost slipped on the hundreds of newspaper pages on the floor, teeming with headlines, obituaries and other information that he had pored over meaninglessly during his big sleep. There were glass and plastic bottles of pills strewn everywhere on the floor and they rolled away from his dragging feet, seeming to hold glimpses of his life in all its entropy. Some burst open and hundreds of large green blobby pills, fat yellow capsules, bright orange saucers raced across the wooden floor; a grey fine powder rose making him sneeze.

Kungu reached the window with his hands still at his sides, his face parting the slips of curtain aside. He observed the obsessive hand of his mother in the neatly tended purple-blue bougainvillea hedge. In the drizzle, flowers from childhood in their wild African colours, in-between orange-reds, yellow-creams brought back Mother's cloying sweetish smell. For a brief moment this drowned the heavy pall of old news, drug-induced sweat and semen in the room. His eyes travelled over the sharply-cut edge of the Kikuyu grass lawn, lush and arsenic-green with life. Their prickly blades made him shudder and a hot itch came over him, making him scratch the back of his neck and upper back with force, his face curling into a rictus of delight. There were several *pangas* lying on the lawn, left by the day workers. A dog appeared swinging with an aimless gait. It licked one of the *pangas* and idly wagged its tail when it sensed his presence at the window. Reaching for the window with its forelegs and failing, it hung there, miles short, with its little pink penis flitting in and out of a piece of skin near its belly.

Kungu sighed and clambered back into bed. Looking at the ceiling brought on an involuntary sob. Somewhere in his chest he also felt a burst of uncontrollable laughter coming on. After a brief struggle, he softly wept for 15 seconds, 'til the drizzle outside turned into a sweeping downpour that lashed at the window-panes. Kungu stopped crying and the rain let up its mocking. The threatening laugh in his chest ebbed away. Yes, leaving here would be easier than living with the welcome everyday thought of killing Mother and destroying the things she had possessed with such greed all these years – his older brother, Morris the banker, lawyer-sister Lois, fat Damaris whose kid, Kiki, was the only thing Maxwell still loved in the family though she had taken over his last-born privileges in the family. Kungu was 37.

When he stepped out of the room at one far end of the large house the corridor was cool and quiet. There was a pile of plates with old food, that looked like mildewed droppings, which Mumbi the maid had forgotten to collect. Kungu listened for noises from childhood but the boards remained uncreaking and the wind in the roof dead to his ear. Other dream sounds from the last six months came from what Mother called his second childhood, the sea of depression that had washed over him. She had laughed off many doctors' diagnoses as indulgences. His melancholia, in her eyes, was a weakness she faulted herself for not nipping in the bud when Kungu had started tugging at her skirts as a child.

The house had been dying slowly. Years ago in the '60s it had been in Nairobi's social magnifying glass. *The Kamande house is one of the proud vestiges of this country's new independence. Delicately balanced like our fledgling democracy, its North Wing looks out into the finest Limuru coffee estates in this country. Mixing leisure and commerce the South Wing gazes across lush meadow and fresh sedge. A small river runs through it. When I jokingly asked Edith Kamande whether they had ever considered opening a small golf course, hubby Augustine Kiereini Kamande looked up with interest…* Once Kungu's father had shrunk to a brittle death from bone marrow cancer eighteen months ago, Mother had boarded up the North Wing, the upper South Wing, and put away most of the furniture. Only the lower South Wing, leeward to the sun, was left open. It held the kitchen, dining hall and three small bedrooms that Mother, Kiki and Damaris occupied.

After Mathare Mental, Maxwell came back, sawed a large hole through the blockboard his mother had used to cut off the North Wing and went into his old room without a word. It was in that far room that he had been living and dying in turns, cut off from the other four inhabitants of the house, Mother, Damaris, old Mumbi the housekeeper, and Kiki – when she came home for the holidays. It took Kungu five minutes to get to what passed for life in the old house. He had to stop for breath after he clambered through the large hole in the blockboard, holding himself up against the dusty comforting walls. Beyond the hole he soon got to the dining hall, the most socially active room of the house, sat down heavily and looked around. There was nothing idle about the room, just four hardwood chairs and the large dining table that once took up to fifteen people.

There were several heavy glass pitchers of coloured water everywhere – on top and inside the cabinet, on the dining table and even on the large window-sills. Every morning, Mother sprinkled the black, blue and green liquid all over the house to ward away evil spirits sent by her enemies. Kungu walked into the kitchen and stumbled on sacks of produce and muddy farm implements. There were several bottles of vodka on the dirty shelves at various stages of depletion. The large clock, one of the remaining pieces of furniture not boarded up in the rooms upstairs, claimed it was 10 pm. Next to it was a large photo of a forbidding looking man, his father with a young woman with a determined chin. It said, *Augustine Obadiah and Edith Kiereini Kamande London. 1951.* Mumbi the maid was nowhere to be seen.

Opening the back kitchen door, Kungu squinted at the large sky, recently visible after more than thirty years. For most of its natural life the back of the South Wing had suffered under the shadow of a copse of impressive blue gum trees. During one of his pre-Mathare impulses, a year ago, while Mother was away, Kungu went into a nearby slum and came back with a gang of men. It took three days for them to bring down the trees. Kungu paid the men in firewood in an over-generous exchange for their labour. He had no idea that blue gum was to furniture-making what *Arabica* was to coffee. The exhilarating after-crash prompted Kungu to slaughter one of his mother's goats for the men. He also got one of the workers to brew *muratina*. In the evenings the men sang, ate and drank, after sawing away at the trees all day with abandon. A few electronics went missing in the house. Half the huge pile of blue gum logs the men stacked in the driveway disappeared in a week, and the rest Kungu sold for a pittance. More than anything else it was this that prompted Mother to call her friends from the Muthaiga Police to 'discipline' him. He spent one week inside, after which he 'cracked' and had to be taken off to Mathare, catatonic and still like the Limuru evenings of his childhood.

Even now the treeless back of the house remained dark and cold. Kungu would never know that his one revolutionary act had not been futile. He had lined the pockets of the farm workers with blue gum cash. He stood there and understood that the back of the house would never acquire the life of the sunny front veranda that had been his father's side of the house. Mother had bolted the front door with his father's passing, impatient with the attention it drew away from the rest of the house. As he looked up into the sky, smelling the rain, Mother appeared on the driveway.

She was a big and firm block of flesh. Her face had turned grey-black over the years, like the aging bark of a *Mugumo* tree. She walked up the *kokoto* driveway crunching stones in black gumboots. She wore a large military sweater and long heavy skirt. A young sapling growing near the wall of the house caught her eye. She strode up to it and quickly and efficiently stripped its slender stem of growth hindering sprouts. Kungu moved away from the doorway at her approach and she trooped inside without a word, dropping the *pangas* from the lawn and flower cuttings at his feet. He heard her rummaging inside for awhile and then she was back. She held a pitcher of black-coloured water in her hand.

He flinched when she grabbed him by the chin to examine his soft, light-deprived face. Her rough and gnarly hands felt like a vice. Her small eyes filled with an ancient mischief when she recognised a new force in him. 'Eh, my boy Maxwell. I see you woken up.' She gurgled softly, sprinkling the black water all over his face with muddy thick fingers. 'Unnnh… so soft and white.' She peered at his stomach, still uncovered, and poked a thick fingernail in it till he doubled over. The sudden intake of stomach almost dropped his pajama pants. 'Mzee, god bless that fool. He would be happy. We eat soon.'

'You can pray in English, Swahili or whatever tongues you been speaking day and night, night and day in that room,' Mother announced when they sat at different ends of the long table. Kungu ignored her. In between them sat a huge pot. Mother muttered a brief prayer and pulled the pot to herself. She ladled a thick stream of boiled whole carrots complete with top, half cabbage chunks and different kinds of seeds, peas, beans, maize, cowpeas, lentils on to her plate. Then she peered inside the pot and pulled something out with a huge clunk onto her plate – an unpeeled *nduma*. This seemed to satisfy her and she let go of the pot. She spooned everything into her mouth without a word, spitting out, twisting and pulling with her hands at everything as a small pile of carrot leaves, cabbage leaves and small husks grew at her side. The *nduma* was left sitting on the plate.

Mother heaved her large frame from her seat and went into the kitchen. She came back carrying an old enormous *birika* and two large tin cups. She poured a steaming gush of milky tea in one cup and sat down. After peeling the *nduma* onto the small pile by her side, she nibbled gently at it and sipped her tea between mouthfuls. Now and then she grunted with pleasure. Kungu sat there till she had finished. When she made to get up, he said: 'I want my money. I want my money and that's all I want.' She sat back and gave him a measured look, releasing an elemental sound from the depths of her largeness, stood up and trumped off, switching off the lights behind her.

Kungu sat there all night. Fog drifted from outside into the house swirling around his still figure. The next morning Mother came in dressed in an old cotton sack of a dress. Now that she knew what he wanted she had a certain swagger. She dipped her finger in the cold pot from last night, put it in her mouth and looked at him mildly. 'Yes I guess you have woken up.' She cleared the pot and the plates, his was unused, from the table and went into the kitchen. She started singing a song about women clearing the forest. He heard her turn on the gas to heat the tea in the *birika*. She came back into the dining room with a loaf of bread, which she cut in huge impatient chunks. 'Your brother and sister will come this weekend and we decide.'

'I want my money.'

'Weekend. You can wait two years. You can go mad. You can have sold my blue gums. You can have been a parkin' man in Tanzania. *Ati* you can have had depression. I don't even know depression for what. Your own mother think… does she even look happy. You can wait till this weekend.'

'I also want the Buru Buru house and one of the cars, even if it is the Mazda…'

'This new government. It has changed things. Now you can have what you want. Nobody wants this any anymore. Moree or *ka* Lois don't.

Maybe Damaris because she is lazy with that barman boyfriend of hers. Things are not like they were before.'

She scooped up the pile of peelings from last night and left him there. 'Back to the river these go. Manure for next year's *ndumas.*'

That Saturday, Morris the banker-brother arrived first. He slammed his car doors shut, ignored the house and went down to the farm. His top-heavy figure, this less-sunny side of fifty, was dressed in a striped shirt and suspenders. Workers stopped what they were doing when he approached. They praised Mother to his face, talked of recent calfings, the size of the coffee berries that year and so-and-so's *Mungiki* son who had been shot by the police. Morris would grunt, remove his non-prescription spectacles and rub his eyes. He refused their offerings of sour milk, black plastic bags full of half-rotten plums and bananas the size of his forearm. Halfway through his tour, he was summoned back to the house. Lois had arrived.

The family met at the table. Mother sat at the head with Morris and Lois on the sides, Kungu sat at the far end. Damaris, whose consequence in the family had flittered way after getting pregnant at seventeen from fucking one of the workers, had not been informed of the meeting. Morris cleared his throat as if to start the meeting but was ignored. Mother started the accusations. 'Remeba that Luo garl you brought home Maxwell. Skinny, like I don't know what. Thin, thin, thin. The kind that white men like to go with in cheap Nairobi hotels and do all sorts of things. What was that? Tell me what was that.' She breathed heavy and deeply. 'But now I wish you had settled with her. Anything would have been better than this.' Lois, the sister-lawyer and the kind of woman who thought that she had to look as ugly as possible for the judiciary of Kenya to take her seriously, and for that matter was not taken seriously, said seriously: 'It is good to see you like this. Wanting things after a long time. It's a good sign.'

'Remember Dad used to say wanting without taking is nonsense. I've always wanted things but you all have always refused me. I'm taking what I want. One of the cars and the Buru Buru Phase 2 house. I also want what is my money that Dad left me. I'm well and I leave Wednesday.'

'Have you been taking your medication?' That was Morris. Kungu walked away finding it difficult to raise his arms from his sides. Mother turned to Morris: 'Go see those Luhyas in the Buru Buru house. Tell them we need it back. We can offer them something else, maybe the house in that other place, Doonholm. Also, go to the bank – the boy will need some money for now. And furniture and things. I'm also giving him the old Land Rover. He looks well enough to me…'

'Edith, I mean Mother. I am totally against the idea. Imagine Maxwell back in the world.' Mother swivelled slowly to him and stared at his forehead, similar to hers. Looking at him she wondered at his stupidity when it came to reading people.

'Moree, keep to your figures and leave understanding people to me. I know the boy. Out there he will soon forget what is his due. And it is not a little sum. The Buru Buru House, a car is nothing. That he'll settle for. His ability to get caught up outside there will be our saving grace. Talk to your friends, those boys in State House – they might get him something in PR. Ten years in advertising should count for something…'

'Mum, I think those people in the Buru Buru house are Kisiis not Luyhas. Or maybe they are Maragolis. Why would Maxie want to live there?' Lois said.

When Kungu made the exodus from Kiambu to Buru Buru, he felt the air around him change and thicken in degrees. By the time he got to Buru Buru he had adapted from the long smooth tree-lined drives of his childhood to the frequent gear-shifts of this new place, crowded with people, cars and activity. He found the Buru Buru house cleaned and laid out simply and comfortably. When he got into the main bedroom upstairs he ignored the bed. He found an old crumpled waterbed in the store, filled it up with cold water and dragged it into one of the empty rooms. He hurled himself onto it and slept for a week. When he woke up he was happy that the windows looked out into the blank colourless face of another building. It was close enough to stretch out and touch.

He had fallen in love with Buru Buru when he had first visited his best friend in high school, years ago. Its informality, the girls who gave it up when they heard he was a Kamande from Red Hill, and the easy movement had for the first time made him aware of the possibilities of class in Kenya. He had spent many a weekend driving around in an old pick-up with Rick, partying it up. That was exactly twenty years ago. Buru Buru, the middle class project, had become an industrial slum over the years – illegal structures had sprung up all over the place like bad teeth. But it was exactly what Kungu felt he needed. He re-immersed himself in the estate's total lack of history, its careless noises and lack of structure. There were no coffee bushes or so-and-so high-profile neighbours. There were no fresh smells, distracting butterflies and flowers. He oriented himself to the estate's 'courts' after growing up with ridges and valleys. Nothing had ever been written about Buru Buru in Kenya's official history outside of Ministry of Housing plans. It was not Limuru or Kiambu with the baggage those places had, the haughty assumptions, country club accusations or land grievances. All Kungu had to do in Buru Buru was float on the waterbed all day, and listen to its strange moorings and urgings.

In the evenings he went for walks between the boxlike structures with orange brick rooftops, ugly and faded in the day but beautifully jaded in the falling sun. Hundreds of antennae reached for the sky. He watched lights come on and go off. Children cried and mothers laughed. Every now and then there were gunshots. Apart from one night when a security helicopter bathed him in light, nobody noticed him. Contact was realised at a distance though people crisscrossed each other every second. Nobody acknowledged his presence in the small lanes that transversed the estates and confused him to no end. But they knew he was new and watched him behind the upstairs curtains of their houses.

He learnt the certain codes of living in an estate, and the look of vague interest exchanged on the pavement. He learnt the language of the small shops and their small concerns. What bread did he want, Mother's Choice or Breadland? What milk did he prefer, Gold Crown or Tuzo? These were things he had never thought of and they charmed him. One of the neighbouring families of his childhood owned Gold Crown.

After about a month he discovered a bar in the nearby shopping centre, in one of the ugly, colourless, plaster buildings and he colonised a quiet corner. It was one of those 'new Kenya' places and was called 'Baada Ya Mateso Hakuna Chuki'. *After The Suffering There is No Hate*. Everyone called it Mateso. *Suffering*. Life in the bar was different and yet similar to the estate. People talked, walked up and down, in and out of the bathrooms, with little contact. To Kungu they seemed to be always reaching to be part of something. They sought a national moment when they all turned to the seven o'clock news on one of the numerous bar TVs. But it was with a puzzled silence that they turned back after they watched the leaders they had elected. In the stream of crises that seemed to be part of the new government they would grimly laugh and sip their beers. Laughter and buzz would build up till Manchester United or Arsenal came on, and a then hush would come over the place.

Kungu grew to like being part of the flickering nothingness of the place, with its ephemeral national moments. He sensed that everyone everywhere in Kenya was doing the same thing, watching politics with hunger, talking Premier League and drinking away the years. He soon learnt not to directly look at anyone in Mateso – after a few flat, hard, challenging stares were returned. He learned to watch people in the bar mirror. And since this had a degree of deniability he got away with it. After a while he became a familiar face at the bar and was nicknamed – 'Chochote'. This was because he never ordered a specific drink but always asked the barman for 'anything you have.' For a long time he thought he was being uncomplicated and friendly. The waitresses, always giggly at his strange lightness and eyes that became big with alcohol, called him 'Brownie.'

One day he heard a knock at the door. The sun had barely come up. It was 6 am. When he opened the door there was a little boy standing there. '*Sasa* Uncle,' the boy said from the nasal depths of his Down's syndrome condition. It was the court's little town crier. Kungu had seen him around greeting everyone and everything with the same loud '*Sasa*.'

'Heeeyyyy, whas your name,' Kungu said.

'Unnhh Unnhh. I want bread. I want T.V. T.V. T.V. I want car. No dog. Heee hee heee.'

'Heeeyyyy, do you go to school? What did you learn yesterday?'

'Mmmm. Bread. I want bread.' Kungu made him some tea and the boy adopted him. The two estate idlers cut quite a pair. A tall, light, moon-faced man with a high forehead, scraggly beard and wild hair, all jangly and awkward with disuse, and a little puffed-up boy with a never-ending stream of snot. The boy's mother always dressed him up in the tightest of T-shirts that failed to cover his protruding tummy and large shorts that kept slipping down his ankles. The little boy was always covered in a thick layer of Vaseline Petroleum Jelly. Everyone in the estate called him Bubu. His head was covered in ugly patches from the pair of scissors his mother took to his hair every several days. Kungu soon bought a T.V. and Bubu spent the long idle days seated on the floor entranced by Cartoon Network.

Since Kungu started going to the bar and sitting in the same tight corner he had on occasion heard a pattern of noises coming up from the third floor of the building. Mateso was on the ground floor and when Kungu asked the barman about the noises, he was told it was mad people jumping around. Kungu assumed it was one of those new churches. It would be quiet when he got to the bar around 3 pm then the noise would pick up slowly by 4 pm. At six, there would be shouts of exertion and some kind of dance music filtering down to his corner. By 8 pm the whole third floor would be lit up and then slowly die down, lights off by ten, when Kungu was going home.

Looking up one day, Kungu stood up and decided to walk up the rickety set of metallic stairs still fresh with ugly streaks of oxy-acetylene flame. The noise came closer as he clambered up the three floors. On the third floor he could hardly hear himself think as he went around a small corridor coming out into a large room. There was a large sign that said *Gym*. Two of the room's walls were large mirrors, and the black rubber floor was full of indignant rubber squeaks topped by a sky-blue ceiling that watched over old men with heaving tits from goat meat and forty years of independence. Kungu saw individuals of all shapes and sizes, dressed in all colours, strained in one form of movement or the other. There were several T.V. screens and on all of them a cheetah chased some kind of hog. When Kungu walked in, he saw a side room with more mirrors and at least thirty women in some kind of separate aerobic activity, moving in unison. Their trainer seemed to be trying to bring the roof down with indecipherable shouts and cheers. Everybody was preoccupied with themselves in the mirrors.

On the further end were large horizontal windows with a bird's eye-view of Buru Buru's rooftops. There was a separate enclosed square space, a barber-shop with two large leather seats with two young barbers hunched over customers. There were five others waiting, seated in right-angled fashion. Kungu saw all this through a reflection in the large mirrors that took one side of the barber-shop. That was when Kungu saw the girl in the mirrors. She sat in the corner, she had a long thin neck and pinched haughty features that cried of boredom and an old wisdom. She laughed at something that was said by one of the customers. The flash of pinkness from inside her mouth was that of a newborn baby. Her face was ageless. Something stirred in Kungu and he felt drawn to this new universe full of mirrors.

As he turned to the floor he noticed that everyone's eyes were glued to the T.V. screens. When Kungu squinted he made out a strange sight on the screen – an elephant was trying to mount a rhino. People gaped, shaking their heads. Then there was a convivial laughter all around. At that moment Kungu decided to sign up. He went up to the desk where a large young man, one of the trainers, sat watching the activity on the floor. Kungu could not tear his eyes away from his large muscled neck as he filled out of the forms. 'Hey, even animals are getting on the programme.

Becoming perverts. Now rhinos and elephants are doing it like you do it on the Discovery Channel. I remember this pig that was always doing it with the dogs in my neighbourhood…' the trainer said with a strange earnestness. His neck rippled when he spoke. Kungu realised how young he was and decided to say something. 'Yeah, that shit is Darwinian – with only a handful of rhinos in the world poor thing probably doesn't have a partner,' Kungu offered. The trainer looked at him incomprehensibly for a moment, then laughed and raised his palm. Kungu put out and the guy slapped it hard.

When Kungu looked up after this exchange and into the barbershop mirror through a glass partition he saw the girl in the corner looking at him with a flat insolent stare. She was washing a customer's head. He put his hand up uncertainly, as if to wave, and the girl with the subtlest of sneers, he was not even sure that it had happened, dismissed him. Kungu felt a sharp pain in his temples. After that he came to the gym every day. He would get onto one of the treadmills and after adjusting the machine to a brisk walking pace watch the girl in the mirrors. When there was no work she slumped in a chair in half a doze with her long legs stretched out, watching the world. Then she would open her eyes in the barber room mirror and catch him looking at her from the mirror in the gym in front of the treadmill. She would stare hard at him till he was forced to look away. One afternoon the intensity of her eyes scared him so badly that he adjusted the levels on the treadmill and started running briskly, as if trying to get away from her.

Within minutes, her image in the mirror started blurring and with a huge pain in his chest he just managed to bang the machine's emergency *STOP* sign before his legs gave away. He stepped off and heaved away for minutes. When he looked up the girl was laughing hard in the mirrors.

On busy days, he observed her as she washed heads and massaged male temples. This was mostly on Saturdays, Sundays and Wednesday evenings and she ignored him completely. He watched her pink mouth laughing with customers and he hated her. On those days he would leave the gym, go downstairs to Mateso and drink himself silly – once or twice he thought of ignoring the turn to his new home and driving back to Limuru. After a few days he would catch her eyes on him and this would bring on a quick recovery. He started arranging his gym schedule around her work patterns. Once he realised she never came in on Tuesdays, he started taking the day off. Mondays and Thursdays, which were extremely slow at the barbershop, became the days he ran flat out on the treadmill

135

under her scornful stare. These became his 250-calorie days.

When she was busy, Kungu found himself unable to summon up any energy beyond a calm walk. He was lucky if he did 100 calories on such days. After two weeks of her scorn, his stomach stopped jiggling. His slow shuffle on the treadmill became a lope and his shoulders and neck seemed straighter. One day, totally lost in himself, drifting in and out of the mirror trying to catch her eye, he suddenly looked at the treadmill gauges and saw the impossible figure of 400 calories. Elated, he looked in the mirrors and caught her eye on him. Her bored look was gone and there instead lingered a curiosity, a frank reappraisal that was gone in an instant. Her features became pinched again and the boredom and haughtiness returned with only the hint of a faint smile at the corners of her mouth.

As the weeks wore on Kungu would lose himself in the calorie gauge of the treadmill machine. Some days he would go on for ten minutes without looking for the barber-shop in the mirror. To maintain discipline he made friends with the trainers and exchanged pleasantries with several of the old men who came to the gym. Most of their stories were the same, they were suits who came to the gym to escape being in their element. After stripping off their shirts, specially adjusted at the girth and neck, they took to the treadmills, x-trainers and exercise bikes with an enthusiasm that quickly faded into sweaty foreheads and heavy puffing. He saw them watching him, hating his slow smooth running figure, a 750 calorie runner. In the sauna, naked and sweaty, the old men talked politics through jiggling stomachs and laughter that chimneyed through the holes in their faces. He declined when one or two invited him for a beer afterwards. He had noticed the girl looking at many of the old fat men with disgusted amusement.

One day as he left the gym, thinking himself cured of staring into the mirrors, he looked up and saw the girl in the corridor outside the men's changing room. She was much shorter than in the mirrors, parts of her face were dry and old. Her arms were covered in bangles. A waft of young sweat floated free from her figure. She looked at him as she passed and whispered: 'Why have you been ignoring me? Who do you think you are?' He went downstairs to Mateso, and sat in his corner. Bees swarmed around his head. 'Buy me a beer,' a voice said next to him, shaking him out of his reverie. It was this old guy everyone called, 'Twenty-five years.' He was a civil servant who started every sentence saying: twenty-five years ago... women were more beautiful, twenty-five years ago... Nairobi was a civilised place...' Kungu gave him Kshs 200 and left.

The next day Bubu appeared on Kungu's doorstep with his head freshly shorn, tufts of hair sticking out of bare patches. Kungu put him in the Land Rover and drove to the barbershop. When he walked in with Bubu everyone stared at them. The two barbers sufficiently recovered and offered a greeting. The girl came over to Bubu, leaned over him and said, 'Has Daddy brought you to get a haircut?' Bubu stood up and hugged her. Everyone in the barbershop laughed. She turned to Kungu and said, 'My name is Kaume.'

Glossary
panga – machete
birika – teapot made of tin
kokoto - gravel
nduma – river arrowroot
Mungiki – local sect

Billy Kahora is the assistant editor of *Kwani?* He is also a freelance journalist based in Nairobi. He is currently working on a collection of short stories and collaborating on a non-fiction book.

Farewell, Robert Redford

Jamal Mahjoub

THERE IS SOMETHING DISCONCERTING about a dead zebra. It had always struck Stanley as a rather curious animal. Never more so than in this particular case. It was not a very large zebra and it was lying in the sand, sightless eyes staring at the sun. Its neck was torn open and flies crowded into the gap; a shiny oil slick bright with seething colour, buzzing with greed. Perhaps it was the contrast of opposites, black on white, the cold logic of geometry, the discipline of lines against the soft blur of the landscape. Rocks, sand, thorns, randomly distributed. How did stripes fit into all that. Still, no doubt nature has its own reasons, about which he could venture little. The point was that this zebra was dead. And there was nothing unnatural about that either.

The view from the rim of the extinct volcano stretched towards the horizon in every direction. The land here echoed with past violence, the history of creation worn down against the hard thumb of the sky. Below, the long, warm length of the crater lake simmered, velvety and green, like a tear that had welled up from a forgotten time.

The German women were still talking amongst themselves and taking endless numbers of photographs. They all had that sturdy, well-fed look that reflected a lifelong diet rich with proteins and lactic products. There were no hollows between their bones, no slack pouches of flesh hanging from their robust cheeks, pink with health. They were clad in the informal uniform of the modern traveller, a kind of semi-military style complete with webbed belts and zipped pockets of every conceivable size and shape. Their English was rudimentary.

'Lion? Is lion here to see?'

Stanley stood up and stepped back to survey the zebra from a distance. He looked at the surrounding vegetation, giant cactus, the camphor trees, the brown, sunburned grass. He shook his head. In all likelihood it was a leopard. This set them all off again, the whirr and snap of cameras interspersed by excited bursts of guttural speech of which he understood not a word.

As they made their way back towards the Camp, the Germans keen not to miss their appointment with lunch, Stanley wondered to himself exactly what this dead zebra might mean in the broader scheme of things. One of the German women asked to take his photograph and so he stood there obligingly and stared back at her and when it was done everyone laughed with relief.

That afternoon Stanley took his bicycle and rode over to see his friend, Henry, who lived by the big lake, about half an hour away. He found him as usual sitting outside his house smoking his pipe. Years ago, Henry's house, like most of those along this side of the lake, was occupied by men who made their living from fishing. But the fish had diminished in number and it no longer paid and so most people had left to find work elsewhere. Henry wasn't most people. He would carry on trying to fish until he dropped dead. This was his home and he was not going to give it up just yet.

He clicked his tongue. 'A leopard, you say?'

'It looks that way to me.'

'Is there anything unusual about that?'

'Not at all. But it set me thinking.'

'Hmm,' mused Henry, his mind leaping ahead. 'The Englishman.'

It was now almost three weeks since the body of an Englishman had been discovered less than an hour's walk from where the two men now sat. The police had declared it the work of a leopard, but Stanley had had his doubts, and their lack of sincere effort to investigate the case made him even more suspicious. The place where the body had been found was not, in his opinion, the kind of territory favoured by a leopard for a daylight attack. It was too exposed and open. But who was Stanley to challenge the police version of events.

The Englishman, a journalist, had come out to here to write a story about the ecological decay of the big lake. The water level had been dropping steadily over the past few years and the use of pesticides in the surrounding land had led to allegedly lethal increases in the concentration of certain chemicals. Hence the lack of fish.

'That man came looking for trouble,' remarked Henry.

The bloodied and torn body of the Englishman had been found beside a remote track. It was Stanley who had first come across the body. The man was splayed out on the ground, face down. His throat had been torn open. He was wearing shorts and sports shoes and had apparently been out jogging.

'Who ever goes running in this country?' asked Henry with a tut of impatience.

The two men had discussed the case on numerous occasions. They had both seen and spoken to the man when he had come around asking all his damn fool questions. On one occasion Stanley had bailed the man out of a nasty situation in the nearby town.

Swollen by almost a hundred thousand recent arrivals, all hungry for work and bitter from too much beer and too little love to go around, the town was stretched to bursting point. The Englishman had gone there to try to find someone who would tell him what he wanted to know when the mob set about him. They ripped his shirt and were trying to take away his camera when Stanley came by. Without thinking he had aimed his bicycle directly at the centre of the crowd. In the confusion he managed to get the man away, at no small risk to himself, one might add.

'Never get involved,' muttered Henry when he heard about the incident.

Stanley had never been convinced that it was the work of a leopard and seeing the zebra that morning had convinced him. The slash of the wounds and the way the body had fallen all indicated some other form of violence. But the case of the dead Englishman had been largely forgotten. The police had been called and duly dismissed the case in no time at all. An attack by a leopard was not unheard of in these parts.

'My love is like a red, red rose,' intoned Henry, recalling a line he was in the habit of repeating in recent weeks. He had once read the line in a book of poetry while still at school, a long and dusty lifetime ago. 'Their love is bleeding us dry,' he concluded, alluding to the irony of the fact that romantic trysts in distant Europe were nowadays accompanied by flowers grown in the nurseries just beyond his house around the edge of the lake. His life was being strangled by the flowers being produced in the extensive greenhouses that surrounded his fishing grounds. The flowers required vast quantities of water, chemicals and cheap labour. They were packed and flown out daily so as to arrive in the cities of Europe crisp with the cold dawn dew still fresh on them. In a decade, the journalist had said, the big lake would be dead and they would be living in a desert. It was already showing signs of shrinking and drying out. Henry knew all there was to know about the lake and its problems.

Coming across the zebra that morning had reminded Stanley that he had never really been convinced that a leopard was responsible for the death of the English journalist. One day he had ridden his bicycle back up to the ridge where the body was found and looked at the brown spot on the ground. Something was wrong about the whole thing. He walked in widening circles around the patch of dried blood until he came across something.

It was a notebook, quite small with hard covers, black with red corners. On the inside of the front cover were the words Made in China, printed in pale blue ink. There was no name inside indicating who the owner might have been, but Stanley was pretty sure it was the Englishman's notebook. Who ever goes running in this country? And who takes a notebook with them? It was lying beneath a sun olive tree (*Dodonea angustifolia*) about fifty metres away from where the body had been found. Stanley was immediately gripped in the fierce clasp of a moral dilemma. He knew that really he should have taken the notebook and handed it in to the police, but Stanley was not particularly fond of the police, and certainly he did not trust Sgt Mwangi and his thugs. Besides, if the police had done their job in the first place they would have found the notebook before he did. Or had they in fact found it and decided to discard it? Stanley decided it would not be unfair for him to take the book home and have a look inside to see if it held any clues.

The first thing he found was a list of names and numbers. The names were all female. Barbara, Susan, Yvette, etc. Alongside each name was a telephone number and beyond that a date, sometimes more than one, ticked in red ink. Even more curious was the little figure drawn beside each date. These were little faces: a circle with two dots for eyes and a line for a mouth. Some of the faces were smiling, while in others the mouth was downturned in disappointment.

Stanley continued his investigation of the dead man's words. Several pages appeared to have been ripped out quite roughly. There was a diary entry for Friday the 23rd, a week before the body was discovered: 'Dinner at Julian Sands' place. Not a bad evening, though for the most part a tedious bunch of people. He seems to choose his friends according to the degree to which they adulate him. Like most writers he is entirely self-absorbed, and allows himself to trot out the most outrageous nonsense while they look on admiringly. He must be unbearable to live with and the look on Anne's face of complete and utter boredom was quite awful to witness. Having no doubt heard each and every one of his rickety theories about the world economy and each tedious anecdote, I cannot understand why she stays with him. Highlight of the evening was meeting Pilar (a name I shall forever associate with *For Whom The Bells Toll*). One of those slightly ditsy types convinced that their mission in life is to save the world. She is a woman of quite stunning beauty, however. Voluptuous is the word that springs to mind. She does not drink and declines each offer with the formal blank response of someone who has been struggling with a problem for quite some time. Still, a first encounter that holds great potential, I suspect. She had just returned from an assignment in one of the Spanish enclaves in Morocco. The fruit of Franco's dream of greatness. They should have been handed back years ago. Apparently there has been a huge scandal there caused by massive assaults on the fence surrounding the town. This is a double barrier some three metres high, and topped with rolls of razor wire. It is meant to keep unwanted people out. The migrants, after having endured weeks of God knows what hardship to cross the desert, camp in the woods just beyond the perimeter of the town. They cut down the trees to make ladders, and then rush the fence in groups of a hundred or more. Throwing up the makeshift ladders as though laying siege to a medieval fortress. As they hurl themselves over the wire the outcome is terrible, people are left literally hanging from their skin, the barbs caught in their arms and legs, until their weight rips them free. Some of them topple from the fence, breaking limbs in the process. Two were apparently shot in the back, probably by Moroccan police. Those who do manage to get through end up in camps from which they are sent back, often to be dumped in the desert in the middle of nowhere. It is, Pilar says in her charming English, a tragedy of our times. Of course, Julian's guests hee-hawed their way off the subject and were soon cackling away at another of his dismal stories. And I am afraid I made a bit of a fool of myself. Seeing she was dismayed by their lack of interest I started chatting to her, telling her where I was off to next and how much I admired Hemingway. One glass too many, I'm afraid. She declared Hemingway a fool who learned nothing about any of the places he ever went to. She sounded rather hurt but I am determined not to be put off and shall call her again as soon as I get back.'

Stanley flicked through the remaining pages of the notebook and found to his dismay that most of them were blank. There were a few notes, times, names, none of which meant anything to him. Had the Englishman been on his way to meet someone when he met his fate? Towards the end of the book he found another passage. This time written in the self-conscious voice of a writer trying to find his subject.

'The rift valley is like a wound that digs deep into the very heart of this very ancient continent. It cuts down through the strata of past ages. What emerges here can tell us much about the state, not only of this continent, but of our world and what is happening to it today.'

The passage ended there.

On his way back from visiting Henry, Stanley found himself thinking about the zebra again. The black and white stripes against the brown grass. It seemed to him that this simple image contained a message. The ordered manner in which the two extremes gave way, folding one into the other in regular order. He had the impression that this was significant, but he could not put his finger on how to explain this feeling.

Stanley was an intelligent man. Most people who met him were struck by the fact that he knew far more than a man in his station in life ought to. He could tell you the latin names for a hundred-and-eighty-four types of bird, but he was self taught and had never attended university. His skills were part of local legend and he moved between the lodges and camps taking visitors on nature walks. He was always in demand.

The lines imprinted on his brain by the dead zebra's hide that morning would not leave him. The distinct nature of black on white, almost like letters, like the script of a language he was no longer capable of deciphering, or a map. He stopped and took out the notebook. On one of the last pages was a series of lines which he had passed over quickly, thinking they were simply the result of an idle movement of the author's pen, but now, as he trained his eyes on them once more he saw that they formed a map. There was the outline of the big lake, here was the path and there was a house. He recognized it instantly and kicked himself for not having seen it before because he knew it well: It was a map of how to reach Henry's house.

By now Stanley had reached the end of the ridge. The German women had settled themselves up on the little flat rock overlooking the camp to watch the sunset. He could see his colleague Miriam puffing up the hillside with a tray of cocktails. They put aside the business of preparing their cameras and waved to him as he approached. 'Isn't this just wonderful,' called one of them. 'Perfect,' said another. 'All we need now is Robert Redford!' and they all dissolved into laughter.

Stanley turned around and began to make his way back down the way he had come. He would have to get back to Henry and warn him that he might be in danger. It would be dark in a few minutes. He heard the sighs of the German women echoing into the air behind him as the sky spun through the spectrum from pink to purple heralding the falling of night. He dropped down the path swiftly, taking a familiar short cut through the forest, seeing out of the corner of his eye as he did so, how the small lake had changed colour, how the failing light now made it resemble the mark of a large feline paw. He rushed on down through the trees, knowing instinctively which way to turn. Something stirred in the bushes, causing him to stop and wheel round. A sound that was familiar, almost like the greeting of an old friend. He turned to find himself facing two glowing discs that burned with a slow, furious heat. They were fixed on him, and drawing ever closer.

Jamal Mahjoub was born in London, where his father was stationed at the Sudanese Cultural Centre. He spent his formative years in Khartoum, Sudan, before being awarded a scholarship to Atlantic College in Wales. He went on to study geology at Sheffield University in England. He returned briefly to the Sudan in search of employment, after which he decided to dedicate himself to writing. Since then, he has lived in a number of places, including London, Denmark and currently Spain, as well as extensive periods in France. Mahjoub has worked in a variety of sectors to support his writing, including telemarketing, catering and futon-making and has also worked as a librarian, freelance journalist and translator.

Mahjoub's first three novels were published in the Heinemann African Writers Series. The main subject of Mahjoub's novels is his relationship to the Sudan, as a migrant with mixed parentage. His first novel, *Navigation of a Rainmaker* (1989), relates the journey of a young man returning to the Sudan from Britain in order to claim his heritage, but it is the height of the famine and the traveller begins to see himself as the embodiment of the same malaise that is gripping Africa. *Wings of Dust* (1994) was followed by *In the Hour of Signs* (1996), which deals with the Mahdist movement in the nineteenth century and the birth of the modern Sudan, and *The Carrier* (1998). *Travelling with Djinns* (Chatto & Windus 2003) won the Prix de l'Astrolabe award in France in 2004. The short story 'The Cartographer's Angel' won the Heinemann/Guardian African Short Story Prize in 1993. His most recent work is *The Drift Latitudes* (Chatto & Windus 2006).

Goliwood Drama

Niq Mhlongo

SOWETO TOWNSHIP. THE TIME WAS 16H00 according to the big watch at the Mangalani BP Garage. If you were not from around that Chiawelo Section, you would definitely think that was the correct time. But the locals were aware that the 'BP watch' was ahead of time by almost thirty minutes. That Saturday afternoon of the 15th of March the sky of Soweto Township was ripped apart by fireworks like never before. It reminded many Sowetans of the day Mandela was released from jail in February 1990 after spending twenty-seven years behind bars.

Thirty-nine-year-old Thami ducked involuntarily from his chair as the first set of explosions went off. His friend Vusi flinched as another cracker was carelessly thrown in the street. Since two o'clock that afternoon, they had been sitting at the balcony on the second floor of their favorite Chiawelo tavern called 24HOURS. They were not drunk yet, but a bit tipsy, although Vusi had bulging and bloodshot eyes that you could easily confuse for those of a drunken man. He was a lawyer by profession and had offices in Joburg City. Thami worked as one of the cabinet ministers' bodyguards. Many people in the township called him 'The Bull' because of his massive body. Besides giving him glasses of his expensive Blue Label whisky that morning, the Chief (as his employer was fondly known) had granted Thami five days off.

There were lots of people in the tavern. But all eyes were glued to the television set that was mounted on the wall. The wall itself smelled terrible because of the new paintwork. There was no music playing this time. The only noise in the tavern came from the wordless voices of the patrons and the television set. Everyone was waiting eagerly. Some people were biting their nails in anticipation. A very important announcement was to be made by the FIFA President, Sepp Blatter. The majority of the people, if not all of them, were hoping that South Africa would be selected ahead of Tunisia to host the World Cup in 2010.

But poor Thami felt alone with his own thoughts and personal misery, even amongst that throng of people. No doubt he looked like he was enjoying his Castle Lager. You could tell by the way he sipped it slowly and licked his thick lips. Of course, he was in the good company of his best friend Vusi. But Thami's heart was heavy. His mind was very busy, racing like a moth looking for a flame. Less than two months ago he had separated from Thuli. She was his common-law wife of eight years. He could not believe that the following Monday he was going to face her at the Johannesburg Maintenance Court. About a week ago, Thami had received summons to appear in Court for not paying the maintenance of his three children.

'Just look at me man, everyone can tell that I'm as black as Africa itself. I cannot be that boy's real father. There is no history of albino children in my family,' said Thami. He paused, and took a drag from his cigarette again. He emitted the smoke through his nose and it lazed upward. 'Thuli probably slept with an albino guy when I was away with the Chief.'

'Oh, good heavens! Stop making a revolution out of it man,' said Vusi while shaking his head. 'These things happen. There might have probably been a biological reason.'

'Heavens, my balls!' intercepted Thami. 'Even my mother knows that that kid is not mine and he's the cause of my separation from Thuli. I'm going to tell the court on Monday that I can't pay maintenance for the kid when I know it's not mine.'

'I've advised you to deny paternity in court on Monday, so what are you still worried about?'

'I have a problem with that date of Monday. I'm going to miss all the celebrations with the big guns of South Africa because of the stupid court case. Everybody from the parliament will be there by the presidential residence if South Africa wins the bid. From the Governor of the Reserve Bank to the Minister of Sports, you name them man.'

A joyful noise suddenly stuffed the tavern. Yes, South Africa had just been declared the host of the 2010 FIFA World Cup! People were hugging, squeezing and patting each other. From the second floor balcony Thami and Vusi could see cars driving past the main Old Potchefstroom Road with their headlamps on although the sun was still bright up there.

'You see, today *baba*,' said Vusi, 'If you want to watch a good movie for free, you don't have to travel too far to town. Our Soweto is like both Hollywood and Bollywood combined. Viva 2010 World Cup, viva!' Vusi announced proudly. He burped loudly after taking a sip straight from his quart of Castle Lager.

'Oh, sure,' Thami answered uninterestedly, while flicking the ash of his cigarette on the floor.

'Come on. Don't give me that worried look,' said Vusi. He looked at his friend with a mixture of pity and disappointment, 'I'm sure you can do better than that.'

Thami did not say a word. Instead he stared at his empty beer bottle as if he was wishing it to be full again. From every direction you could hear the deafening noises from the vuvuzela plastic horns of soccer lovers. Most of them donned the jerseys of the national soccer team. The hooting of cars along the road also disturbed the peace in the whole neighborhood. At the nearby traffic lights at the Mangalani Complex some thugs started spinning their BMWs. A huge crowd of people, young and old, watched in amazement. It looked as if the whole of Soweto Township had come to the street to celebrate.

Ten o'clock Monday morning was the court date. That morning Thami was driving along the M1 North freeway in his Honda Ballade towards the Joburg city centre. The traffic was moving very slowly as usual. Thami looked at the watch on the dashboard. It was half-past nine. He began to panic. His friend Vusi had warned him a number of times about that particular magistrate at the maintenance court. 'She is a feminist. She will not hesitate to hold you in contempt of court for not showing up on time.' Vusi's words rang in his mind again.

To Thami's relief, the traffic started to clear next to Gold Reef Casino. Cars moved faster. The road was like that until he arrived at the Johannesburg Magistrate court four minutes before his case was due to start. The benches along the corridor were full of people. Most of them were women. As he entered, Thuli was already sitting on the bench along the corridor. Her face was almost beautiful. But her flat nose spoiled whatever beauty she might have had. Her hair was well braided and her Police sunglasses were pushed back on her forehead. She wore a fake Gucci leather jacket. In her right hand she carried a leather handbag of the same design. Big silver round earrings were shining from both her ears. She could not hide her anger as she saw Thami approaching. She stood up. Her squinting eyes warned him that she was angry. There was an obvious tension between them.

'And you call yourself a man. I don't think so,' Thuli said out loud. She then shook her head. 'Do you want me to tell you what real men do, heh? Real men support their children. They put the bread on the table every day for their children. Real men pay for their children's studies, and they make sure that their children have shelter. You are not a real man because you do not support your three children.'

'Yes. Tell the bastard how useless he is,' said the lady who was breast-feeding a baby on the opposite bench.

Thami was tight-lipped. Everyone in the corridor was looking at him. He felt humiliated. He hid his face in his hands for a few seconds. But his heart was pounding furiously in his chest. He cleared his throat in a sound of disapproval. Thuli clicked her tongue twice and wrinkled her nose. There was an expression of bitterness on her face.

'Just look at you!' She eyed him sharply.

The outer corners of Thuli's eyes had mascara on them. She pointed her finger at him as if it was a gun. They had long nails that were painted red.

'You are not even ashamed of yourself!' she continued. 'You are here wearing an expensive suit and nice shoes but your three children are naked and bare-footed at home. I would be ashamed of myself if I were you.'

'Divorce the bastard and get on with your life, Girl. You are still young and there are lots of men around that can kill just to be with you,' said another lady who was sitting at the far end of the bench. The lady leaned forward and snapped her fingers. 'Just like that! Dump him like a hot potato, Girl. But you must make sure the bastard pays heavily for wasting your precious time. He doesn't deserve you at all.'

Thami pinched his nose in embarrassment. Many thoughts were going through his mind. He felt tired of being around all those women. His friend Vusi was right. He had warned him that all women inside the Johannesburg Maintenance Court Building belonged to one organisation called MAPS (Men Are Pigs Society). He had thought that Vusi was joking. But now he was convinced that MAPS was not one of his friend's exaggerations. To him it existed as a secret society that specialised in hating men like him. He was also sure that competing with those women would be like cutting his own throat. They were all giving him a stare that he could only interpret as hatred.

'Your friends think you're a man because you are President Mbeki's bodyguard.' Thuli shook her head again, 'I don't think so. The only thing that makes you a man is that useless stick between your legs. Yeah, real men don't go around fucking and making babies, leaving them to starve like you do. You are a useless son of a bitch with a heart of stone. I wonder what came into my head the moment I spread my legs for you.'

Her statement hung around Thami like a bad smell from the toilet. There was laughter, and it came from most of the women who were sitting on the benches. Thami was tempted to throw back some nasty words. But he remembered his friend Vusi's advice not to do that. At the same time, the door to one of the offices yawned open. A woman in black pants and a blue shirt appeared. She stopped at the door frame. On the door was written: 'Ms Dube, Marriage Counsellor'. All the noise in the corridor subsided.

'Mr and Mrs Maphela!' the woman in black pants called out while standing at the doorway of her office, 'Come to my office please.'

Thuli and Thami followed the woman inside. She pushed the door shut with her right leg without turning. Again without wasting time she gestured to them to sit on the two chairs that were there. Above the woman's head on the wall was a poster that read: 'Stop the Violence against Women and Children'. On the other wall was a framed photograph of a woman shaking President Thabo Mbeki's hand. Thami realised that it was a picture of the same woman that was sitting before them.

'Well, as you might already know, my name is Sylvia Dube,' she said. There was a tone of authority in her voice, 'I am the marriage counsellor. I can tell that it's a difficult period between the two of you. I also know that for the sake of the children, Mrs Maphela here has laid a complaint against you for not giving your three children some financial support,' she said, while moving her eyes from Thuli to Thami. 'I understand that you are at your job and earning the same amount as when you were paying your maintenance about three months ago. But what made you suddenly stop doing that Mr Maphela? Why are you not supporting your children anymore? I think the problem is not about money here?' Counsellor Dube looked at Thami with accusatory eyes. They possessed the power of asking questions, although they were small and serious.

Thami thought for a while. He felt some great demand in Counsellor Dube's question.

'Yes, you are right counsellor. My problem is not about money at all. I am denying paternity of the last born. I don't believe I fathered him,' he

151

said, with a forced calmness in his voice. The reply was very slow in coming. But he regretted what he had said the moment it came out of his mouth. He loved his two other children and wondered how the whole thing might have affected them. He did what he did because of that last-born albino baby. That is what he had come to contest in the court. He wanted to know the truth.

A shockwave passed through Thuli.

'What?' she demanded angrily, and without a blink in her eyes. It was as if she was not expecting those words from Thami. She then gave a derisive laugh, 'Ha, ha, ha. You want to tell me that all these eight years that we've been together you did not trust me? You also want to tell me that you had no balls to face me, and that you were just waiting to say it in court? Is that right?'

Thami remained calm. He did not say a word. But a puzzled expression jumped into Counsellor Dube's eyes.

'Hold on! Let me get this straight,' said Counsellor Dube while demonstrating with her hands. Thami and Thuli's eyes followed her. 'What you are saying is that you are here to contest paternity of one child amongst the three, is that right?'

'Right.'

'Are you sure about this?'

'Yes, I am. In fact my intuition tells me that the last-born child is not mine, I want to clear it up once and for all,' said Thami without looking up.

'What about the other two children, why are you not supporting them?'

'I think that for those past two months my mind was not working well. It had affected me a lot.'

'Did it affect you to the extent that you failed to support your own children?'

'Yes. I guess so.'

'That's a tough one,' said Counsellor Dube. She sounded unconvinced. 'So you want the blood test to be done?'

'Yes. That's what I want to do and I'm doing it for the sake of the children and myself. I want to clear my doubts. And if in fact I am the father, I will happily support my child,' he answered, avoiding eye contact.

'You are a liar! You are doing it for your ego and not for the sake of the children,' interrupted Thuli angrily. The way she looked at him it was like she could plunge her long nails into his face.

'Mrs Maphela… let's…' Counsellor Dube could not finish her words.

'Please call me Thuli. I no longer want to be associated with his surname.'

'Ok, Thuli. We assure you that the court will do everything in its power to make it a point that your children are well looked after,' said Counsellor Dube, as she tried to calm Thuli down.

Counsellor Dube clasped her fingers. A large gold ring was shining on one of them. She looked at Thami for a second. 'But do you know that this might have serious consequences for your relationship with the children?' she asked.

'Yes. It is a risk that I am willing to take.'

Counsellor Dube widened her eyes and nodded her head. About thirty seconds passed without a word from all of them. Thami looked at Thuli. Her face was already frowning a warning. She was not sure that going for a blood test was a good idea. There were some few mistakes she had also made in the past. The blood test might expose that, she thought.

'Yah, why are you running away from your responsibilities?' shouted Thuli impatiently, her eyes searching Thami's face. 'You might as well forget about it. I don't need your money. You can keep your dirt anyway. The children and I can survive without your help like we have been doing all these days. You must forget about us, we don't need you in our lives anymore.'

Counsellor Dube looked at her watch. She stood up with some papers in her hand. 'I'm just going next door to consult the magistrate. I'll be back in a minute. I want you two to behave when I'm gone. Don't shout at each other inside my office,' she said as she opened the door and stepped outside.

The tension between Thuli and Thami continued. There was no single word spoken between them. They shied away from looking at each other. Thami's eyes remained downcast with his chin balanced on both his hands. Thuli tapped her fingers on the table rhythmically. They remained like that until Counsellor Dube came back about ten minutes later.

'Well, both of you will be appearing before the magistrate in Room Four in about thirty minutes,' said Counsellor Dube in a new tone of voice. 'I had thought that your problem was only about paying the maintenance. Unfortunately, it seems it is more complex than that. I don't have the authority to ask for your blood samples. But the magistrate has, and that is why you have to go in there. Oh, again the unfortunate part of it is that all five of you,' she said, as if to soften her words, 'I mean you and your three children, will have to undergo that blood test. We want to compare all your DNAs and make sure that the outcome of the blood test is a hundred per cent correct. Is there any question that you two would like to ask?' she concluded while looking at each one of them with a feigned smile.

Thuli shook her head. 'No. I can't subject my children to such torture because of him. What would they think?' protested Thuli.

'But believe me; it is for their own benefit,' said Counsellor Dube. 'Besides, the matter is now in the hands of this court. We have to be fair. This court is required by law to solve this matter in the best interest of the children. And since the matter is already brought to this court, we are not allowed to leave it hanging. We must solve it. Oh, one more thing: you Mr Maphela will be the one who will bear all the costs incurred for the blood test. But most of that will be confirmed by the magistrate.'

Thami and Thuli watched each other, not moving, and their eyes met. They both stood up and carefully slid their chairs under the table. Thirty minutes later they appeared in front of the magistrate. The case lasted for only ten minutes as Thami maintained his original position. A court order was issued by the magistrate saying that Thami and Thuli, as well as their three children, must go to the nearby Braamfontein Laboratory to have their blood taken. The next court date was in two weeks' time.

Inside 24HOURS Tavern, Thami tried to catch the waitress's attention by waving his right hand. He was thirsty for another beer. As soon as the waitress came, he gave her a fifty rand note and ordered two Castle Lager quarts. Most people were watching a derby soccer game between two South African teams: Kaizer Chiefs vs Orlando Pirates.

'Pirates have to win this game if they are serious about winning the league trophy this year,' said Thami.

'I think today is Pirates' day, man. They are playing very good.'

The waitress came with four beers and put them on their table. Vusi opened a bottle with his teeth.

'The next round will be on me,' said Vusi.

'Thanks man. Very soon I'll not afford to buy you one beer my friend. All the money will be going towards the maintenance,' teased Thami.

'When are you going to know about the outcome of your blood test?' asked Vusi, a glass of beer in his hand.

'Day after tomorrow in Court.'

'What are you going to do if it turns out that all the children are yours?'

'I'm ready for any results, man. Whatever comes, I'll have to act like a man.'

Magistrate Zodwa Khumalo presided over the court proceedings that Friday morning. Thuli and Thami arrived early before the start of their case at nine o'clock. Thuli was accompanied by her mother and her friend. Thami had come with Vusi. There were already about twenty people seated on the benches inside the courtroom. Everybody remained quiet.

'This is the case of paternity between Thami and Thuli Maphela,' said Magistrate Khumalo after clearing her throat. 'May the two parties step forward please?'

Vusi gave his friend a big wink and raised his thumb. Thami and Thuli stepped forward in front of the magistrate.

'We will start with Leleti Maphela, a female, born on the 17th of July 1997. For the case of paternity you brought before this court, you are excused. You are not the father,' said the magistrate while looking at her files. Thami's palms were already sweating. 'The second child is Zolani Maphela, a male, born on the 10th of October 2000. For the case of paternity, the court excuses you as the father. The third child is Zandi Maphela, a female, born on the 2nd of January 2003. For the case of paternity, you are the father. You are therefore required by this court to maintain your child by paying the amount of R750 every month.'

24HOURS Tavern was crowded that Friday evening. Thami and Vusi sat at the corner next to a large speaker that was blurring out Kamazu's popular old song called *Korobela*.

African woman, why give me korobela
Oh, korobela

Thami sang along to the song. His head was moving rhythmically with the song.

'This song speaks to me, man. I think Thuli gave me the love potion to blind me with love. How come I didn't see that she was cheating on me all along?' said Thami as soon as the song ended.

'I don't blame you, man. It's difficult to see this *korobela* ointment. I heard that most of the women use *korobela* to control their men. My father told me to be careful because most of the women apply it on their arms, thighs, genitals and chest before sex. When a man is busy dancing between his woman's legs and enjoying it, the potion is transferred.

'You see me married again, you cut my throat. I have had enough of women,' Thami said in a drunken tone of a voice.

'You just chose the wrong woman, man. Thuli was a bitch, man. I felt for you that day when you two exchanged your vows in the church. I

155

think that you should have said to her, *I'll be with you until further notice* instead of the usual *till death do us part.'*

Niq Mhlongo is the author of the novel called *Dog Eat Dog*, published by Kwela in 2004. His novel is also translated into Spanish. He also writes short stories, one of which is translated into German in the anthology called *Yizo Yizo*. Niq is also a film maker and lives in Soweto, South Africa.

Dancing With Life

Christopher Mlalazi

TODAY, AS THE BELEAGUERED PRESIDENT is once again flying East, Mxolisi is also flying, but west – over a low wire fence and into a yard.

Dressed in green overalls, he lands nimbly on the other side, and races past the house, headed for the back, the soles of his sneakers flashing orange behind him. As on most afternoons, a steely sky tightly lids the township, as if it would suddenly lift and let out a puff of steam and the stink of decaying dreams into the beyond, then a shovel is prodded in and flips this life over onto a fresh and purposeful side.

'Stop!' A policeman, mounted on a bike, shouts at him from the street in a harsh voice that has been highly trained to instil fear and, once, instant obedience. But today, the voice, like the country's much touted myriad economic turnaround programmes, fires another blank. Mxolisi is clambering over a tall brick wall behind the house – he disappears over it into another yard. The alarmed cluck of chickens from the other side greets his disappearance.

The policeman, unable to follow on his bike, races along the street to cut off Mxolisi on the other side of the row of houses.

Mxolisi appears from a gate into the street this side of the houses, walking slowly, and now dressed in black sports shirt and a white vest that reveals a sinewy body. He is whistling a 'Third Chimurenga' song, whose lyrics he has never bothered himself with, like most disillusioned urban youngsters these days.

At twenty-one, he has a small, funny, spade-like head which, uncannily, resembles that of a lizard, hence his nickname, Mpankwa, meaning lizard in the Ndebele language. His eyes are protruding and are always bloodshot

157

from the *mbanje* which he chain-smokes – just like those of *ntikoloshi's* from stories grandmothers scare unruly children with at night. An ex-university student whose laugh can make any person want to laugh too, Mxolisi tossed honesty over his shoulder a couple of years back, after that infamous elections scam that perpetuated, as he often curses, 'official looting'. Now he dances with life daily outside the township sports bar peddling *mbanje* and, with a shrewd squint in his right eye, providing articulate overviews of the country's political scenario to other loafers, the majority of whose intellectual scope is limited to petty gossip and just farting around.

Mxolisi had found the policeman behind Figa Sports Bar assaulting his best friend Juluka with fists and boots for drinking a scud in public, and, from a distance, had shouted in his most taunting voice: 'Wena! Leave that man alone! Can't you see he is not a white farmer?'

'Ah!' the policeman had gasped in astonishment. Then he had picked up his bike lying on the ground, leapt on it, and, without much ceremony, the chase of the week had been officially launched.

Suddenly, the policeman races around the corner in front of Mxolisi, who whistles the Chimurenga song louder.

The policeman brakes to a stop in front of him.

'Did you see a thin fellow in green overalls?' the policeman asks, wiping sweat off his brow, one brown-booted foot balancing on the ground, the other cocked on a pedal. He is younger than Mxolisi, but is fitter, and taller.

Mxolisi points up the street, his lips pursed in whistle. The policeman races in the pointed direction, bent on national retribution, his neon police bib shining brightly in the sun.

A stray dog, as emaciated as drought-prone Tsholotsho infants, leaps out of a yard and chases after the bicycle, barking fiercely. A few steps away, it turns back and disappears into another yard, satisfied that it has expressed its displeasure at whoever killed the country's economy and made food scarce from the township bins it scavenges from.

Virginia watches the policeman cycling hard towards her, and the chasing dog turning away from him. Behind him, Mxolisi is walking in the opposite direction, making hard for the corner of the street, now and then darting looks over his shoulder.

Virginia hates Mxolisi. She also wishes him ill. Two weeks back, he had been intimate with her in the public toilet behind Figa Sport Bar, and, afterwards, in the faeces-smelling darkness, had given her a roll of money.

She had charged him two hundred thousand dollars, because, she had hotly argued when he had tried to haggle, his pants around his knees, things were going up by a thousand per cent every minute in the country – just look at the cost of sending a child to school now! She had a daughter at primary school.

Back inside the dimly-lit Sports Bar, standing at her favourite corner in front of a large mirror that enabled her, now and then, to turn her back to the room so the patrons could see her abundant posterior, her strongest marketing point, and see their faces in the reflection, she had counted Mxolisi's money, and discovered that it had all been counterfeit. When she had confronted him outside the Sports Bar where he peddled his *mbanje*, he had clicked his tongue at her: '*Nx*! If the state is daily printing money that does not buy anything, who are you to complain about my money? You can go and make a report to the police right now if you want – your *gorilla* was not even nice.'

She dare not report him. She knew she would be charged for soliciting. Just last Friday, she had come out of the Sports Bar at closing time only to discover, to her shock, policemen ambushing all unaccompanied women at the door and bundling them into a waiting police van. They had all been carted to the police station, where she had spent an unpleasant night in a crowded cell, and in the morning was made to pay a fine for soiling the respected name of the country's newly introduced currency, the bearer's cheques, by making men ejaculate inside her in order to fill her bra with them. To add to the insult, the bearer's cheques even had the highly esteemed Reserve Bank Governor's signature on them too!

When the policeman reaches her, she points over his shoulder back at Mxolisi, who is almost at the corner.

'That's him,' she whispers to the policeman. 'He has taken off his overalls.' Her face is concealed by a floppy sun hat and large dark sunglasses. She has a good body, revealed by tight pink pants and a matching vest that leaves her belly button in the open. A small patch of curly dark hairs trails from below the navel into the pants.

Mxolisi, nearly at the street corner, darts another look over his shoulder. The policeman is bearing down on him, seeming to become larger and larger on his bike. Behind him, he can see that bitch Virginia standing watching him – he breaks into a run.

He turns the corner, his feet flying. Everything is now a blur, the houses, the people he passes.

'Mpankwa!' he hears a familiar voice call, but he has no time for it. He cuts into another corner, darts into an open gate, around a house, and comes to a stone wall. He stops running, his shoulders drooping in disappointment. The wall has jagged pieces of broken bottle lining its top, embedded in the concrete.

There is the thud of boots, and the policeman bursts into view.

A hard clap cracks into Mxolisi's right cheek — he blocks a fist centering for his stomach.

'What's happening here!' a shirtless man shouts in an angry voice from the corner of the house. 'Please get out of my yard. I don't want any dead bodies here!'

Mxolisi is now in handcuffs, and the policeman drags him around the house and out of the gate. A crowd has gathered outside, so many people, especially kids and women, and some still pouring from the surrounding houses, just like mice out of a burrow flooded with hot water.

'Leave Mpankwa alone!' somebody shouts. It is Juluka. 'He is my friend, he has done nothing!' He is holding an empty scud container.

'Yes, release him!' a woman also shouts.

More and more people appear running.

'The country is being raped by men with big stomachs and you are wasting time arresting people spending their honestly earned money,' a man, carrying pestles which he sells around the township, cries out. 'This is your thank-you to us for providing your salaries!'

The policeman and Mxolisi are now surrounded.

'Open the way please!' the policeman says. 'Don't start something you are not going to finish!'

'We are going to finish it!' The crowd roars back in defiance, and a puppy barks from its midst.

Suddenly, four other policemen, all mounted on bikes, cut into the crowd, and it withdraws.

'It doesn't matter how many of you there are!' Juluka shouts from the safety of the back of the crowd, waving the scud container in the air. 'We are not your wives! Go and fuck somebody else in your cells!'

One of the policemen throws his bicycle down and leaps for Juluka. He trips on a stone, and falls down in a cloud of dust. The crowd roars in laughter and catcalls. The policeman leaps up and races after Juluka, then suddenly stops and turns back, his hand on his belt. His eyes are on the ground, searching.

'What is it?' another policeman asks him.

'My handcuffs,' the first policeman replies in a low voice.

The four policemen, watched by the laughing crowd, search the ground, kicking over the soil, especially where the first policeman had fallen, but no handcuffs are to be found. They finally give up the search, and lead Mxolisi away.

'It's me who showed the policeman Mpankwa,' Virginia is telling Juluka as they sit on stones under the shade of the thorn tree behind Figa Sports Bar. 'My thing is not forged like his money, even big shots know that, and the money they give me, Juluka!'

Juluka pulls on a joint, then pinches his nostrils closed, his lips and eyes also closed. He keeps the smoke in for a few seconds, then opens his eyes, releases his nostrils, and blows the smoke out in a steady stream through his mouth. He passes the joint to Virginia.

'It will never end,' Virginia says, smoking. 'I don't forget that easily. Nobody puts his stick into me for free and gets away with it!'

'But you enjoyed also,' Juluka says, his eyes on the curls under Virginia's belly button.

'He is selling shit too,' Virginia says. She holds the joint up. 'What is this?' She takes another pull. 'Guava leaves are even better. Is he not ashamed of himself?'

'Bring the handcuffs,' Juluka says.

Virginia pulls the front of her pants open, revealing the handcuffs sitting on her crotch over a pair of red knickers with a white heart on the front. She takes them out and covers herself again. 'They are for sale,' she says. 'Find a buyer *tshomi*. I need the money.'

'Who can possibly buy handcuffs?' Juluka asks. 'Throw them away, they are as useless as our MP whom we only see driving past in a nice twin cab – how I wish I could only wash that car!'

'Go and wash your mother's behind first.' She returns the handcuffs into her crotch, and passes the joint to him. 'I will keep them at my place, they are a donation from the state to poverty.'

'Arrest poverty,' says Juluka, his eyes dreamy. 'Lock it in hand-and-foot cuffs, dump it into a cell and throw the keys into a very deep river!' He laughs in staccato in bass, his chest sounding like a burst drum from phlegm.

'*Wuwi!*' Virginia adds a loud soprano laugh, and passers-by turn to stare, some shaking their heads, for they can never understand how productive young people can spend their days loitering at a liquor outlet when so much needs to be done.

A handcuffed Mxolisi trots along a path in a bushy area of the township, headed for the police station. Behind him slowly cycles the policeman who had arrested him. The other four policemen had left them to go and prowl somewhere.

'Stop,' the policeman growls behind him.

Mxolisi stops and turns around. The policeman has dismounted from his bicycle and laid it on the ground.

A slap cracks into Mxolisi's cheek.

'Repeat it,' the policeman says, and slaps him again on the same cheek. Tears spring into Mxolisi's eyes. Another slap. 'Repeat what you said, damn you!' the policeman shouts, his eyes on fire.

A lizard darts into the path from the undergrowth, stops, and it cocks its head their way. It stares at them for a brief moment in serpentine contemplation, then darts across the path into the undergrowth, startled by the crack of another slap on the human with a head almost similar to its own. He must have been one of us in a past age, it is thinking.

The policeman slaps Mxolisi twice more on both cheeks. 'I feel pity for you,' he says. He takes out a key from his trouser pockets and unlocks Mxolisi's handcuffs.

'Go!' he says, and boots him on the buttocks. Mxolisi flees into the forest away from the path, leaping over bushes, the policeman shouting behind him: 'If I catch you again…!'

'He is not a white farmer!' Mxolisi shouts back, now running hard. He falls into a gulley that has sewer water flowing in it, scrambles up, and runs on, his clothes dripping wet, and finally disappears behind an outcrop of rocks.

The policeman, swearing in a low voice, takes out a crumpled cigarette pack from his trouser pocket. He shakes out a half smoked joint from it, lights it and has a smoke. A few minutes later, he is mounted and cycling away, scowling deeply.

'What is this?' maNdlovu shouts at Mxolisi as soon as he enters the sitting room from the kitchen. He has used the back door. She is holding up a plastic 2 kg sugar bag. Inside it are twists of *mbanje*. On the table in front of her sofa is a pile of stacks of money, and next to it are Mxolisi's crumpled green overalls.

'Somebody wants petrol outside,' Mxolisi mutters to his mother. His clothes are wet, and flies are buzzing around him. He opens his bedroom door and disappears into it, leaving behind him the stink of raw sewage.

'One day I am going to kill this dog!' maNdlovu shouts to an empty room, her nose wrinkled against the stink. She places the *mbanje* on the table, just as Ngulube comes in from the kitchen. He has a kitchen knife in one hand and a tomato in the other.

'Did you ask him about that money?' he asks maNdlovu, wiping his sweaty brow with the back of the hand carrying the tomato.

'Just because he has grown a beard he thinks he owns this house,' maNdlovu says. She is a huge woman with big hunched-up shoulders that make her look as if she is going to throw a punch at any time. Her head, like her son's, is also spade-like, but her eyes not as big. 'I do everything for him, but still, it is useless!' she rages. Her cheeks are covered with a rash from a childhood skin disease.

'It's him who took that money I tell you, but you keep saying it's me,' Ngulube is handsome looking, but in a weak way.

A car hoots sharply outside.

'Shut up and go and attend to that customer!' maNdlovu snaps at him, taking a stack of money from the table and beginning to count it. 'And I don't want to hear anything about that money again. I try to help people, but...' she shrugs her shoulders, her lower lip curled down. 'They will learn about life when I am no longer there for them.'

'But I am cooking, honey,' Ngulube wails.

'You now want to go back to your wife? Can't you see I am counting money?'

Without replying, Ngulube lays the knife and tomato on a side table and walks out of the front door.

A cellphone crows from the table. MaNdlovu picks it up.

'Hallo?' she says into it.

'Inspector,' a voice says into her ear. 'This is Sergeant Nkomo at the station. A hot tip has just come in. Somebody is selling black-market petrol...'

'Enemies of the state!' she promptly declares into the mouth piece. 'Wait for me. I am coming over right now – we are going to pick up the swine.'

Ngulube is busy cutting a tomato into a pot on the four-plate stove, which is full of meat. He stirs it with a tablespoon, then, finished, closes the pot. A spicy smell fills the kitchen.

'Where is mother?' Mxolisi asks from the sitting room door. Ngulube closes the pot, turns and looks at him, wiping his hands on a dish cloth. Mxolisi is now dressed in clean clothes – jeans and a t-shirt, his face fresh from a bath.

'She has gone on duty, but she will be back soon.' Ngulube does not look at Mxolisi's face. Mxolisi goes to the refrigerator and takes a Coke bottle from it.

'Why did you tell her I took that money?' Mxolisi asks, opening the Coke with his teeth. 'Don't think I didn't hear you. Is that what you came to sleep with mother here for?'

'What kind of a child are you?' Ngulube is bristling in anger. He is older than Mxolisi by twenty-five years, but they are of the same height.

'Gives you status to be the boyfriend of an inspector doesn't it, *chef?*'

'No wonder they chased you out of university. You have a very dirty mind.'

'Ah, so says the wife-deserter.'

'I will hit you if you disrespect me!'

'I will hit you if you dithrethpect me!' Mxolisi echoes him with a lisp, his mouth twisted. 'And I will phone the police station and make a report to the inspector!' He drinks the Coke halfway in one thirsty swig.

Ngulube is now very angry. Mxolisi sees his hand straying to the knife on the table, and throws a last punch:

'Your *shamwari* has gone to *buy* more petrol for both of you to make more money out of, whilst your wife and children are queuing at Social Welfare for free mealie-meal.'

Mxolisi disappears from the kitchen door into the sitting room, still carrying the Coke.

'Gecko!' Ngulube mutters to himself, and looks out of the kitchen window. Directly facing it is the ex-chicken coop, a low brick affair topped with wire mesh and roofed with asbestos. This is where the black market petrol is stashed. And now it is empty. He remembers that there had only been one full twenty-litre container remaining. He dashes out of the door into the back yard. The house is enclosed in a red brick wall. He looks in the chicken coop. The gallon is no longer there. He sees the five empty ones lying outside the coop. He races around the house to the front gate, opens it and goes out. He sees Mxolisi walking up the street, one hand in his pocket, the other carrying the coke. Suddenly remembering the pot on the stove, Ngulube dashes back into the house. He is now frightened. What is maNdlovu going to say when she comes back?

Mxolisi finds Juluka standing at the street corner. It is now twilight, the cloudless sky an eternal blue-grey, just waiting for darkness and God to flip on the stars, and mankind their vices. A cool wind is blowing away

164

the heat of the afternoon.

'Where is it?' he asks Juluka, taking a sip of Coke.

'In the maize field next to the bus stop. You took long to come?' Juluka holds his hand out to Mxolisi, who gives him the nearly finished Coke.

'Should I have taken a shorter time?'

'I heard you telling him through the kitchen window.' There is laughter in Juluka's eyes. He finishes the Coke, and hands back the empty bottle to Mxolisi. 'Ta.'

'Did I tell him any lies?'

'Only the truth, and enough to make him not look behind him out of the kitchen window. But Mxolisi, what about your mother?'

'If she wants to report the theft of black market petrol, let her go ahead. At least you and me will be together in the cells. Let's go and look for a buyer.'

'Ngulube took your overalls from my father who saw you hide them in our bin through the door when the policeman was chasing you. Did he give it back to you?' They are now walking in the direction of the bus stop.

'I don't know what I should do about that squatter,' Mxolisi replies. 'I don't want him at home. His family needs him more than my mother. Tell me, Juluka, how can an old woman like that like sex so much? And to make matters worse,' his voice lowers, 'you know my father died from AIDS.'

Glossary

Scud – a local traditional brew, cheaper than clear beer.

Mbanje - Marijuana

Tshomi – colloquial Ndebele for friend.

Shamwari – Shona for girlfriend incorporated into Ndebele colloquial.

Christopher Mlalazi is a product of the Crossing Borders Creative Writing Project. He writes adult and children's fiction, poetry and plays. He has been published in three anthologies and online and premiered six plays. In 2004, one of his short stories was accorded the Highly Recommended citation in the Sable Arvon 2004 Short Story Competition.

Aunty and Ma

Muthal Naidoo

ASHES TO ASHES AND DUST TO DUST, so why all the fuss?

Yislaaik! A corpse is a horrible thing to look at; like some weirdo's rotten attempt to create an image of you. Man, I look grey, washed out. As for that fucken garland around my neck – marigolds on shit! Everyone who enters the marquee feels obligated to look at this dead thing in the coffin that isn't me anymore. Some even kiss it. Gross! They all shed crocodile tears. Even my mother. She's really glad I'm dead but she sits there with waterfalls gushing out of her eyes. Putting on a show! Why? Nobody expects it. Now that I'm gone, she hopes it's all over but of course it's not. I don't know why but I know it's not.

'And you should be ashamed of that.'

'Pa? What the heck are you doing here? Don't tell me you came to pay your last respects? That's a laugh.'

'Don't call me Pa. I am not your father. You are not my son. All that is irrelevant now.'

'So what must I call you?'

'Don't call me.'

'I didn't. So why'd you come to my funeral?... I didn't come to yours. I didn't want to get involved in all this shit. Did you see Vasi in the house having his head shaved? He's going to be doing all that shit with lamps and camphor and stuff.

'You should be grateful.'

'*Ag*, you still mad because I ran away from your funeral. I didn't want to be involved in this mumbo-jumbo.'

'No, you went off to get high instead.'

'Chill out Pa, you're dead. You're a ghost. Let it go. If I had a joint now I'd give it to you. That would calm you down... Hey, how come you're still hanging around here?'

Pa ignores me. He is looking straight at Ma who is talking to Aunty from No. 46. Both the old birds are in a state. What's the matter with them? They look like they're hiding a stash somewhere. 'Now Aunty's a miserable case, if you want to know.'

'I don't.'

'Look at her, Pa. A miserable, shrivelled up old *parti*. She's Ma's best friend now. Lives with her son, Morgan, and his wife, Devi. Morgan brought his old lady to stay with him when his old man died; he didn't want to lose the money. Once he got his mother to put her thumbprint on all the necessary documents, Morgan had control of all the money and bought the mansion at No. 46.'

'Look, I know all about her.'

'But Pa, you died before she moved here, how do you know?... You haven't been walking around here for ten years, have you? Surely not? Pa? Pa! I don't believe it! Didn't you go to heaven or hell?'

'Don't talk rubbish. There's no heaven or hell for Hindus.'

'So what happens then? For God's sakes, Pa! Do we just hang around like zombies?'

'If your soul is pure, you merge with the supreme creative force – that is *moksha*. If you are still carrying *karma*, you are reincarnated.'

'Then why are you still here? You should have merged with the whatever or you should have been born again. So what happened?'

'I don't know. I don't know.'

'Man, you're like a prisoner on death row. I can see why people convert. It's much simpler if there's a heaven and a hell. So what do you do all day; hang around watching over Ma?'

'I can't watch over her; I just watch her. It's been terrible to see how much you made her suffer. Thank God, you can't torment her anymore.'

'You don't know anything. Ma understands me. Hey, were you here the day I died? I don't remember what happened. My heart was beating too fast, I was desperate for a fix... Pa?... Were you here?... Okay, okay. Ignore me. I just asked because I don't really know what happened. I know I can look backwards and forwards in time now, but that moment escapes me. I don't know why, but it does.'

Pa is standing next to Ma stroking her hair. What for? She can't feel a thing.

Vasi and the *poosari* have finished mucking about with lamps, flowers and sprinklers. The caterwauling stops: it's time to take the body to the crematorium. Family members lift the coffin off the table, carry it out of the tent and, with the crowd following behind, proceed to the front of the house where the hearse is waiting. As they slide the coffin into the vehicle, a mechanical wailing fills the air. Somebody pinches my sister, Saras, whispering to her to scream and roll on the ground. Even though she can get quite carried away at these rituals, Saras just gives the aunty a dirty look. Thank goodness! I know Saras cares for me, not like my other sister, Punjee.

A couple of years ago, Punjee and her husband, Gopal, took me away to stay with them. Nobody asked me. They just took me. I mean I wasn't a kid: I was twenty-seven. The whole family was behind it, except for Ma of course.

The day they took me away, her in-laws, wealthy, upper-class snobs who didn't try to hide their contempt, came to visit. I swore, cursed, told them all to go to hell, picked fights and threatened them. They gritted their civilised teeth but their eyes were cold. They said not a word. But when I took an interest in Gopal's teenage sister, lovely girl, they went ballistic, thought I was going to rape her or something. They couldn't wait to get out of the house.

Punjee was mortified.

The next day, they put me to work in Gopal's paint store. Me! I had never worked a day in my life.

I had to be up by seven, go to the shop, dust the shelves, put out paints, sweep out the store and help customers load stuff in the boots of their cars. It was like being in jail. After living a carefree life, here I was slaving like a kaffir.

At work, all I could think about was dope.

Every time I thought of my last high, I got the shakes. I didn't have any money; the bleddy family had cut off my allowance. Ma didn't have money because the family stopped giving her cash, they gave her groceries 'n stuff, no cash. I wasn't staying with her so I couldn't get at her pension money. When I asked Punjee for an advance on my wages, she refused. Damn slut! I could have killed her.

Instead I went home, had a fight with Ma, beat her up good for sending me to live with Punjee, and then searched the whole house for money. I pulled off the covers on Ma's bed, looked under the mattress, looked in the jars in the kitchen, turned out the drawers in the bedroom

– I trashed the whole house but couldn't find a cent and the next pension day was two weeks off.

I was desperate, my body was a mass of pain; I felt like every part of me was being crushed in a giant vice. I couldn't stand it so I went back to the shop, found thinners in the storeroom but they didn't quell the craving. I went to Punjee's house; she wasn't home. I searched her bedroom, found a couple of hundred and sped off to Skoon Blokkies, to Boetie, my supplier.

When Punjee arrived at Ma's with a supply of groceries and found her bashed up, she bundled her into the car and took her to the hospital. Ma came back bandaged like a wounded soldier, her arm in a sling. It seems Ma's collarbone was broken. Punjee was ready to report me to the police for assault and battery. But Ma began crying as usual, 'Please give him another chance. This is my boy, my only son. It will be a terrible disgrace.'

'Stop protecting him Ma, he *is* a bleddy disgrace. Everybody knows how he treats you. How many times haven't the neighbours called the police? He'll kill you if we don't stop him.'

'No, no. He doesn't mean it. Leave him, leave him. He's really a good boy.'

They are always trying to poison Ma against me but I know I can depend on her.

'That's the trouble; you spoil him rotten. Your boy child! Well, he's useless; a high school drop-out, a bleddy drug addict, selling dagga to school children to support his habit. He's a burden on all of us. I'm going to call the police.'

'If you do that, I'll kill myself. Just leave Poovy alone.'

All this was too much for Punjee.

She had taken me in thinking she could control me but I showed her I wasn't a pushover, like her husband, Gopal. After just one day she was desperate to get rid of me.

But she definitely didn't want me back with Ma.

She called a family council that night, got all the relatives to put money together and sent me to the rehab centre in Cape Town.

Boy, was that place harsh! Like a maximum-security prison.

After they tortured me there for a couple of months, they said I was clean so I came home to Ma.

Now that I am dead, of course, that solves Punjee's problem.

She doesn't hide the fact that she's glad. She's walking around smiling and joking with everyone like she's at a party. She put herself in charge of the cooking to avoid being involved in the funeral ceremonies.

People are getting into cars to go to the crematorium. Ma and Saras are in the first car. Even though she's not family, Aunty gets in with them. Poor old sod, she's got a band-aid on her forehead. Her daughter-in-law threw a punch at her this morning.

Punjee doesn't get into any car. I'm not surprised.

If I'm going to be hanging around here like Pa, I'll make it my business to haunt her.

Pa and I get into the car with Ma, Aunty and Saras. We sit on their laps as we ride off together. I don't know why I am here. Maybe it's because a dead person has to watch his funeral before he goes off to wherever. Man, I hope I don't end up stuck here like Pa. I better be born again.

Aunty, Ma and Saras have been quiet up till now.

They don't seem to be at ease: Saras keeps frowning; Aunty and Ma scrupulously avoid looking at one another.

Then Saras bursts out, 'Ma, what happened when Poovy died? Punjee told me she found the two of you lying on the floor. You had passed out and Poovy was lying in a pool of blood with a gunshot wound to his chest. But they didn't find a gun. What happened Ma?'

Ma covers her face. Pa puts his arm around her in a futile attempt to hold her close.

Aunty chimes in, 'Saras, your mother burying her son today, her only son. This is not the time. Why you don't wait 'til after the funeral?'

'You're right, Aunty. I'm sorry, Ma. I suppose even a bad son is still a son. It's so hard nowadays. You don't know how your children are going to turn out. I talk to my Vanitha and Nishen every day about drugs or AIDS. I pray, I go the temple; I'm doing my best to keep my children safe.'

I can't help laughing. Saras thinks she takes part in temple ceremonies because she's helping others; actually she just loves being involved in the rituals. She's really doing them for herself. Gives her a sense of purpose, makes her feel good sitting with the ladies at the temple gossiping, cooking, decorating lamps and statues. That's how she gets her high. After I am reincarnated I'll teach her the pleasures of smoking a joint, of getting a real high.

Pa turns to me, 'That's just it. You can't go back. I see it now.'

'What do you mean?'

'You made me see it. It's an addiction. You have to give it up.'

'What are you talking about, Pa? I've given up everything. I'm dead.'

Pa's eyes are light. 'I see it now. You have to give it up.' His translucent arms flow out from around Ma. 'Mundane reality. It's an addiction.' He

171

shines at me, smiling. 'Thank you.' Then poof! He's gone.

Outside the crematorium, which is at one end of the cemetery, they lower the coffin onto a few bricks on the ground. Vasi and the Poosari resume their performance: lighting lamps and so on. When they finally close the coffin and take it to the oven, it is time for eulogies.

Nobody comes forward. Nothing is said.

They just sing songs for the dead as they watch the coffin enter the flames. Then the oven is closed off and that's that.

Except it isn't. Not for me. Maybe for them but not for me. What the fuck am I supposed to do now?

They cremated me a week ago but I'm still here, hanging around in the marquee, which stays up until the *karmathi*, the sixteenth-day fire-raising ceremony, when they smoke me out of the premises. So I have a few more days to wait before my soul is released from its earthly bonds. At least I hope it's only a few days. Man, I don't want the same fate as Pa. It wouldn't be so bad if I could smoke some crack or a joint but dammit I don't crave those things anymore. I want to but I can't. Before I died, if I just thought of coke, my whole body would anticipate it. What the hell did Pa mean, *Give it up*? I don't have a body now.

Sitting around here, watching the passing parade is tedious. I know everything that has happened and is going to happen. The world has become a bleddy boring set of TV reruns. I watch people popping in to commiserate with Ma. I watch my sisters come in and out getting things organised for the *karmathi*. Am I gonna be a couch potato for all eternity? Watching others? Not having a life of my own? Yislaaik! What a horrible thought.

I go to the front of the house and what-do-you-know, it's time for the next programme, a local soap opera starring two old ladies, Aunty and Ma. What a laugh! Here comes Aunty, rushing like a mad woman, making a dramatic entry like that first time Ma took her in. Poor old lady! Devi really hates her. Tortures her, swears at her, hits her, starves her. Until she met Ma, Aunty was always running down the street screaming and crying. One day, when Punjee was bringing Ma home from the hospital, Aunty came running towards her. Ma put her arms around her and took her inside. That was the beginning of their friendship.

What a life! Watching two senile crazies who should be dead instead of me! This is even worse than the lousy programmes on SABC.

Now Aunty has come to Ma with a nutty story.

Aunty knocks loudly on the door. As soon as Ma unlocks, she bursts in sobbing wildly. Ma settles her on the sofa, then comes back to lock the door again.

Ma has her arms around Aunty, trying to soothe her.

'They going to kill me. I know it. I'm going pass the dining room, I see Devi with two visitors. Two black ladies. They sitting together, drinking tea. I know they talking about me. I hear the black ladies saying they will take care of me. They signed the papers and she give them money. They say they coming for me next week. When I hear that, I run out. Can you see what she's doing? She's hiring those people to kill me, like that gambler lawyer, Moosa, got two blacks to hijack his wife, chop her up and throw her body in the veld.'

'It can't be. Your son will never let her do that.'

'She rules him. She tells him what to do. I don't know why he married such a woman. Why did they bring me to stay with them if they don't want me?'

'How you know those two black ladies are killers?'

'They must be. I never seen black people sitting having tea in the house before.'

The old lady is definitely off her rocker. Devi is a bitch, but this is nonsense.

Ma takes Aunty to the kitchen to make her a cup of tea. Aunty calms down. Then, as she sits there, she turns to Ma, a determined look hardening her eyes. Suddenly, Ma is at the fridge looking for something to cook. She's trying to avoid Aunty. I feel some kind of tension between the two old birds. I don't really know what's going on. Why? Now that I am dead, I can see everything past, present and future. What's blocking me here?

'You can put me up a few days? Till I can get in touch with my sister in Ladysmith? I can't go back to my son's house.'

'Of course, you can stay. You stay long as you want. I alone now. After *karmathi*, it will be very quiet. But you must forget about Devi. I can't help you with that.'

'But I helped you.'

'No, I can't do it. I'm sorry.'

'My daughter-in-law is a terrible woman. One day she will kill me. I know it. They say her mother's death wasn't an accident.'

'Forget about her. You come stay with me. Punjee will make sure we are all right.'

On cue, enter Punjee. She sets a box on the table, kisses Ma and Aunty, 'I brought some of the brassware we need for the *karmathi*. Aunty, after the ceremony, I want you to cook your fabulous mutton *biryani*. I am so tired of this vegetable diet. I don't know why we have to punish ourselves for my rotten brother. We should have been eating *biryani* every day to celebrate his passing.'

'Punjee, I want to go to my sister in Ladysmith. I might not be here for the ceremony.'

'Aunty, you can't run away. What will Ma do without you?'

'I can't stay here no more.'

'Yes you can. You can stay with Ma.'

'No, they won't let me. I'm not safe here. I must go away.'

'But Aunty, you have to report these people. You must talk to the social worker. I'll arrange it for you.' Aunty is silent. Punjee looks at Ma who just shrugs. 'I am going to call the social worker. You can't keep quiet about it. You have to report it.'

'No. No social worker!'

'Don't be like Ma. You see what happened here; Poovy nearly killed her. So many times I told Ma, he'll kill you, himself or both of you. Luckily he only shot himself.' Aunty looks at Ma who is very busy rinsing spinach. Punjee picks up her cellphone. 'I'm calling the social worker.'

'No, no. Don't do that. This my business.'

'You're just like Ma. She was always making excuses for Poovy and look what happened. I don't care what you say, I'm calling the social worker.' With her cellphone to her ear, she goes into the lounge.

Aunty turns to Ma. 'You know I don't need social worker.'

'Maybe it's for the best.'

'I know what is for best. You know it too.'

Punjee comes back. 'Mrs Patel can see you tomorrow morning. Now Aunty, you must tell her everything. She's a social worker. She won't spread it all over the neighbourhood. She will help you. Don't be foolish like Ma.' Punjee picks up her bag and leaves.

Aunty stands up to go. Ma turns pleading eyes on her. Aunty's look is stony. 'I must go home. If you won't help me, I'll do it myself.'

'No, no. Stay. Don't go back there.'

'I won't see social worker. I'm going.'

'No, no, you can't go. Stay here!' Aunty starts to move off. 'All right, I'll help you.' Why does Ma sound resigned? Aunty and Ma stare at each other for a long moment. 'I promise. Let all this *karmathi* business be over. I will help you.'

Now I know.

Here in the empty marquee, I'm forced to take stock because I know. My Ma and her friend! Two old women!

It all came back to me in the moment that they looked at each other. So now I am reeling back to relive my demise.

As the sun begins to rise on the morning of the last day of my life, I lie on my bed wrapped in agony. Pain, seeping through my skin, twists every cell in every muscle, crushes every particle in every bone, and sets up a terrible tattoo in my chest. I crawl out of bed; stagger off to the kitchen, into the pantry where my stash is hidden. With trembling hands, I search for my parcel. There's nothing.

Must get to Boetie before I die.

I turn the kitchen and pantry upside down looking for money; there's nothing, nothing left to sell either. No gadgets, no electrics, no decent pots or dishes. I rush off to Ma's room, kick open the door, dash over to the bed and grab the old lady by the neck. 'Where's your money, Ma?' Gasping convulsively, she can't say a word. I smash her across the face a couple of times and shove her back on the pillow before I start searching. No money, no jewellery, nothing I can sell; all gone. Still I empty all the drawers, desperate to find something, anything.

All I find are papers. Papers! What's Ma doing with papers; she can't read.

I glance at them. Title deeds! These are the title deeds to the house. I'm saved. Thank you God. Now I have something to sell, something big! I can get enough crack to last months. I throw on my clothes and dash over to Boetie's.

I bang and bang and bang on the door.

Clutching a blanket over her shoulders, Boetie's wife, peeps through a crack. 'Hey, you know what time it is? Go away.'

'I must see Boetie.'

'He's sleeping. Come back later.'

'I can't. I'll die if I don't get some dope.'

'I don't know what you talking about. Go away!'

Man, can't she see me here shaking like a person in a trance. What's she giving me this bullshit?

Then my legs go; I'm falling.

When I open my eyes, I'm on the sofa in Boetie's lounge.

Boetie wipes his brow, 'Man I don't know what I would have done if you died here. You know how long you been out?'

I try to get up. My legs don't move but the shuddering won't stop. 'Damn it man, gimme a hit.' Boetie gives me a little crack to smoke. After a few pulls, the pain begins to ebb. Soon, I'm floating on a cloud. The world comes back into focus. I smile at Boetie.

'You smiling, you bastard. This's gonna cost you. You know the rules; you can't just come to the door like that.'

'I would have died.'

'You're a bleddy burden.'

'I can't help it; the stuff wears off quickly. Give me a stash before I leave.'

'Pay up first.'

'I don't have cash but I have this. It's worth a lot.'

Boetie takes the title deeds. He shakes his head as he reads. 'This is no good. You can't sell the house. It's not yours.'

'Listen man, it's officially my Ma's, same difference. When Ma dies, it will be mine. So the property is practically yours. It's worth thousands; you'll be able to supply me months, maybe years.'

'It's no good. These are not title deeds. They are transfer papers.' What the hell is Boetie talking about? The house belongs to Ma; Dad left it to her. 'Didn't you read these papers; your Ma transferred the property.'

Grabbing the document out of Boetie's hand, I scan the pages.

What a shock! Ma has betrayed me; she's put the house in my sisters' names. Damn you, Ma. I'll kill you; I'll kill you. But she wouldn't do such a thing to me. I'm her son, her only son. She has more time for me than her daughters. She would never do a thing like this. She's not smart enough. They put her up to it. That bleddy Punjee; she must have masterminded the whole scheme.

When I get home, Ma is in the lounge lighting the lamp. I grab her and push her against the wall, shoving the papers in her face. 'This is my house. You had no right to give it away. You tell Punjee and Saras to give it back. Don't tell me you can't do it. If you can give it away, you can get it back.' I drag Ma to the phone, dial Punjee's number and push the receiver against her ear. 'Tell her to bring the title deeds back.' Ma begins to protest. I twist her wrist. My legs are not steady; when I lean on the phone table to support myself, Ma tries to get way but I put a neckhold on her, 'Tell her! Tell her!'

Ma doesn't say a word.

I slam the phone down. My hands are shaking and drums are going in my chest. If I don't get some dope now, I am going to die. I drag Ma to my room; she'll run away if I let go of her. Holding onto Ma with one hand, I reach under the bed for the handgun I have taped to the base. Shoving it against Ma's head, I drag her back to the lounge. 'Phone Punjee now! Tell her, I'm waiting.'

But Ma is paralysed with fear.

'If you don't call her, I'm going to kill you.'

As I release the safety catch, a python coils itself around my chest and begins to squeeze the life out of me. My arm slides over Ma's shoulder and as the gun starts to slip from my fingers, Aunty who has been watching from the kitchen, darts forward to grab it. Ma, suddenly galvanised, puts her hands over Aunty's, shoves the gun against my chest and pulls the trigger. The discharge throws them backward and my body falls to the floor. When Ma sees the blood that gushes from the wound, she falls down in a dead faint. The gun, still in Aunty's hand, sends her screaming out of the house in a mad panic. No one takes any notice of her. They are used to seeing her careering down the street like this.

I look down at my body; at Ma lying near it and I am distraught.

Ma pulled the trigger!

She deliberately shot me. She wanted me dead! My own mother wanted me dead. I thought she loved me.

She thinks she killed me but my heart gave out before she fired.

It doesn't change the fact that she wanted me dead.

Nobody can understand what happened.

Nobody connects Aunty with the shooting or thinks to look in the shoebox under her bed for the gun.

Aunty and Ma have not spoken of the event, not to each other, not to other people.

But today, after Aunty saw her daughter-in-law paying off the two black women, she wants to emulate Ma. What remains in her memory is Ma resolutely pulling the trigger. Under the terror of the moment, there had been pure admiration.

Ma had become her hero.

Now, Aunty wants to be able to free herself in the same way. And to honour Ma, she wants her to share the moment as they had done when Ma shot me.

Nothing will come of it, however. Morgan is sending his mother to an old age home. The two black women that Aunty saw drinking tea with Devi are nuns from Immaculata Home for the Aged. After Morgan and Devi dump Aunty there, she will never see them again.

177

And that's the end of the story.
In death, I am clairvoyant in all respects but one.
I don't know what is happening to me?
Why am I still here? Fuck. Why are my eyes filling with tears?

Muthal Naidoo, a retired teacher, is the co-founder of the Shah Theatre Academy in South Africa. She has been involved in theatre for a number of years as an actor, director and playwright. Most of her theatre work was done in Durban between 1977 and 1983 and her plays include *We 3 Kings, Ikhayalethu* (originally *Coming Home*), *Of No Account* and *Outside-In*, as well as a number of other short plays and revues.

Of No Account and *Coming Home* were nominated for the Critics' Circle Award in Durban. In 1983, her revue *The Master Plan* – a satire performed at UDF meetings in the Durban area – was banned.

The play *We 3 Kings* was published by the University of Durban-Westville in 1992 and in 2002 *Outside-In* was published in an anthology entitled *South African Indian Writings in English*. Last December, Muthal's book of short stories, *Jail Birds and Others,* was published by Botsotso Publishing.

To a Cartoonist

Tolu Ogunlesi

YESTERDAY MORNING I SEWED UP the bloodied heads of seven men. When I finished I looked at the bandaged scalps and imagined how I would feel if I had a machete interred in my head – as punishment for something I do not know anything about. The swish of rusty metal through the air, the interruption by bone and a thin slice of flesh, the bluster of blood, the pain hurtling down to the feet, more and more impudent by the second. Those bloodied heads were a consequence of riots accompanying the publication of your cartoons. Those cartoons were not published in Nigeria. No one would have dared do that. Hours after my encounter with the injured men, Aishat, my fiancée, is about to leave me, because of the cartoons. It is for this reason that you, the cartoonist, begin to loom large and wild in my thinking, almost like some obsession.

A colleague tells me the cartoons can be seen on the internet. I remember a 'tragic' incident involving my older brother many years ago, involving his painting of the Prophet Mohammed. My curiosity is stirred. I decide to go to an internet café. Very discreetly I download the cartoons onto a flash disk to have a better look at home. I do that often; download stuff at internet cafés, to read later on my computer, since I do not have internet access at home. I return home and load the cartoons onto my computer. And then I get an emergency call – which happens to have to do with the arrival of more broken bodies from the riots – and rush out.

Hi, I say, when I return to the house, hours later. I am worn out. She's sitting on the couch facing the TV. No answer. At first I assume it is one of her usual moody spells. The TV is off. She is not asleep. I move over to sit beside her on the couch. There are some papers on the glass stool

179

beside her. I pick them up. Printed copies of the cartoons.

'Where did you get this?' I ask.

'Where did you leave them for me to find?' she answers, folding her arms across her chest. 'I always knew that someday one of us would do this to the other,' she says. I sigh. Whenever she's in a bad mood that's how she talks. She starts a conversation as though we were in the middle of one.

'What were you thinking when you did this?' she picks the papers up and waves them in my face.

'When I did what?' I say. My voice is raised, defensive. 'Can't you see I got those from the internet?'

'And you thought it was a great idea not to leave them there…'

'I wish I could swear I understand what you are saying.' I sound like I'm whining, a little child battling to open a jar of biscuits.

'I wish I could tell you I understand why you did what you did,' she says.

'Wait a minute… what are you accusing me of doing?' It is difficult containing my frustration. I want to bang my fists on the table and tell her I have had enough. Enough of what? I don't know. That's what anger does to you; you speak without knowing why you say what you say. 'Why did you print them out?'

'If you had wanted to dump me and move on to some other girl, at least you could have done it like a man. Like a man. You should just have told me you were tired of me, not run off to work and left these behind to do the dirty work!'

'Don't be silly! How can you think like that? You should be ashamed of yourself for thinking like that!'

'You are sick!' she spits. I flinch at the bitterness in her voice. Her arms are still folded across her chest, the muscles of her neck taut with anger. 'You keep these on the computer and ask me how can I think like that!' I sit there watching as she storms out of the house. As I write this letter, twenty-four hours have passed since Aishat left the house. Her phone is switched off. That really bothers me. It is very unlike her.

I mentioned an incident involving my older brother. He was nine at the time. He made a painting for my maternal grandfather's birthday. It showed grandfather side-by-side with a bearded man labelled 'Mohammed', both men standing atop a huge book labeled 'Koran'. He walked over to where my grandfather sat surrounded by fellow Imams and with as much of a flourish as a nine-year-old could muster unrolled the painting for the admiration of his audience. Instead grandfather's face (and all the other dozen or so faces there) grew dark and pinched together, mean as the clouds on a stormy day, beard quivering like a fevered bird. A shame-laden hush sat upon everyone in the room. My grandfather stormed out of the room bellowing for my mother. I stood there, a seven-year-old mass of terror, wondering what had gone wrong. My mother came up to my brother, grabbed him off to the balcony and in a voice that was filled with equal measures of irritation, shame and an attempted kindness of speech, told him that it was a SIN to draw the Prophet Mohammed, and that grandfather was very upset. I did not understand why an 'act' of water-colour would fall into the same category with lying or taking what was not yours. At that point I remembered the painting of a feasting Jesus and the twelve disciples that hung above our dining table, the one that had *The Last Supper* inscribed fancifully at the top. I wanted to mention the painting to my mum, but I saw that she really wasn't in the mood for a lesson in theology. It must have been embarrassing for her that day, with all these learned Muslim scholars who were eyewitnesses to the sacrilege perpetrated by the grandson of a much-respected Imam. I wonder what my grandfather said to my mum, that day. *See what you have done to me.* I assume that is what he told her – because those were the only words she uttered to my brother in the car on our way home. I pitied him greatly on account of his misfortune, and remember saying a prayer of thanksgiving to God that I was not the 'scapegoat', because it dawned on my seven-year-old mind that it could have been me and not my brother. We never mentioned that incident after that day, and I'm not sure my brother ever painted anything again after that. When Aishat left the house in anger yesterday it occurred to me that my twenty-seven-year-old thanksgiving prayer had perhaps arrived at its expiry date.

Just before the men with the bloodied heads left the hospital, one of them said something to me. He said: *God bless you.* He said it without a smile. Perhaps that was to show that he meant it, he wasn't joking or just being polite. He held out his hand. I hesitated for a moment, then clasped it heartily – and guiltily – to make up for my hesitation. For a moment I tried to imagine which 'God' he meant. It was supposed to be a prayer. Whether it is or not depends on whether there is a God or not, and if there is, which one we're talking about. The 'Danish' God, whom I can swear is a myth with a capital 'M', or Aishat's God, or my own 'God' (which would be more like a United Nations Assembly of Principles). I've never been to Denmark, but from what I know, a good number of you are atheists. It's not your fault. In your part of the world, you guys really don't need God that much. In Nigeria we employ God mostly to do such stuff as cajoling the power company to sustain the power during the Nations Cup finals, or blinding the eyes of policemen to the fact that your vehicle particulars expired last year, or fouling up the chances of the two-hundred other folks also applying for the job you want. God is some kind of handyman, you see, he comes in very handy in getting all sorts of miscellaneous tasks accomplished. But in Denmark, God, in my opinion – and I've got no apologies for this – is obsolete. Public power supply is never in danger of vanishing, you don't have to do two dozen interviews to get one job, and even if you don't get this job, you've got welfare, and I presume the pay's not bad. You see, if I were God, I'd blot every country with a per-capita income above a certain figure out of my files, and channel my attention to those ones whose per-capita income figures would resemble the Eskimo headcount in Saudi Arabia.

Now, my point is simply this, those cartoons had to come from someplace like Denmark, and from someone like you. Don't be shocked. I haven't met you, we can both testify to that, but I have this feeling that I know you. Most probably atheist, middle-class, middle-aged, no, somewhere between twenty-five and twenty-nine, most likely gay, but then maybe not, grossly dissatisfied, wondering what to do with his life… I think I can bet my stethoscope on my guesses about who you are. Which leads me to the heart of the matter. Which is that while I do not give a damn about what you choose to do with your pen or pencil in far-away God-on-sabbatical-Denmark, I think it was not fair that you published those cartoons. At least it was not fair on me – the man with a bloodied heart – and I daresay it was not fair on the men with the bloodied heads. While I am not a fan of censorship, I believe in common-sense and fairness. If I were you and the Muse descended on me, you know, '*This is my beloved cartoonist in whom I am well pleased and I want you to draw so-and-so cartoons,*' I wouldn't disobey the divine call. No. I'd smile and immediately start work upon the cartoons. But the instant I finished, I'd summon the muse to inspect them, even admire them, and then without wasting a second I'd set fire to them, every single one of them – not insensitively inflict them on the world. It'd be between the Muse and me, our private joke. Anything to do with religion is like underwear – essential, perhaps, but generally meant to be kept out of sight.

Unlike most – if not all – Nigerians, I do not belong to any classifiable religion. I'm neither Moslem nor Christian, which are our two largest religions. And I'm not an atheist – if you gave me a questionnaire to tick my religion from a list, I'd probably skip to the bottom of the page and add 'All and None of the Above' to the options. But I happen to hold God in high esteem, simply because He/They is/are all around me, in the lives of friends and family, on television, at work, stickered onto cars, everywhere.

My father used to be Muslim, then Pentecostal Christian, and then ended up Anglican. My mother was the daughter of an Imam. She fell in love with my father – a former Muslim. In the opinion of her father, falling in love with a non-Muslim was despicable enough, but choosing an ex-Muslim was the height of rebellion. In an (unsuccessful) attempt to appease him she got my father to do an Islamic wedding. He unearthed a long-forgotten Muslim name, and did a revision course in Islam. We came on the scene, my siblings and I, and for a while, we were spared the burdens – and liberties, if any – of religion. I guess my parents decided to take a sabbatical from religion; they had bitten off a huge chunk during their courtship and needed time to chew and digest it afterwards. And then, when they resumed, we kids found ourselves bundled to Sunday school with my father every week. First it was Pentecostal Sunday school, where we met a Jesus who was quite hip, who didn't mind fast dancing and didn't mind jeans and might have spoken slang for all we knew. Then my father discovered another Jesus, in a Baptist church almost opposite our old church. So we had to get used to this new Jesus, who disapproved of 'worldly' dancing and didn't like to see girls leave their hair uncovered, and always required that we asked ourselves 'What Would Jesus Do?' before we made any decisions. But somehow, as is the way with kids, we only mourned our old Jesus for a while and settled down quickly with the new one. Not long after I left home for university, I decided to spare Jesus the burden of taking full care of me. My mother on her own part remained a Muslim, shifting in and out of a commitment to the religion. One year she'd adhere strictly to the Ramadan fast, next year she'd act as though Ramadan were a pagan ritual, not to be touched with a long pole. She never went with us to church.

Aishat's mother is from a well-known Muslim family in Lagos, and has been on *Hajj* a lot of times. Aishat has been to Mecca once. We have been going out almost a year. And we have lived happily ever after, until now, that is.

I didn't draw those cartoons, I didn't publish them, I didn't put them on the internet, I didn't forward the internet links to everyone in the

Address Book of my email account. There was no impulse in me to laugh when I saw those cartoons, I swear! Definitely not when I remembered the incident involving my brother. I did not call Aishat to come and have a look at them, though I am sure she had heard about them. But now, because of one split-second action (File – Save As – OK); a seemingly innocuous last step in a thoughtless chain originated by you, thousands of miles away – I am on the verge of losing (or am I being irrational?) the woman I hoped would be my wife. And those are your supposedly harmless cartoons, aren't they? Those cartoons seem to love their liberty as much as you love your own liberty to produce them, that seems to be why they've been having a season of wild fun all over the world, conquering lands from Islamabad to Maiduguri.

I have a strong feeling that at this point, you'd want to bring out your pencil (the most blasphemous one in your collection) to scribble a reply to me at the back of one of the cartoons (the most blasphemous of the lot). A very short reply of course, you wouldn't want to waste any more time on some delusional, anti-Danish psycho.

Dear Doctor,

Has it occurred to you that your woman might just have been looking for an excuse to leave you?

Yours Truly

My answer to this is that that's impossible. There's no way I wouldn't have suspected – had Aishat been fed-up, and desirous of an exit – it's not possible, believe me. She was not looking for an opportunity to leave me.

Did I imagine that the images would be offensive to Aishat? If there were some kind of balance that measured 'Religious Sensitivity', on a scale of 1 – 10, I would expect Aishat to measure a '4'. If you asked me, having gone out with her for almost a year, if I would ever have imagined she'd react that way to the cartoons, I'd say no. Agreed, they are blasphemous stuff, insulting to her religion, but would you not expect her to wave them aside as the work of some depraved mind, and ignore them completely? To be candid, I have come to the conclusion that she was being very illogical thinking the way she did.

I thank you for reading on till this point. Before I go I've got some final words of advice for you – a few words and you will never hear from me again. The next time the Muse alights on your head like a dove and wants you to do *that* sort of art, I think that Jesus might be a more willing subject. I presume you do know that, and that you deliberately draw the Prophet Mohammed because you want to be naughty for naughty's sake. As I have argued, God is probably just some intellectual concept to you, so it's difficult to blame you. Something's occurred to me, a chart kind of thing, you know, a line dividing a page into, say, two columns, or more, one column for each religion known to man, to be published and distributed all over the world – *Religious Trivia for (Danish) Dummies*, or *The Danish Cartoonist's Guide to Gods* or something of that sort. A sample chart is below, you know, just a sample. The third religion is *The Sacred Imperialist Order of the Star-Spangled Banner*, which I'm sure you have not heard of. The founder is an American who likes to be known simply as 'The Great Texan Cowboy'; The patron saint, Uncle Sam, is also American. On a wall in a tiny English seaside town is graffiti that reads – *Saint Sam is a wanker* – most likely the handiwork of an English infidel threatened by the fervid spread of an American religion. Just goes to show how far we have come from the days of the itinerant English missionaries who went around the world taking the gospel of salvation to the heathen. It's the Americans who now evangelise to the English, and to the whole world. The English graffiti seems to be a similar brand of protest to the ones that have rocked the world on account of your cartoons.

You may of course enlarge the chart to your taste. Though I have a feeling that in your hands, such a chart would just turn out to be another joke, a tool for further assault on innocent religious sensibilities.

Islam	Christianity	The Sacred Imperialist Order of the SSB
Does not permit depictions of Prophet Mohammed	Does not mind depictions of Jesus	Encourages depictions of Uncle Sam, especially in foreign countries
Allows up to four wives	One man one wife	One man one warfare
Forbids homosexuality	Forbids homosexuality	Forbids homosexuality (If you disregard Abu Ghraib)

Now, a letter should have a Beginning (Introduction), a Middle (Body), and an End (Conclusion). This is the 'END', included so as not to mortify my fifth-form English Language teacher, who might stumble upon this letter – should your enviable respect of the 'fundamental' freedom of speech and weird sense of humour, push you to publish it as a foreword to *Best Blasphemous Cartoons in Danish*.

Once upon a time, there must have been only one God. Or even maybe no God at all. Don't expect me to tell you Confucius said that. No. I said it. It's my opinion. If you open to the first chapter of the book of human existence you will find that *one* God. Then you flip to the last chapter, you know, to see how the action ends – and you are shocked to find that there are as many Gods as there are men. But wait a minute. There is a problem somewhere. The chapters in between – which form the bulk of the book – are missing. So no one knows how one God became many. Or how No-God became Many-Gods. Cloning? No, I don't think so. That's a fairly recent human indulgence. Now, get this clear. I am not a philosopher, no, and I have no aspirations of that sort. I am just a doctor as well as a thinking human being. Thirty-four years of living have tipped the question-answer balance of my life in favour of questions. Which, in my opinion is what growing up is all about – exchanging answers for questions. This compels me to end this letter with a question. If you were me, in my shoes, at such a turbulent period, what would you do to get your woman back?

Tolu Ogunlesi is a pharmacist currently living in Asaba, Nigeria. He is the author of a collection of poetry, *Listen to the Geckos Singing from a Balcony* (Bewrite Books, 2004). His fiction has appeared or is forthcoming in Wasafiri, Pindeldyboz, Times Arts Review, Crossing Borders magazine, PEN Anthology of New Nigerian Writing and Weaverbird Anthology of New Nigerian Fiction.

Green Apples

Pravasan Pillay

PINKY PILLAY BALANCES ON THE NARROW SILL outside her second-storey bedroom, and smokes a cigarette. She's twelve and has been out on the sill, smoking, for three consecutive nights. It's ten-fifty and everyone else in the house is asleep.

In two hours, Pinky will jump from her window and break both her legs. She will explain to her parents, when they discover her crouched underneath the washing-stone the next morning, that she had thought that their semi-detached council house had caught fire. Mr Pillay will not believe her story, though, at the time, he will say nothing to her on the matter. A week later, Mr Pillay will install iron burglar guards on Pinky's windows. He will cite rising crime as his reason for doing so.

She inhaled until the flame melted into the filter, and looked out onto their rectangular backyard, identical in size to all the others in the neighbourhood. It was unevenly cemented and featureless, save for a washing-stone planted at the furthest end and sagging clothing lines running through the middle; a red dishtowel hung crookedly on one of them.

The yard used to be sandy before her father hired a workman to cement it over. That had been two years ago. Before the man came she would play there often with her little brother, wetting the soft dirt and moulding it into mud-cakes.

She held onto the window frame and tossed the crumpled filter up to the roof. In just over an hour she had smoked seven cigarettes, one after the other. The previous night it had been four in roughly the same time; and the night before that, three.

Now she felt thirsty.

She stepped back inside her room and drank from a glass of water resting on her dressing table. It tasted stale. It had been sitting there since yesterday.

She held the water in her mouth, picked up a small mirror from the table, and stared at her bloated cheeks. She looked like a fish, she thought, a black fish, with a hooked nose, saucer eyes, and short curly hair.

A toby.

She kept the water in her mouth for a while longer, until her cheeks began to ache, then gargled, walked over to the window, and spat it out. In the quiet night the splash below sounded as loud as a toilet flushing.

She stood still, a sliver of spit trailing down the side of her mouth, half-expecting someone to wake. The house remained silent, save for the hum of the geyser. She unhooked a towel from the back of her bedroom door, wiped her lips on it, then rolled the towel up, and placed it at the foot of the door; then she took out a damp tissue from her pyjama pocket, tore off a piece, and stuck it expertly into the keyhole.

She switched on her bedside lamp and lay down on the bed, her elbows propping her up. In front of her was a dog-eared exercise book labelled 'Composition'. The book's cover was littered with hand-drawn shapes, mostly circles, each meticulously coloured in, some so thickly that the covering had begun to fray. She opened it and read what she had written a few hours earlier:

23/09/1985

War

It was the Boer War and evil aeroplanes were bombing Montford.

She bit hard into the top of her pen and stared at the lone sentence, her feet swaying above her; then wrote the following in a tiny irregular hand:

When the aeroplanes finished blowing holes in all the houses the evil leader sent his killer army to kill everyone. Everyone fought very nice but they all died in the end. Blood was everywhere. It was a sight. It was a very sad sight and many people cried. War is indeed evil!

She counted the lines, mouthing the numbers, and then snapped the book shut and tossed it aside. Then she sat at the side of her bed, sweeping her foot lazily along the floor. Her bedroom shared a wall with the neighbours; a man's snoring started-up.

It was regular around this hour.

She stuck her forefinger into the air and began to mimic the rising and falling of the man's breathing, her finger moving, conductor-like. At a louder snore she would raise her finger high above her head and stretch

188

her arm until it could reach no further.

After the third or fourth such snore, she dropped her arm to her side, and clicked her tongue at the unpainted wall. She looked over her shoulder at the exercise book, sniffed, got up decisively from the bed, opened her door, and stepped outside.

She walked noiselessly downstairs to the kitchen where she removed two slices of bread from the bread-tin and poured herself a glass of water. In the lounge, she disconnected the telephone, and tucked it under her arm.

Only when she was back in her room and had laid everything out on her bed did she realise that she had forgotten to bring a knife. She sighed, then returned to the kitchen, fished one out, and started up the stairs a second time.

A small dark figure blocked her way at the top of the stairwell.

It was her six-year-old brother.

'What you doing?' he asked, through a protracted yawn. 'What time is it?' His hair was long, and his fine-boned features were identical to hers. He was dressed in pyjama bottoms and a creased white t-shirt, torn underneath the collar. His dark shiny skin showed through it.

'Nothing. I'm doing nothing... come you must go back to sleep,' she answered, in a hushed voice, holding a finger to her lips. 'It's still night-time.'

He looked at the knife clasped in her hand. Instinctively, she tucked it into the seat of her pants.

'You having a house picnic, isn't it? I know it,' he retorted, his eyes now wider and his voice dropping noticeably. 'I can come too?'

She knew that he was excited because she had woken him many times in the past to eat treats in her room. She glanced nervously at her parents' door, then led him back to his room, and sat him down on his bed.

Her brother's room was smaller than hers and sparsely furnished. Only half of it could properly be said to be his. His half contained a children-sized single bed, a kitchen chair that served as a night table, and a pine-finish wardrobe – atop of which lay a large cardboard suitcase. The other half of the room was used by their mother for ironing. An ironing board was propped up against the front wall. Pushed against it was a square plastic basket, filled with clothing.

'Sorry for getting you up...' she started, sitting down beside him, and drawing her arm loosely around his shoulders.

He shrugged, then repeated: 'I can come...'

'I'm not having a picnic I promise you...' she replied, her arm gripping his shoulder, as if to confirm that she was speaking the truth.

He looked unconvinced.

'Why you got a knife then?'

She bit her lower lip, thought for a moment, then drew him closer.

'I'm making a tunnel in my room to outside...' she said finally, her mouth now centimetres from his doll-like ear. 'Like in that videotape we saw... remember that videotape we saw in Uncle Vijay's house, about that prisoner?'

She knew he would remember. The two of them had watched the video – the only one their uncle owned – obsessively over the two weeks that they had spent there during the school vacations. In the end, their uncle had to hide it away from them.

'*Ja*, but they caught him, isn't it... they caught him when he came out the other side. Isn't his friend was on the crooks' side?' he said, his words coming so quickly that they seemed to merge into one another. 'That's why they caught him. His friend was a crook.'

Then suddenly, as if he had forgotten that she was in the room with him, he picked up a tin of Vicks that had been sitting on the chair beside his bed and began tossing it up into the air.

She watched his, mostly futile, attempts at catching it for a minute or so before interrupting.

'*Ja*, he wasn't a good friend,' she said, grabbing the tin in midair and throwing it back onto the chair; it spun around a few times before coming to rest, the wrong side up. He tried immediately to reach for it. She stopped him.

'Right, you must sleep now... you must go school tomorrow,' she continued.

'You too must go school... not only me,' he replied, though disinterestedly. His eyes were still on the tin.

'*Ja*, but I had my sleep in Geography class today,' she said, taking his face in her hands and narrowing her eyes.

He stared at her without comprehension for a moment, then smiling, pushed her shoulder lightly. She fell exaggeratedly onto the bed with a muffled cry. He giggled and followed her so that they lay on their backs, alongside each other. She felt the knife dig into her back.

'Since when you got so strong... looks like bluffing everyone you got asthma,' she said, staring up at the ceiling, and twisting a lock of thick hair around her finger. The ceiling was flecked with mildew at its corners and around the bare light bulb. It had been worse, but her father had painted it over. Then a few months later the mildew began to return. 'The roof must be got a hole,' she had overheard her father say to her mother.

'Pinky…' he whispered, breaking the momentary silence.

She grunted, still staring at the ceiling.

'I can see the tunnel you making.'

She considered the ceiling for a few more seconds before replying.

'I can't show you now boy… only when I'm finished I can show you. It's secret okay… you can't go tell Ma or Pa or anyone,' she said, sitting up on the bed, before continuing, 'You know if you tell them they'll go cover it or something.'

He looked at her seriously, and nodded his head in agreement. She got up to leave but felt his hand on her wrist.

'Why you digging a tunnel? You going away from here?'

'I'm not going nowhere. I'm just digging it for an emergency… just in case I must get out from my room quickly,' she replied.

'For an emergency?'

'*Ja*, for an emergency'

'You'll show me when you finish isn't?' he asked.

'As soon as I'm finished you the first person I'll show.'

She noticed the curtain billow. The window was slightly ajar; she walked over and shut it. 'You know you not supposed to leave it open.'

He placed his fingers over his eyes. It was a common gesture, pulled out whenever he had done something wrong.

'Sorry…' he said, before sliding his hand from his eyes to his mouth, muffling his words. 'Pinky, you'll buy me a Coke tomorrow for first lunch break? Everyone in class said they buying tomorrow. Ma them don't want to give me any money… Coke is so cheap…'

'Why you want to do what all the other children do?'

'They my friends how. Anyways, it's only twenty cents… fifteen cents if you got your own bottle and Kese said he'll lend me his bottle when he finish drinking.'

'I'll buy it for you if you go to sleep okay?' she said, trying to hide her smile. 'Come and see me in first lunch break by the change rooms.'

'Night Pinky,' he replied almost immediately, pulling the blanket up to his shoulders.

'Night Apple's Brother,' she replied, under her breath, using the name everyone in the neighbourhood called him by. She herself had been called Apple when she was around his age, though no one called her that anymore. She had got the name after throwing an unripe apple against their front window, shattering it, and breaking several of her mother's vases. As punishment her father had made her stand outside, staring at the broken glass, and eating the same apple that she had thrown.

Back inside her room, she plugged the telephone into the wall socket, placed the receiver to her ear, and waited for a connection. She then let the telephone at the other end ring five times before cutting the call.

She glanced at her wristwatch, then reached under her bed and took out a squat object wrapped in foil. It was a can of condensed milk that she had opened about a week and a half ago. From experience she knew that she had a day or two more before it went bad. She peeled off the foil and upturned the can over the bread.

As usual the thick liquid fell slowly enough for her to shape a rudimentary house. It was a trick of hers that had always pleased her brother though recently he had grown tired of houses.

'At least put a chimney,' he had told her the last time.

She admired her work for a few seconds, then pulled apart the slices, and spread the liquid evenly. She licked the knife clean, folded the bread, and took a generous bite. Still chewing, she picked up the receiver and dialled again. It rang twice before it was answered.

'I thought you said it was going to be three rings from now,' said a girl, sounding out of breath.

'Sorry Faye…' she answered, swallowing the bread, and placing her head on her pillow. 'I forgot. I…'

'It's late now…' Faye interjected.

'You was sleeping?' she asked. Her head lay opposite the telephone set. It smelt strongly of furniture polish.

'No, but I was falling off to sleep. I'm so tired. I had long-jump practice today,' Faye replied. 'Mr Samuels made us run everywhere carrying medicine balls.'

'He must be trying to kill you or something… murderer.'

'He said all the top long-jumpers do the same thing,' Faye retorted, then seemed to hesitate. 'Pinky, you think I can talk to you tomorrow morning? I can't keep my eyes open this side.'

'Talk for five more minutes please. I'm so bored over here… I think I'm going to die or something. I think I got a fever or something,' she said speaking flatly, taking a quick sip of water. 'You finished Mrs Naidoo's composition?'

'*Ja*, I finished it when I came from school,' Faye replied, then tacking on as an afterthought, 'You?'

'I still got thirty-one lines to do… I don't know what to write

192

about… did you write the whole thirty-five lines?'

'*Ja*, you have to otherwise she won't take it.'

'That's not right… I can't write thirty-five lines… why she don't let people who can't write thirty-five lines write ten lines? Ten lines is not nothing,' she said. 'I think she hates people who can't write thirty-five lines or something.'

'She don't hate you,' Faye said, her voice wavering as though she were searching for the right words. 'You just don't do her homework.'

She responded quickly: 'I don't care. I'm only going to write ten lines… I don't care what she do me… she don't know I like standing with my nose on the board.'

Faye laughed: 'Must see if you carry on like this you going to fail this year. Then you mustn't come cry by me.'

She snorted. 'You said I'll fail last year and I'm still over here.'

'*Ja*, but you came out last from everyone, Pinky.'

'Someone must come out last. If I didn't come out last then Rajen should have come out last and you know he'll start crying or something,' she said, switching the receiver from one ear to the other. 'Anyways you don't need school if you want to be a dressmaker,' she continued. 'How my auntie she only went Standard One and she makes dresses for everyone?'

Faye paused. 'Since when you want to be a dressmaker?'

'I was just thinking last night… I couldn't sleep nice. Anyways you don't have to worry then… you'll get free miniskirts for the rest of your life… and real ones too… not like now how we have to staple the hem,' she said.

'But you can't sew and plus the other week you was saying you want to become a singer.'

'I can't sing anymore… I'm smoking too much,' she said, making her voice hoarse, and coughing a few times.

Faye stopped her. 'Carry on joking. If your father catch you then you finished.'

'I'm already finished.'

'What you did?' Faye asked, for the first time her voice showing genuine interest.

'Nothing. I just…' she managed to get out, before Faye interrupted her again: 'Wait… I think someone woke up. Just hold on.'

'Okay…' she said, listening to the receiver being set down. She went over to her dressing table and felt underneath for the pack of cigarettes taped there. She pulled it out and removed a cigarette, then straightened the tape and refastened it. She carried the telephone to the end of her bed, nearer to the window, and lit the cigarette. She took a few drags before placing the receiver to her ear. She could hear voices on the other end. A minute later the phone was picked up.

'My mother woke up to drink some water,' Faye began, by way of explanation. Her voice was raspy.

'She never say nothing?' she asked, drawing on the cigarette, and tapping the ash outside.

'No, she just asked me what I was doing. I said I was coming from the toilet.'

'You lucky... if they catch me awake here they act like I'm making a bomb or something,' she replied.

'Anyways you didn't tell me what happened. What you did?'

'I didn't do nothing... I'm just bored... there's nothing to do over here. Everything is the same... like if you have a bath or play snakes and ladders or eat or anything. It's all like one thing.'

Faye waited before replying. It was clear she was expecting more. 'I don't know what you saying... are you in trouble at home?'

'No, I'm not in trouble. I'm just talking nonsense... don't worry about it. I think I just want to sleep... you can't even sleep in this place. Listen over here,' she said, leaving the cigarette on the sill, and walking to the wall she shared with the neighbour. She placed the receiver against the wall. 'You can hear?'

'Every night it's like this,' she continued, picking up the cigarette, and drawing. The tobacco crackled as it burnt.

'If you bored like that why you don't come and join the long-jump team? How many times I told you you must come. You don't take part in nothing that's why you bored every time,' Faye said.

'*Ja*, maybe...' she replied, her voice trailing.

'Then we can take part in interschool together... that's not boring Pinky... I promise you. They let you go in a bus to another school and plus you get a half-day off.'

'*Ja*, maybe I'll come and watch you. But I'm not carrying medicine balls... if Samuels wants to kill me, he must have me a fair fight,' she said.

'Come tomorrow, you'll like it,' Faye insisted.

'I'll come if you can guess what I'm eating,' she teased, taking a large bite from her sandwich, and chewing loudly into the mouthpiece.

'You always eating the same thing when you phone me. And must see if you carry on you going to rot all your teeth.'

'Never mind my teeth get rotten… at least then I don't have to smile at Mrs Naidoo,' she said. 'Come on. Guess.'

'Gold Cross,' Faye replied, with a hint of resignation.

'That's why you my best friend,' she said, dusting cigarette ash off the sill. 'You know my can is nearly finished… maybe tomorrow we can go after school to buy another one.'

'But tomorrow is long-jump practice… you coming right?'

'*Ja*, no I'm coming. Forget it. We'll go another day.'

Faye yawned: 'Anyways, I must go sleep now. Must see tomorrow night after practice you'll be tired like me, then you won't have any problem sleeping.'

'Okay… I'll see you,' she said quickly, then stopped herself. 'Faye, why you don't call me Apple no more?'

'Why you want know that?'

'No I was just thinking.'

'What's wrong?'

'Nothing. I was just wondering.'

'I don't know Pinky,' Faye replied. 'We not small anymore… and plus you don't do mad things like that no more.'

'Thanks. I was just thinking.'

'You okay isn't?'

'*Ja*, no I'm okay. I'll see you then.'

'See you,' Faye ended, cutting the call.

She placed the receiver down and disconnected the telephone. She drank a bit of water, opened her exercise book and scratched out all that she had written. Then she walked back to the sill, stubbed the cigarette out, and tossed it onto the roof.

Pravasan Pillay was born in 1978 and lives in Durban, South Africa. He writes poetry and short stories.

The Absence

Véronique Tadjo

'BUT I KNOW YOU,' SHE SAID. 'I know you so very well! We have the same tastes, the same passion. When I went to your house, I knew that for the first time in my life I had met someone I could truly connect with. Everything in your home talked to me.'

She recalled the memory of their first encounter with fondness. She had been swept over by his presence. Everything about him pleased her.

She made a point of remembering every little detail because she knew that one day, if she stopped doing this, his face would disappear entirely and she would be left with nothing, or at best with a blurred picture.

So, when she went to bed at night, she would force her mind to go back again and again to the many phases of their life together. From beginning to end. She would replay the same scenes over and over until she fell asleep.

In her dreams, she travelled to where he was. She would knock on the door of his chamber to wake him up from his deep slumber. But it was always with great anticipation. Was her call going to be answered? Would he let her in? He had many reasons not to.

In spite of this every night they would stay together until the early hours of the morning, talking, making love and holding hands. Then he would gradually withdraw from her touch, swallowed by the light.

Waking up in an empty room she felt so lonely, the walls looking down on her, ready to fall and crush her body. She wanted to pull the cover over her head, bury herself in the hollow of the bed.

'Where are you, where are you?'

On her bedside table, she could see the photograph showing them together on a beach in Cape Town. It was a happy scene. The sky was endlessly blue and the sea looked truly glorious. But she did not want to look at it anymore. It made her sad, as it seemed too much like a distant time in a place that may have never existed after all. Between the photograph and her life today there was his absence and it wiped out everything, tore away every bit of hope.

He wasn't part of her waking world anymore. During the day, he could not mingle with other people who had no knowledge of death, no respect for it. He couldn't remain her husband.

One day, as she was walking in a busy street, she caught sight of someone who resembled him. She actually believed it was him. So she followed the man for a long time, afraid of what she was doing while at the same time, desperate to get closer to him. But then he turned round unexpectedly and their eyes met for a fraction of a second, enough to make her realise how terribly mistaken she had been. She quickly entered the first shop she could get into and stayed there until her heart resumed its normal rhythm and her hands stopped shaking uncontrollably. She bought a few items and left.

'Living without you,' she whispered to herself, 'living without you is a long melancholy, a descent inside the corridors of darkness. Learning to understand again the space that surrounds and oppresses me from all sides. Learning to comprehend my fears and my longing in this world devoid of warmth and recognition.'

The wind was blowing outside. Hard. She could hear it hissing, trying to get inside the house. To find her where she was hiding away.

Only a few months ago, they were still together. She remembered the afternoon on the Coast when they went to walk along a cliff. The sea below them was dark green. She wanted to dive between the rocks, to fly for a few seconds over the ocean and enter that immense womb, that matrix from where we all come. She was just looking for a tiny moment of eternity; holding time by the neck and making it kneel down in front of them. She wanted to set her eyes firmly on the horizon and then enter the water in a thunderstorm of laughter and despair.

But instead, they had sat on the soft moss that covered the rocks and had marvelled at the beauty of what they saw.

'You have to come to the edge of the land to realise you are in a prison from which you cannot escape,' he suddenly remarked. 'Look at it again,' he urged her, pointing at the line where the sea met with the sky. 'We are all surrounded, trapped in this circular cell. Really, the earth should flip over so we can fall into the air, fall past the birds, past the fluffy clouds, past our conscience and our dreams until we reach the bottom of the sky.'

She had not understood him at the time. She had been afraid of his words.

But now, she was aware that the loneliness taking hold of her so intensely had been born long ago. It had crouched with her inside her mother's womb.

'I need to dig with my own hands at the root of my restlessness,' she thought with anguish. 'I have so little patience, so little tolerance. I cannot sit and wait for better times to come my way. I have to hear the music of my body for fear of becoming deaf. I have to look inward for fear of becoming blind. I have to direct my scream towards a form of creation or else its sharp thorns will slash my throat and tear my soul. I have to withdraw in myself if I want to open up to others.'

Yes, she could not forget him although there were moments when she wished she could. She felt she would never get over the pain. Yet, in the end, it passed. She was left with anger and with this enormous impatience. She desired nothing. She was not interested in anything. Why did he go?

They told her his body was found in his hotel room when the maid came in. He was stretched on the bed, fully dressed. The television was still on. No sign of fighting. No medicine lying around. No handwritten note.

She received a long-distance phone call, a voice with a strong foreign accent telling her that her husband was dead.

Then she had to get his body.

She took the first flight and once there, she did all the paperwork, signed the documents to release him and organised the final trip back home. Only when all was done, did she become aware that she was losing her mind.

Inside the airport, she kept telling herself: 'Now, I must control my fear, really control my fear.'

Standing on the escalator with her suitcase, she felt as if she were climbing higher and higher. Yet at the same time she thought people were walking above her head. Her body was swaying dangerously. She was going to fall backwards, she was certain. She gripped the side of the escalator with all her strength. No, she was not going to fall. The landing was just a few seconds away and in the departure hall there would be many travellers like her. Anonymous people. Just like her. All she had to do was to control her fear. She was not going to fall backward.

Suddenly she was projected into a crowd. Someone smiled at her. She was relieved. But what was happening to her?

She remembered the day before he left. There had been an argument.

'I've had enough,' he said raising his voice, 'enough of your changing moods and of your coldness towards me. You never seem happy these days.' Then he added, his voice breaking slightly: 'And you don't like making love any more.'

'How can you say that?' She protested.

'Well, at least, not with me!' came the sharp answer.

'Are you trying to say something?' Her tone was defensive.

'Don't play games with me. I know something is going on. You can't deny it. You have changed.'

'Listen, it's not about you. It is just that...' She had a blank look on her face, incapable of finishing her sentence.

He cut in: 'I am not sure I can trust you any more, you know. You are not being honest with me. You have put up a barrier between us. I can't reach you.'

It hit a nerve, throwing her off balance. Was her attitude so obvious? She thought she was good at hiding her feelings but to her surprise, there he was, reading through her.

'Please, don't talk like this,' she pleaded. 'It's not as bad as it looks.'

But he had already stiffened.

He was deeply hurt, hurt in a way that made her sad because she had not meant to cause any suffering. Where had all the lightness in their life disappeared? She wondered. Everything was so hard nowadays. She felt confused. She did not know which direction her life was taking and it scared her. She wanted change, that was sure, but how much of it, she had no idea. She avoided his gaze, afraid he would be able to sense what was going on in her mind.

'I wish you would be more sincere,' he continued. 'Do you expect me to carry on like this?'

Now, there was outrage in his voice, a sense that she had not respected his feelings. She could see how much he felt deceived. He had probably thought he knew her well but now it dawned on him that she had kept great chunks of her life away from him.

She started panicking sensing that they were getting off limits, entering a dangerous territory. She wasn't ready for it, wasn't ready for big revelations. Too many doubts assailed her.

To appease him she tried to give him a kiss. But he stepped back abruptly and walked away.

And that was it. They went to bed not saying one more word to each other.

They were still not talking the next morning when he climbed into a taxi to go to the airport. She watched him behind the bedroom curtains. Just before the car started, he looked out of the window as if he wanted to catch sight of her. All of a sudden, she had this urge to run out of the door and say goodbye. Instead, she drew the curtains wide open and made a big gesture but he was already gone and all she could see was the back of his head in the car.

She had thought a lot about that bad morning. She had thought about it many times. What would have happened if they had properly kissed each other goodbye? Would he still have been with her? She believed fate was made of a series of events that locked into one another. Change one link in the chain and something totally different might happen. Yes, she was convinced she could have altered everything that morning – she could have prevented his death with a simple kiss.

'The aim of life is death, and looking backward, inanimate things existed before living ones.' The first time she heard this line by Eugene O'Neill was in the big university amphitheatre where she was taking a drama course. Now it came back to her with an acuteness that was painful. Our whole existence was driven by death and not by life. It was towards this goal that we were striving.

She could not help crying over the wasted years. But she wiped her tears, got up from her desk and went to the window. Night was approaching. She wanted nothing. She stood there watching darkness getting thicker. The sky was turning purple. Everything seemed silent. Branches were swaying, leaves trembling in the chill of the evening.

She wanted to give away most of his clothes. She only wished to keep a few of his shirts. He loved his shirts. Each time he went on a trip, he would buy himself one. They came from all sorts of shops and also from markets, cut in the fashion of the countries he visited. She did not know what to do with the shirts now. When she was tidying his closet, she took out, cleaned and ironed every single one of them. She found a fifty-dollar bill in a breast pocket. She laughed when she saw it. 'He must have forgotten he put it there.' she thought. 'He'll be happy to get it back.' And then she remembered he wasn't there anymore. She couldn't talk to him about her lucky discovery. He had briefly made contact with her but he was already gone again, leaving her stranded in the house full of memories.

After the funeral ceremony, she talked to some people about his shirts. She told them she wasn't prepared to put them in a box or to give them away to a charity, unknown people. Each time she opened his wardrobe and saw all his clothes neatly hanging there, she felt like he was still alive. But listening to her, the men remained frozen on the spot not knowing what to say or what to do. Frozen by what seemed like fear or guilt at the realisation that, although he had been their friend, deep inside, they did not want to have anything to do with the dead man's shirts let alone wear them. Nobody volunteered to take them.

'My world has been broken. Our house has crumbled down. I used to love its walls, its floor, its windows and its roof. I used to like its smell, the way it caught the sun in the morning, the light never wanting to leave the side of the garden where the tall trees stand strong and protective. I used to think it was the most peaceful place on earth. Hours would go by undisturbed by anything other than the ticking of my own clock; my own breathing, my own mind humming quietly.

I am a pauper now begging for an end to my misery. I beg for a respite.

Where are you? What are you doing? Are you all right?

You have left me here to watch over your legacy. But where is my strength?

As I advance further and further, the wound of your absence becomes deeper and deeper. I feel that I am leaving you behind, digging emptiness around me. I close my eyes but I find nothing inside me, just the confines of my body. And like a bird in a cage, I try to find the opening that will free me, that will let my soul escape to a wider space, fields that go across the lands and beyond the horizon. I am flying over the mountains and over the seas, slashing the air with my wings and suddenly veering towards the sun until I am one with the intensity of its fire.

But I remain a prisoner of my own jail, stuck to the earth, rooted by gravity. I can't touch you. I can't speak to you. I can't write to you.

And it is your voice that draws me back to you in waves that come and go, washing the sand with its thousand and one stories. It is you, singing in my ear.'

Deep in her mind, a sharp secret stabs her heart, a pestilent truth, an untold reality. Pus oozes from the wounds, blood thick and nauseating, turning into a brownish colour. Suffering has lost its meaning. Indifference has covered everything from the earth to the sky. Nowhere to hide. Nowhere to stop and rethink. Time is out of hand. Pain is a silent cry.

Who are we that we have lost our souls? That we have let these things happen?

Chaos standing up. Chaos ready to pounce. Chaos eating up our flesh.

Who are we that the weakest among us die a silent death while shame floods the sky? Clouds carrying rain, preparing for the storm that will wash away the richness of the land.

Could she have rebuilt the trust had she been given another chance?

Nothing stands on its feet anymore. Her soul is shattered. No emotion is worth its weight.

A dark flame burns her conscience.

Véronique Tadjo is a writer and painter from the Ivory Coast. Born in Paris, she grew up in Abidjan where she attended local schools and subsequently became a lecturer at the National University until 1993 when she took up writing full time. She has lived in several countries and is currently based in Johannesburg. Her latest book, *Reine Pokou*, is on the subject of Queen Pokou, founder of the Baoule Kingdom. She also writes for the young.

Rules

The Prize is awarded annually to a short story by an African writer published in English, whether in Africa or elsewhere. (Indicative length, between 3 000 and 15 000 words.)

'An African writer' is normally taken to mean someone who was born in Africa, or who is a national of an African country, or whose parents are African, and whose work has reflected African sensibilities.

There is a cash prize of $15 000 for the winning author and a travel award for each of the short-listed candidates (up to five in all).

For practical reasons, unpublished work and work in other languages is not eligible. Works translated into English from other languages are not excluded, provided they have been published in translation, and should such a work win, a proportion of the prize would be awarded to the translator.

The award is made in July each year, the deadline for submissions being 31 January. The short-list is selected from work published in the five years preceding the submissions deadline and not previously considered for a Caine Prize. Submissions should be made by publishers and will need to be accompanied by twelve original published copies of the work for consideration, sent to the address below. There is no application form.

Every effort is made to publicise the work of the short-listed authors through the broadcast as well as the printed media.

Winning and short-listed authors will be invited to participate in writers' workshops in Africa and elsewhere as resources permit.

The above rules were designed essentially to launch the Caine Prize and may be modified in the light of experience. Their objective is to establish the Caine Prize as a benchmark for excellence in African writing.

The Caine Prize,
The Menier Gallery,
Menier Chocolate Factory,
51 Southwark
Street, London SE1 1RU.
Telephone: +44 (0) 20 7378 6234.
Fax: +44 (0) 20 7378 6235.
Website: www.caineprize.com